M000200528

Praise for Howard Odentz's Dead (A Lot)

"A fun and witty zombie apocalypse narrative that will bring a smile to your face as you discover (or remember) how the teenage mind operates in times of difficulty. The dialog is clever and the characters are realistic."
—ScaredStiffReviews.com

"Right out of the gate, the plot is fast-paced and action packed (like any good zombie book should be) and infused with some great humor. It's a fun and entertaining ride and I was sad when it [came] to the end."
—BookandCoffeeAddict.com

"Howard Odentz does an impeccable job writing about this world turned dead."
—BeautysLibrary.com

What We Kill

by

Howard Odentz

Bell Bridge Books

This is a work of fiction. Names, characters, places and incidents are either the products of the author's imagination or are used fictitiously. Any resemblance to actual persons (living or dead), events or locations is entirely coincidental.

Bell Bridge Books
PO BOX 300921
Memphis, TN 38130
Print ISBN: 978-1-61194-836-3

Bell Bridge Books is an Imprint of BelleBooks, Inc.

Copyright © 2017 by Howard Odentz

Published in the United States of America.

All rights reserved. No part of this book may be reproduced in any form or by any electronic or mechanical means, including information storage and retrieval systems, without permission in writing from the publisher, except by a reviewer, who may quote brief passages in a review.

We at BelleBooks enjoy hearing from readers.
Visit our websites
BelleBooks.com
BellBridgeBooks.com
ImaJinnBooks.com

10 9 8 7 6 5 4 3 2 1

Cover design: Debra Dixon
Interior design: Hank Smith
Photo/Art credits:
Woods (manipulated) © Smileus | Dreamstime.com

:Lwkw:01:

Dedication

For David

1

IT STARTS LIKE THIS.

2

"WEST? ARE YOU awake? Weston?" A far off voice calls my name but I'm nestled in clouds. I don't want to open my eyes.

"Holy Christ," Anders gasps. Anders Stephenson is my best friend. I've always known him. He lives across the street in the persimmon-colored house. I only know the name of the paint because his mother goes out of her way to tell everyone she used a fancy color.

Mrs. Stephenson is typical Meadowfield.

"What . . . what's happening?" I hear someone else cry. That's Marcy Cole. Marcy is beautiful. She has curly auburn hair and blue eyes. She also has a thing for Anders that's been brewing since the third grade. As cool as we all are, I don't think that Marcy and Anders are ever going to happen. When we graduate next spring, Marcy is going to be a mess. Anders wants to take a year off and go visit relatives in Norway. I'm hoping I'm in college by then. I don't want to be left behind to pick up little Marcy pieces.

That puzzle is a little too abstract for me.

"Earth to Weston Kahn. Earth to Weston Kahn," Robbie Myers says. "Come in Weston Kahn." Myers is my other best friend. Me, Anders, Marcy and Myers have all grown up in sight of each other on gently sloping Primrose Lane. Myers is kind of a mess in a nerdy way. If I were to point fingers, I'd point them at his mother, but we all have our little issues.

No one is perfect, even in a town as perfect as Meadowfield.

"What the hell?" cries Anders. I slit open my eyes so little that they might as well not be open at all.

The sun is shining overhead, fractured in a zillion pieces.

Branches.

We're in the woods.

"Shit," Anders cries again but this time he sounds almost hysterical.

"Oh my God," gasps Marcy. Her voice is husky. "Is that blood?"

What does she mean, *blood*? Where's blood? Who's bleeding?

"West?" It's Myers again. His black hair and Chiclet teeth momentarily blot out the sky. He's leaning over me and his hot breath is assaulting my nostrils. "I think . . . oh no . . . I think Weston might be dead."

I take a deep breath. "Shut up, Myers," I murmur. "I'm not dead." I open my eyes a little more. Only then do I realize that my arm is stinging. The more sleep falls away, the more insistent the pain becomes. I squeeze my eyes shut and feel tears dripping down my cheeks.

"It *is* blood." Marcy chokes out, and this time she starts to sob.

There is so much promise in letting myself slip away again, but I know that I can't. Something's not right. As a matter of fact, something is very, very wrong.

I sigh, reach up and push Myers away. "Move," I tell him through a mouth that might as well be filled with cold oatmeal, and struggle to get to my elbows because my arm really does hurt.

"Sorry," says Myers. "I thought you were dead." He leans back on his bony knees. There's something weird about how Myers looks, other than his scrawniness and his dorky tee-shirt that says 'Master Baiter' with a picture of a worm on a hook, but I can't quite put my finger on it. My head is all full of cotton. Besides, any thoughts of Myers fade away as soon as my eyes begin to focus.

We *are* in the woods, and everything is all too familiar. This is Prince Richard's Maze, the stretch of forest at the edge of Meadowfield that towers over the highway and the Connecticut River beyond. My fingers dig into the ground and October leaves crunch beneath my hands.

Marcy is still crying and Myers starts to cry, too. I hate when he does that. No wonder he gets picked on so much at school.

"Why is there blood?" Marcy blubbers, and this time Myers joins her.

He says, "Anders, there's so much. What . . . what did you do?"

I roll to one side and wince. My arm stings like a son of a bitch, but it doesn't even occur to me to look down and find the source of the pain. I'm too busy gawking at Anders.

There's blood alright. There's blood everywhere, but it's only on him. His blond hair and square jaw are dripping with it. His tall, ropy, basketball frame, covered only in a tee-shirt and jeans, is sloshed in red. Anders looks like Carrie White—not the new one but the old one played by that girl with the stringy hair and the flat face who is older than my mother now.

Anders is painted in blood.

Myers and Marcy are crying, and we're in Prince Richard's Maze, but I don't know why.

"My eye," Myers suddenly screams. "Where's my eye?" I know that sounds like a bizarre thing to say, but Myers has a glass eye. I can't pull my muddied gaze away from Anders because of all the blood, but suddenly I realize why Myers looks weirder than usual. He's missing his eye. All that's left is a droopy, crusty hole in his head. He always forgets to clean it out and it's gross. "Shit," he cries. "My mother will friggin' kill me if I lose it again."

"What's happening?" blurts out Anders with his hands held in front of him and the whites of his eyes popping out of his crimson colored face.

"I don't know," I say, then wince. The stinging, burning sensation on my arm becomes so insistent that I simply have to look. I glance down and my eyes grow wide. There is a tiny triangle, way smaller than a penny, burned into my forearm. The skin around its edges is puffy and pale.

A triangle.

"Marcy?" whispers Anders. "Marcy?" I've never heard Anders Stephenson sound so small or so weak. He's not weak at all. He's our jock buddy. He's the one who sticks up for us when nobody else does. "Marcy?" he says once more, but his words are barely a whisper.

"Um, Marcy?" says Myers through his tears. "Where . . . where are your pants?"

I look back up and see Myers without his eye, Anders covered in blood, and Marcy wearing only a torn top, dirty panties, and no shoes.

Marcy screams.

For that matter, so does Myers.

We're in some sort of dream. We have to be. I must be dreaming and at any moment I'm going to wake up. If I'm not, there is no reason why the four of us should be in The Maze.

There's no reason for so much blood.

Suddenly, a long, deep wail pierces the forest and we all look up. The otherworldly siren is the Meadowfield fire alarm. The sound cuts through town like a sickly fog horn, unable to be ignored. The alarm blares away for a good thirty seconds, and Myers starts hiccupping in the middle of crying. He's hyperventilating. Myers is a junior volunteer for the town fire department, but he's not going to be able to show up for the alarm because he can't find his eye.

Anders is covered in blood.

Marcy's lost her pants.

I have a burning triangle on my forearm.

What's more, if this isn't a dream, then I can't for the life of me remember how we ended up in The Maze.

Frankly, I don't even remember last night.

What the hell is going on?

3

"GIVE ME YOUR sweatshirt," I tell Myers. The gray fleece sleeves are tied around his thin waist because it's been so warm lately. This October's schizophrenic weather has made our little corner of the world the poster child for global warming. The temperature has topped 70 degrees most days this past week when the thermometer should really be hovering in the forties.

"Why?" he sniffs and rubs one dirty arm across his face, which is getting increasingly hard to look at. His fleshy eye socket seems huge even though it's not. I force myself to ignore the hole. Instead, I tilt my chin toward Marcy, and he silently mouths, *'Oh.'*

Myers quickly unties the sleeves and tosses his sweatshirt to me. I get up, my head still reeling and my arm burning, and stagger over to Marcy, who is totally lost in a puddle of curly auburn hair and tears. Her hands are trying to cover as much of herself as possible. Even in the early morning light I can see that her cheeks are burning red.

"Here," I say, and toss Myers's sweatshirt in her lap.

Marcy says something under her breath about how she's mortified. I try not to roll my eyes. I'm not even sure I have the strength to roll them, anyway. Every square inch of my body aches, and the pain in my arm is searing.

"You'll be fine," I tell her. Being mortified isn't a permanent condition. Besides, she doesn't have anything we haven't seen before, and now there's a more urgent issue.

Anders is becoming totally unglued.

First he starts shaking. Then he climbs to his feet and takes off running with his arms stretched out so maybe he won't get any more blood on himself.

"Stop him," I snap at Myers, which is like telling a Chihuahua to stop a mastiff.

"Wait, what?" he stammers as he watches Anders barrel through the fall foliage away from us.

"Damnit," I cry and try my best to follow after him, still imagining my knees rubbing together as I run, which they don't do anymore. I know where he's going but I don't have time to explain to Myers or Marcy. She's too busy holding a pity party for herself.

I dive into the woods after Anders, but he's fast. Anders has always been fast. He's always been the captain of this or a varsity player of that. I'm not a jock. People like me aren't jocks.

"Anders, you prick. Stop already." What I really want to say is *'Anders, you prick. Don't let anyone see you. If you're seen covered in blood then we're all royally screwed.'*

Thankfully, we know The Maze. We've played in these woods for years, even after the town put up the *'No Loitering'* sign and hung a chain across the entrance so that desperate, horny men wouldn't park their cars inside at night.

Finally, I burst through the brush onto one of the well-worn paths. Although I'm really groggy, I'm pretty sure this one is Little Loop. Big Loop is wider and goes all the way out to the bald patch that looms over the highway. We used to watch fireworks there with our families on the Fourth of July. Little Loop only goes as far as Turner Pond.

A few yards in front of me I find Anders' bloody tee-shirt in a ball on the ground. I scoop it up and keep following Little Loop. About a hundred feet farther down are his bloody jeans.

From somewhere up ahead I hear a splash.

When I finally catch up to him with my lungs burning deep inside, I find Anders chest deep in Turner Pond, naked, except for his socks and underwear. He's scrubbing at himself with his fingernails, probably doing more harm than good.

"Get it off me," he keeps wailing over and over like he's being sucked dry by a leech.

"Stop it," I cry. I want to wade into the water after him, but I'm not the kind of guy who does stuff like that. Anders is the one who does stuff like that.

Not now, though. Now he's just a mess.

"Get it off me," he screams again. "Get it off me."

Suddenly, Myers is at my side, eyeless and a little clueless. I think his head is all filled with pudding like mine. Seconds later, there's a blur and a spray of water.

Marcy has run right into the pond and splashes her way out to Anders.

"Anders," she cries and grabs him by both shoulders. "Anders, STOP."

Just like that, Anders falls to pieces right in Marcy's arms. She's probably dreamt about this happening every night for years, but not like this.

Never like this.

Anders sobs like only a guy can sob when something truly awful has happened. He sobs like guys only do once in their lifetimes.

Marcy pulls Anders to her and buries her beautiful, curly head in his collar bone. He wraps his arms around her and holds on tight like if he lets go, he'll plummet to the bottom of Turner Pond and then keep on going, sinking into the muck, and the filth, and the secrets way down deep.

"Shhh," she whispers to him. "It will be okay. Honest. Everything will be okay."

Meanwhile, back on shore, Myers stares at Anders and Marcy in the water with his mouth hanging open. "Some things you can't ever unsee," he murmurs, his face slowly going pale.

"Really?" I say to him. "Seriously?"

He slowly nods his bobble head up and down on his turkey neck, with his black hair and his "Master Baiter" tee-shirt.

"That's the best I got," he says. Then, like a total douche, he quickly reaches up and rubs his good eye with his fist. "Wait," he stutters. "I think my other eye just went blind."

4

MEADOWFIELD ONCE appeared in a joke book about preppies as one of the hundred most desirable suburbs in the country, but that was decades ago. Still, our town—along with Longmeadow, Littleham, and a few other places where there are enclaves of McMansions—is prime real estate in Western Massachusetts.

Everyone here wears plaid and untucked oxford shirts. Most families own golden retrievers, big black labs, or hypoallergenic designer dogs.

Some of us are Jewish, like me and Myers, but being Jewish these days has turned from a religion to just another reason to get gifts at the holidays like all our non-Jewish friends.

Most of our parents have been divorced at least once, and they all think they're cool by telling us if we're going to drink or get stoned, we should do it at home. They won't judge.

Parents lie.

We all go to college after we graduate high school unless there's some fancy-ass reason not to, like Anders has about going to Norway for a year.

We all perform community service and think of our grades in terms of percentiles.

Bad things don't ever happen in places like Meadowfield, or at least that's what everyone likes to think, but it isn't true.

Bad things are happening right now.

The four of us sit next to Turner Pond in the morning chill, all shivering. Marcy has put on Myers' sweatshirt, but now her panties are soaked from the pond. Anders is curled in a ball, mostly naked except for his wet underwear and socks. His splotchy sneakers are almost buried in dead leaves at the water's edge. He won't put on his bloody clothes. He won't even look at them.

His head is in Marcy's lap, and he's staring into space like it's a tangible thing. Behind his vacant gaze is complete darkness, and I'm afraid for my friend.

Marcy keeps rubbing his back, her face empty, too. Meanwhile, Myers can't stop staring at them, and I want to say something really juvenile like *'take a picture, it will last longer,'* but I don't because there's a dense fog in my head, and I'm not entirely sure any of this is real.

Finally, Myers reaches up and wipes his droopy socket.

"I have to find my eye," he murmurs like he's already been yelled at for losing it by his mother.

"Needle. Haystack," I say. "It's probably in the woods, and if it's in the woods, it's gone."

"Pffft. All gone," Anders whispers, not moving his head from Marcy's lap. Goose bumps pop up on my arm. I'm almost positive he's not talking about Myers' eye at all. He's talking about something else, like childhood or innocence.

"Shhh," says Marcy and runs her fingers through Anders' blond hair. Unless there's something I don't know about, this is the first time she's ever had access to it. "Sorry," she whispers to Myers about his eye but all our words fall on deaf ears.

Myers deflates, even though there isn't much of him there to begin with. He looks even scrawnier than before. Finally, he turns to me and motions to my arm. "Let me see it again."

This time I actually do roll my eyes. "Whatever," I say and hold out my left arm. The new isosceles scar is still burning, and I wince. Myers leans in and stares at the puffy little triangle, the one that I'm never going to be able to explain.

He whistles. "That's what they do," he says. "They mark you."

"Oh my God, shut up already," I snap at him.

"It's true," he says. "The government wants you to think it's not, but it's true."

"Seriously," I tell him. "You need to stop." I don't want to hear any more about Myers' obsession. Aliens don't exist. They don't abduct people in the night and stick magic wands up their butts. They don't leave strange scars on their victims after wiping their memories.

That's only on TV, and it's not true.

Marcy's eyes fill up with tears but she refuses to blink them away. Instead, she lets them overflow and run down her cheeks. "I don't remember anything," she says. Anders is silent. He continues his creepy, blank stare. His GQ face is as hard as a brick.

"I don't either," I grimace.

Myers opens up his mouth, presumably to drive home his alien theory, which would make so much sense in an alternate universe where aliens *do* exist, then closes it again. Finally he says, "I should remember my own eye falling out." He hooks one finger in his mouth and pulls it out with a pop. My stomach does acrobatics. Silence drapes over all of us again, and we sit quietly, nursing our collective wounds.

Suddenly, I become acutely aware of an empty feeling in my pocket and realize that my phone is gone.

"Crap. I don't know where my cell went."

"I'll call it," Myers says, but quickly realizes that his phone is gone, too.

"Pffft. All gone," Anders whispers again, but this time he splays out his long fingers like a magician who's done a cool trick.

It's not cool at all.

Marcy takes a deep, ragged breath, and more tears drip down her face. She should be happy. She's finally gotten what she's always wanted. Anders is right there with his head in her lap. Still, even I know that she doesn't want a broken Anders. She wants a bright and shiny Anders who winks at her from the basketball court after making a shot, or steals tater-tots from her tray during lunch in the Meadowfield High School cafeteria.

I reach down and rub the little triangle on my arm and try to blot out the pain. I can feel the perfect angles under my thumb like skin Braille. Burns like this one never go away. I'm branded like a cow. I'm branded for life.

Baa. Baa. BAAAAA.

A chill runs up my spine. Somewhere in the back of my skull I hear that sound—sheep crying.

Baa. Baa. BAAAAA.

Baa. BAA. BAAAAA.

BAA. BAA. BAAAAA.

Without warning a wave of nausea smashes into me with such force I almost topple over. Dark visions swim across my brain.

I see eyes—big, black eyes, looming over me, boring into me. If I didn't know any better, I'd say they're alien eyes like in Myers' stupid TV shows. Bile rises up my throat. I almost puke, but I don't. Puking right now would be the worst possible thing in a long list of really awful things.

Besides, I'm convinced those eyes aren't real. If they are, I'm not sure they're even human.

I puke anyway.

A lot.

5

"ARE YOU OKAY?"

Myers is standing next to me as I sink my feet halfway up to my shins in the muddy waters of Turner Pond. My stomach won't stop twisting and turning around my insides and little beads of sweat pop out on my forehead.

"I'm fine," I say to him, which is such a monumental lie that he looks at me with his one good eye like I've gone crazy.

I hug myself with my burning arm. "I'm fine," I say again as the cries of sheep echo in the back of my mind.

Off in the distance, a faint wail pierces the morning. I squint and look up into the sky. This time, instead of the town fire alarm, I hear the sound of police car sirens, which are completely foreign in Meadowfield.

Ours is a good town. We're good people. We don't hear police car sirens or see flashing red and blue lights, not unless it's during Meadowfield Days on the town green and there's a parade or something.

I turn and look back at Marcy, with her soft curls and beautiful face, and Anders' head in her lap. She matches my stare, so I try my best not to let my eyes do a once over. I don't want her to feel even more self-conscious about only having panties and Myers' sweatshirt to cover herself.

"Anders is bloody." I say. That's not entirely true anymore. He's still splotchy, but the water got most of it off. His clothes are another story. If he's smart, he'll bury them, but he's not anything now except close to catatonic.

"Yeah," says Myers. "And you're pukey." He reaches up and rubs his head, not where his eye is supposed to be, but along his temples. "I have a killer headache."

I step out of the water, reach down, and wipe the pond scum off my legs. Meanwhile, Marcy tilts her head up to the sun. Her nostrils flair a tiny bit. "I don't understand how we can't remember anything," she says. "And I feel awful."

I lick my lips. "Try puking," I say, being totally honest. "I think I feel a little better." Of course my brain is still all fluffy but it doesn't do any good to state the obvious.

Another police car siren slices through the morning.

"I should be there," says volunteer fire-nerd Myers, even though none of us even know where *'there'* is. Something's happening outside of The Maze—something not right—but something's happening inside The Maze, too, and I suddenly feel an urgent need to get away from Turner Pond, Prince Richard's Maze, and all the dead leaves.

I want to feel pavement underneath my feet.

"I'm going to get something for you and Anders to wear," I tell Marcy. Then I look over at Myers. "There's an eyepatch on a coconut in my bedroom," I tell him.

"The creepy pirate one with the painted teeth?"

"Yeah," I say. "The creepy pirate one with the painted teeth."

"But what about my parents?" he whimpers. "I'm so screwed."

"Tell them the truth," I say. "You lost your eye. That's the truth."

I take a deep breath and slowly let it fill up my insides. I do it again, three, maybe four times. A third siren swirls through the morning, this time high and fast. It comes and then it's gone.

We all look at each other, and Anders closes his eyes really tight and puts his hands over his ears.

He's broken somehow. Someone or something has reached inside his brain and scooped out the part that's supposed to be Anders Stephenson, leaving him a mushy mess.

Pffft. All gone.

"I'm going," I tell them all. I roll my shirt sleeve down over my arm, mostly to cover the burning triangle, and start walking away from them down Little Loop.

"My parents are gone for the weekend," Marcy calls out after me, like I don't already know that the Coles went to the Indian Casino down in Connecticut for their anniversary. They decided that Marcy was finally old enough to stay alone and not get into any trouble. They were wrong. "You know how to break in?"

I don't turn around as I keep walking. "In the garage," I say loud enough for her to hear. "On the ledge under the steps." Then I keep going, wanting to get away from my friends, Turner Pond, and everything.

Five minutes later, after some twists and turns, I reach the chain that crosses the exit to The Maze and Meadowfield Street beyond. There are cars going back and forth, because to the left of the maze is the entrance to the highway and Springfield's dinky skyline off in the distance. I take a deep breath, step over the chain, and take a right onto the sidewalk.

It's almost three miles to home. I walk quickly, but not too quickly.

I don't want anyone wondering why I'm out for a stroll on a Saturday morning without my friends and with a confused look on my face.

I snort.

No one in Meadowfield would even care about me or what I'm doing.

As I walk, my thoughts wander back to the sheep. We don't have farm animals in Meadowfield. We're a big, square patch of suburbia where you can't even have a rabbit hutch in your backyard. I only know that because Myers had a pet rabbit a couple years back that stunk up his basement so much that his parents made him keep it outside in a wooden hutch. His next-door neighbor, Mrs. Horowitz, complained to the town that it was unsightly. Myers ended up having to get rid of the hutch, his rabbit, and everything, and he moped around for weeks.

But sheep?

There aren't any sheep for miles—not until you cross over the border to Connecticut and hit Tobacco Alley where all the farms are.

So why are they in my head?

Why?

I close my eyes and start walking a little faster, but not too fast. In a town where everyone knows everyone, I feel paranoia clinging to my insides like I did something wrong and now everyone knows what I did.

I can't keep my eyes closed, though. When I do, I see big black orbs staring at me again.

Huge.

Thankfully, I don't scrunch up my face when I start crying. The tears start to flow. For all I know, they're glistening on my face in the sunlight, and I look like one of those diamond-covered vampires.

That, or some other kind of monster.

6

I MANAGE TO MAKE it almost all the way home—down Meadowfield Street, past the library, through a cluster of neighborhoods where the wealthy of the wealthy live in big brick colonials, alongside Elm Knoll Park, and almost in sight of Meadowfield High School before the inevitable happens and I run into someone I know.

"You look like shit, man," says Grafton Applewhite. He's on a mountain bike, wearing soccer cleats and a Meadowfield soccer uniform. It's Saturday morning. There must be a game.

"Whatever," I say. I can't think of anything else worthwhile to let slip from my lips. I'm not friends with Grafton Applewhite, but he plays sports with Anders, and Anders has made it crystal clear to anyone and everyone that his friends aren't to be messed with, no matter what.

Grafton used to be a total dick in junior high school. I remember he labeled me *'lard ass'* once, then called me out to the dunes after school because he said he wanted to beat the fat out of me.

Back then, I almost shit my pants. I didn't know how to fight, but when you get called out to the dunes after school, you have to go. If you don't, you're a pussy for life.

I remember hiding in the bathroom during F Block—Social Studies—afraid to leave the building once the bell rang. Thankfully, the ceiling started echoing with the sounds of a downpour outside. By the time last period ended and I got up the courage to leave the bathroom and school, I knew full well that the dunes would be empty. Everyone who normally gathered there wasn't interested in seeing blood drain away in the rain.

The next day, with my heart pounding in my chest most of the day for fear that the dunes were still looming in my future, Anders got to Grafton Applewhite in the gym locker room before Grafton ever got to me, and punched him in the head.

Grafton never bothered me after that.

But today, of all days, he seems like he wants to be friends.

"I mean, you really look like shit," he says. "Just saying."

"Bad night," I mutter and keep walking. Grafton pumps his bike a couple times to keep pace with me.

"No kidding," he chuckles. "I saw you at The Stumps last night. You were pretty wasted."

The Stumps.

The Stumps?

We were at The Stumps?

After the freak storm in 2011, there were so many downed trees that the town took the far end of Miller Road, where it dead ends near the dump, and piled everything there. After a while, the woods behind the enormous pile of uprooted debris became known as The Stumps—a prime party spot.

"I don't remember being at The Stumps," I tell Grafton as I reach over with my right arm and rub my left. It's true. I don't remember anything about The Stumps, or last night, or being hammered like Grafton says I was.

Grafton bursts out laughing, and all of a sudden I want to be back in junior high school again so I can be the one to call *him* out to the dunes and beat his face into a bloody mash. "No doubt," he snorts. "You, Anders, that weird kid you hang out with and . . ." Grafton licks his lips. "And Marcy Cole."

The burning in my left arm starts throbbing, and I bite my lip.

"Okay," I say, trying to figure out a way to tell Grafton to get the hell away from me. I'm confused and in pain, and all I want to do is get home and find clean clothes for Anders and Marcy, and a coconut's eyepatch for Myers.

"Must have been something good," he says. "Share next time." Then he pushes on the pedals of his bike, speeds up, and heads off toward the high school parking lot and the playing fields beyond.

I watch him go, still all gummed up and confused.

The Stumps.

We were at The Stumps.

The four of us—me, Marcy, Anders and Myers—aren't exactly part of the popular crowd. Anders has his jock friends, and I'm sort of friendly with some of the kids in chorus, but Marcy and Myers stick to themselves or to us. We're not Stumps-kids. We may want to be, but we're not.

Still, even if we were at The Stumps last night, and even if we were wasted, there would be something in my head telling me it's true. There would be a little electrical synapse firing off a tiny loop of brain-film that would play over and over again, making me realize that, yeah, we were there, and we were partying like the jocks and the cheerleaders and anyone else who considers themselves part of the popular crowd.

But there's nothing.

All there is inside my fuzzy memory is big, black eyes and a soundtrack right out of a slaughter house.

My tears start to bubble up again and I let them have their way.

Drippity drip.

Drip.

Drip.

Drip.

7

BERYL KAHN IS A therapist, but she's not, really.

Beryl, which my mother demands that I call her instead of *'mom,'* is an intuitive counselor. That's a fancy way of saying she's a psychic, at least in her own mind.

She also has a fancy way of parenting, meaning she doesn't parent at all. She's too busy getting high, or meeting with desperate clients, or meditating, to worry about something as trivial as a kid.

We have money. Everyone in Meadowfield has money, but Beryl Kahn's money comes from a trust fund that my grandparents set up a long time ago. If not for an endless supply of cash from my dead grandma and grandpa, we wouldn't be living on Primrose Lane.

We'd be living in a shelter.

As I slowly walk up Primrose Lane to our sprawling ranch house with the curved driveway and the purple door, and pumpkins strategically placed on the front porch because Halloween is Beryl's favorite holiday, I briefly wonder how I'm going to explain to her where I was last night.

Then I realize that no explanations will be necessary. We have a *'don't ask, don't tell'* policy in our household. It's really more like a *'don't ask, don't care'* sort of thing.

The front door is unlocked. I'm hoping that I can quietly slip in and hang a left down the bedroom hallway without having to stop and engage Beryl in any kind of conversation. Hopefully, she's all the way in the den so she won't hear me.

Hoping is for suckers.

Beryl is in the kitchen, drinking her millionth cup of coffee for the day. All her holistic vitamins are spread out on the table in front of her next to her giant pill box. Her hair is rolled up into a ball on the top of her head, with fabric and chopsticks holding it together. I don't know what you call the outfit she's wearing. It's tie-dyed, flowy, and psychedelic.

She looks like a carnival gypsy.

I at least have to say *'hi,'* to her. Niceties are still upheld in our household. There's no reason to be rude.

"Good morning," she says absentmindedly before I have a chance to greet her first. She picks up an amber bottle and shakes out a handful of vitamins. "One, two, three," she murmurs as she drops them into her huge pill box which should probably be used for nails instead of pills.

"Beryl," I say back, and slightly nod my head.

My mother and I are random talkers. Nothing we ever say to each other is too deep. She doesn't look at me. Instead she picks up another bottle of pills, lowers her trendy, progressive glasses, and stares at the label. After a moment, she tilts her head backward and holds her arm out as far as she can.

"St. John's Wart," she muses. "I wonder if St. John knows his legacy is an ugly growth?" I don't say anything back. Beryl is bizarre. I don't feel like being bizarre this morning. "Oh, well," she shrugs. Then she unscrews the cap and shakes another handful of pills out onto her palm.

In most households, someone my age staying out all night would probably constitute at least a *'where in the hell have you been?'* or an old fashioned *'you're grounded.'* That doesn't happen here.

Nothing happens.

I slowly shift from one foot to the other, searching for words to fill her awkward lack of interest. Finally, I come up with something. "I heard the town fire alarm," I say. "And police cars."

"Hmm?" she mumbles. She's no longer with me anymore. She's lost in whatever fucked-up labyrinth is inside her head. "Yes," she says. "Coffee is on the stove."

I'm used to her perpetual attention deficit disorder so I mumble a thank you, turn, and walk out of the kitchen, rubbing my triangle-burned arm again. I don't even stop in the pink-tiled bathroom to strip off my clothes, pee, and weigh myself, which has become an obsessive morning ritual over the past year.

It would be great to say I have a love affair with the scale because of sports.

It's more about fat.

I was—fat.

I probably still am. Everyone says differently, but I don't care about everyone. I care about the scale.

Somewhere down deep I can intellectualize that I've already reached and surpassed that magic 70-pounds-lost mark and I'm going to have to stop soon. If I lose any more, I might get lost along with it.

Certainly the idea of slipping away would be a welcomed relief today, but the strange turn of events that have occurred since I first opened my eyes in Prince Richard's Maze are weighing heavily on me.

I can't even begin to imagine how they must be weighing on my friends.

My bedroom door has a 'Keep Out' sign on it. My mother encourages free expression. Lately, her indifference to the fact that we share the same air has caused me to express myself a little too overtly with that sign. I don't know why it matters. She doesn't care.

She never has.

Once inside my bedroom, I turn and lock the door. Beryl says that every human being deserves their own private space. To that end, she installed a lock for me a long time ago. Maybe she knows what it is that I do behind that locked door at least a dozen times a day, or maybe that's why she put the lock on in the first place.

What does it matter?

With a locked door between us, I slowly sit on my bed.

The mattress is dented from too many days eating Tasty Cakes in the exact same spot, but there is less of me now, so the dent doesn't press down to the springs like it used to do.

The stinging on my arm starts calling attention to itself again, right as I hear another police car off in the distance.

What's going on? All I know is that I can't stay here and wallow in brain fog with my friends stuck in The Maze. I get up, go to the shelf, and pull down the pirate coconut that my grandparents gave me when I was little. The eyepatch it sports is held in place with a black, elastic cord. I easily peel it off and fold it into my pocket. Then I make a mental note of what I need—something for Marcy to cover herself with and clothes for Anders.

I stand up and go over to my desk, piled with books for school and applications for next fall. I'm going to leave Meadowfield and Beryl Kahn and go someplace far away for college. I'm thinking Stanford. Beryl went there and Grandpa went there, too. Palo Alto is so far to the left of Meadowfield, Massachusetts that it might as well be in another country.

Of course I'm not worried about the grades, and thankfully I'm not worried about paying for college either.

Beryl's not the only one with a trust fund.

I have one, too.
Thanks for thinking of me, old dead people.
Thanks for giving me a way out.

8

TWO MINUTES LATER I'm in the pink bathroom again, throwing up and dizzy. I guess that's why I don't hear the phone ring. By the time I wipe my mouth and gargle, Beryl is on the other side of the door.

"Mrs. Myers is on the phone," she says.

Something ugly crawls out of my stomach and lodges itself in my throat.

"I'm in the bathroom," I mutter.

"I told her. She's insistent."

I pull open the door. My mother is standing there, thinking about lint, or kittens, or her next client, and obviously bothered that she had to expend the effort to answer the phone.

I take it from her and gingerly put it to my ear because I'm starting to brew another headache.

"Hello?" I say.

"Weston, this is Mrs. Myers, Robbie's mother." Right off the bat, I cringe. I've known Mrs. Myers my entire life. I've known Myers my entire life. I don't understand why his mother needs to announce herself. She's so goddamned proper, it's unnerving, especially when she's not proper at all.

"Hi," I say, then wait for an onslaught to pour out of her mouth. Nothing is ever easy with Myers' mother. Everything is an ordeal. Everything is high drama. Propriety can disappear in a heartbeat.

"Can you please tell me where my child is?" she snaps. I can feel the hair on the back of my neck start to prickle. To say that Mrs. Myers has an anger management issue is like saying that a shark has a carnivore issue. Anger is a way of life with Myers' mother. That's how she copes, I guess.

It must be so hard to be a doctor's wife.

"Um . . ." That's about all I get out before the bubbling pot of anger on the other end of the line starts to clink and clatter and just plain explode.

"You're supposed to be his best friend, Weston. I don't know what the rules are in your home. I don't know what Beryl is thinking, but the rules in my house are that my child is supposed to be under my roof by 11:00 at night, no exceptions, and if he's not under my roof then he better have . . ." Her voice starts rising in octave and pitch. "He better have a fucking good reason for not being here, because I fucking do everything around here and no one helps, and the least thing my fucking child can fucking do is to have the fucking courtesy to call me and tell me where the fuck he is."

I stand there in the doorway to the pink bathroom, my arm burning and my head aching, waiting for her tirade to end. Her outbursts are usually short and punctuated with four letter words that would make most truckers blush. Still, I have to listen to the litany of profanity spew out of her because that's how she deals with life.

Fuck. Fuck. Fuck. Fuck. Fuck.

"Um . . ." I say again, but she barks back at me lightning fast.

"Are you there, Weston? Are you even listening to me?"

"Myers told you we were all staying at Marcy's house," I hear myself lie.

"What?" she snaps, and this is the part I'm an expert at. The truth is, Mrs. Myers is about as effective as Beryl at keeping track of things.

"At Marcy Cole's," I say as quietly and evenly as I can, even though I can feel that it would be so easy to tell Myers' mother to go shove it along with her sewer of a mouth. "We told you yesterday," I continue, conjuring up an image of exactly what Myers' mother was doing yesterday after school when I stopped by his house a few hours before my memory disappeared. "We told you while you were making cookies for his Boy Scout troop."

She had been baking several batches at once when Myers and I walked into the kitchen. She immediately starting yelling that she didn't have enough and we couldn't have any, and that we were making a mess of her kitchen and had to leave.

Poor Myers.

I hear a deafening silence on the other end of the phone as Mrs. Myers tries frantically to remember the nonexistent series of events I laid out for her, then weigh whether or not she actually spaced what I told her, and she's wrong.

Not that it matters. She's one of those people who will never, ever admit to being wrong, so I sit and wait on the phone for her manic brain to do whatever machinations it needs to perform so she can say what comes next.

"You tell my child to pick up his goddamned phone," she hisses at me.

As muddied as I am, I'm quick as a whip. "I think he might have turned it off," I tell her. "We stayed up really late last night. I only stopped back at home to get a change of clothes."

She's quiet on the other end of the line. I know Myers' mother well enough to know that she is rapidly moving from anger, to denial, to some sort of state where the events of the last minute never happened in the first place.

I'm right.

Her voice softens and slows. "So how are your college applications coming?" she asks like she didn't just swear at me a zillion times.

"I'm sorry," I say. "My mother needs to talk to me. I have to go." Then I hang up on Mrs. Myers with a click of a button, which at the moment is about as satisfying as taking a good, long dump. "Bitch," I mumble under my breath, hoping that releasing that little observation will somehow paint over how terrible I feel.

It doesn't help.

I need some of her special four-letter-words to do the trick, but even then, I know that all the swearing in the world won't fix what is going on with the four of us.

Maybe nothing will.

9

I'M ALMOST OUT of the front door when Beryl says, "Why are there sirens?" She is back at the kitchen table, her pill bottles in front of her, looking out the kitchen window at Anders' house across the street.

"I don't know," I tell her as I roll my shirt down to cover the Band-Aid I've put over the tiny triangle on my arm. Little dabs of Neosporin are still seeping out from underneath. No matter. They'll dry soon.

"Must be a fire," she says dreamily with her eyes half-lidded.

"Must be," I echo, waiting for Beryl to say something else, anything else. Maybe I'm waiting for her to reach down deep into her pool of nonexistent psychic energy and ask me why there is a triangle burned into my arm.

Nothing.

"Hmmm," she says.

"Hmmm," I reply. Then I'm out the door.

I'm carrying my backpack that I bought last year from L.L. Bean with the money my mother gave me for Hanukkah. We don't really celebrate the holidays at my house, mostly because there's only the two of us. We light the candles, though, and say meaningless prayers in Hebrew that we don't even know how to translate. Then, on the last night of those very long eight nights, Beryl usually gives me a check for $250.

That's what I used to buy the canvas and leather backpack that I'm now carrying. It's empty, except for the eyepatch that I took out of my pocket.

I'm wearing a different oxford shirt from last night and a different pair of jeans, but I look the same.

I wish I could say that I feel the same, but I don't.

I walk over the grass on our front lawn, perfectly kept by our lawn man, Mr. Rozelle, and cross the street to Anders' house. My brain is still filled with clouds and I don't know quite what I'm going to say to his mother, but Mrs. Stephenson is so preoccupied with her own life that I probably won't have to say much. She's not like Beryl in the absolute absence of the knowledge that she has a child. Mrs. Stephenson is more consumed with the fact that someone in her socio-economic status should be dating in the Ivy League pool.

In truth, she's more apt to be screwing the guy who's cleaning the pool.

Ever since Anders' dad left, Mrs. Stephenson has dated a lot. Non-bloody Anders often jokes that his mother probably owns stock in many of the dating sites on line. Bloody Anders probably just wants his mommy right now.

That's a scary thought.

As I walk across the front lawn of Anders persimmon-colored house, I hear the gravelly sound of tires on pavement and turn to see Mrs. Stephenson's red corvette maneuvering up the street and into her driveway.

She watches me watch her, her oversized sunglasses covering three-fourths of her thin face framed in blond. I stop, not quite sure what's going to come out of my mouth once she gets out of her car. There are the unlikely scenarios in which I blabber all over the place that Anders is stuck in The Maze with Myers and Marcy, and all he is wearing is underwear because his clothes are covered in blood, all the way to a litany of colossal lies, each one more improbable than the last.

What finally comes out is this: "Is Anders home?"

Mrs. Stephenson is a talker. She's always been a talker. She completely evades my question as she gets out of the car, reaches in the back seat and pulls out a huge plastic bag filled with dry cleaning.

I don't even know why she gets her clothes dry cleaned. It's not like she works.

"West, have I told you how good you look?"

"Thanks," I say, feeling a little uncomfortable. I don't want to have this conversation again.

"I mean, really," she says. "You were getting quite out of hand." In translation, that means she is fully aware that I was enormous and approaching the point where one of those shows about fat teens might be interested in me.

"Thanks," I say again. Any more than one word responses might get Anders' mother talking more, and I don't want to talk. "Is Anders home?" I ask again. It's a woefully poor attempt to try and hide the fact that Anders isn't home at all, and hasn't been since yesterday, but I hit pay dirt, like I did with Myers' fuckity-fuck-fuck-fuck of a mother.

"I'm sure he's still sleeping," she tells me, then winks. "I didn't come home last night."

If Myers were here, he'd grumble something to me about going deaf. No one wants to hear that Mrs. Stephenson *'got some'* last night, least of all her son's friends. A messed up image of two raisins smooshing themselves together bubbles to the surface.

Gross.

I don't know how Anders can stand it. His dad isn't much better. Every time Mr. Stephenson comes into town, which is becoming less and less of a habit, the women on his arm are getting younger and younger.

I guess some guys would think that's cool. Anders doesn't. He's embarrassed by his father. For that matter, he's embarrassed by his mother, too.

"Can I go wake him up?" I hear myself say.

"Good luck," Mrs. Stephenson says as she tosses me the house key dangling from a pink, rhinestone-encrusted fob. I'm totally unprepared and not even a little coordinated, so the fob hits me in the chest and falls to the ground. "Sorry," she laughs.

A real mother—a mother who is more concerned about her son instead of finding Mr. Right for the second time—would realize that it's Saturday morning and Anders has soccer practice on Saturday mornings.

I tuck that little tidbit of knowledge away because I'm going to need it soon.

Inside Anders' house, I dash through the foyer and down the hallway to his bedroom. I wrinkle my nose. His room reeks of sweat and guy shit, like the locker rooms at school. With seconds to spare, I shove my arm into the depths of his laundry basket and pull out a change of stinking clothes then stuff everything into my backpack and turn around, just in time to meet Mrs. Stephenson in the hallway.

"I'm so stupid," I say pulling the virtual tidbit back out. "He's at soccer practice."

A dim expression passes over her face. She knows that she's supposed to be on top of things like that, but she's not.

"Oh," she says and shrugs. Then she gets this wistful look in her eyes. I guess she's thinking that she could have gone a couple more rounds with Mr. Whoever-last-night-was, instead of coming home for nothing. What did she think she was going to do for Anders, anyway? Make him waffles?

"I'll catch up with him later," I say as I hand her back the house keys and leave before her brain can even come up with the notion that

Anders never came home last night in the first place.

As the brisk morning air slaps me in the face in front of Anders' house, a funny thought slips through my head.

It must be hard to be a good parent. It's too bad that most of ours will never know.

10

WE'RE COVERED for last night.

Beryl couldn't give a shit where I was. Anders' mother was too busy getting laid, and Mrs. Myers bought the whole idea that he slept over at Marcy's with the rest of us. As for Marcy's mom and dad, they're down at one of the casinos.

No one will ask where we were, why we didn't come home, or if blood washes out of clothing easily.

Dodging a very large and potentially ugly bullet, I cross back to my side of the street and walk up the gentle climb of Primrose Lane to Marcy's house.

The Coles are actually pretty cool. They're involved, but not too involved, and they hover, but not too much like Myers' parents. Marcy has just the right balance of parental supervision and freedom. That's why her parents let her stay home alone this weekend even though there's some sort of stupid law in Massachusetts that says you can't leave your kids home overnight and unattended until they are seventeen and a half.

Marcy had her seventeenth birthday this past May so she's close enough that her parents gave her a free pass last night.

Mr. and Mrs. Cole trust Marcy and they trust me, Myers, and Anders. We're the good guys. We're safety in numbers.

Marcy's house isn't a sprawling ranch like some of the others on Primrose Lane. The dark, wood-stained structure is set back from the road and covered by overgrown bushes, but the foliage still can't hide the paradox behind it.

Sometimes it hurts my head to look at Marcy's house. I can't really tell what shape it is. There's a huge, round room on the second floor that hangs out over the first floor like one of Myers' fictional flying saucers perched on top of a beer can.

Mr. Cole is an architect. I think he designed it.

Mrs. Cole is a therapist, like Beryl, but that's where the comparison ends. She's actually a real psychologist, with a real job, and real clients who have issues, like cheating on their spouses or drinking way too much. I'm only privy to some of the gory details because Mrs. Cole shares the crazier ones with Marcy, and Marcy shares them with us.

How else would I know that old Mrs. Easterbrook, my middle school Social Studies teacher, refuses to put her dementia-ridden husband, who's prone to wandering, in a nursing home? Although nobody realizes it, she's been using her dog's invisible fence to keep him from leaving the yard.

I think she puts its collar around his ankle.

That's messed up, but there are a lot of messed up people in Meadowfield. Coked out dads, bored housewives, cheaters, cybersex addicts, you name it, they live here. You don't have to dig too deep to find them. They lurk right beneath the surface.

Around the back of the Coles' garage is a door that's almost hidden by all of the shrubbery. The door is never locked, so that's where I go.

Inside the garage is Mr. Cole's BMW and Marcy's beater car. I guess a friend of Mr. Cole's sold it to Marcy's dad really cheap, so she has wheels. It's big, way bigger than most cars these days, and probably older than me, but it's perfect for Marcy. She's usually our designated driver when we go out—not because we party, but because her car is large and roomy. Even if we did party, she would probably be our designated driver anyway.

She can't drink because of the stuff she takes.

'*I saw you at The Stumps last night. You were pretty wasted,*' Grafton Applewhite said. '*You, Anders, that weird kid you hang out with and . . . and Marcy Cole.*'

His words slip inside one ear, momentarily coil around my brainstem then slip out the other. There's no way Marcy could have been hammered last night. Her meds are way too important for her to screw up everything with drinking. She's too diligent about things like that.

As I stare at the dull green hood of Marcy's monster car, I try to remember being chauffeured around town last night, but I can't. There's a gaping, black hole in my memory where we should all live, partying at The Stumps and getting wasted like Grafton Applewhite said.

Nothing comes except for the faint mewling of farm animals and a vague flash of deep, dark eyes.

I lick my lips, turn, and almost fall over as another wave of dizziness rolls over me, not quite as strong as before. The room tilts sideways. My legs get wobbly for a moment, but I manage to steady myself against the hood of Marcy's car.

Crap.

My triangle burns.

I have to get back to my friends at Prince Richard's Maze.

I have to get Anders and Marcy some clothes and Myers an eyepatch.

I have to not feel like shit.

As the wave subsides, I manage to bend down next to the three short steps that lead to a door into the house. Behind them is a little ledge, and on the ledge is a key. I've known the key has been there since forever. That's one of those shared secrets between the four of us.

Another is that Dr. Myers keeps vintage dirty magazines filled with girls dressed in skimpy nurse and cheerleader uniforms in his sock drawer underneath dozens of colored socks rolled into doughnuts; and Beryl always, always, always has pot in the cookie jar in our kitchen. I'd love to say that Anders' mother has secrets too, but she's way too much of an open book and that's one novel that none of us want to read.

I curl my fingers around the Coles' house key, stand, and slip it into the lock. The door clicks. Seconds later I'm inside the lower level below the saucer-shaped second floor.

11

NORMALLY, ANYONE stepping into Marcy's house would immediately freeze after one look around, strain to hear if a burglar is still creeping around in the upstairs space ship, then frantically scramble for their cell and call the police. Normal, however, isn't exactly normal in Marcy's house.

Marcy's parents are slobs. They don't have tuna fish sandwiches hidden under the pillows in the lower-level rec room couch, or cat poop everywhere. They're just messy like you wouldn't expect adults to be messy. In the gloom of the Coles' rec room I see piles of unfolded laundry, stacks of books, and Mr. Cole's NordicTrack, which Mrs. Cole calls his coat rack. There are shirts hanging on it and a couple of boxes overflowing with papers and cardboard tubes leaning up against the underused equipment.

Marcy's goldfish, Tyrone, is floating in his goldfish-shaped bowl on a stone coffee table in front of a lumpy leather couch. The couch used to be upstairs but there are so many burn marks marring the leather, it now lives down here. The current version of Tyrone in his bowl has been around for about two years. There's always been a Tyrone, but even Marcy knows that Tyrone the first, the second, and the third were all discretely flushed and replaced over the years in an elaborate scheme to ignore death.

There are a few pictures of Marcy's brother, Tate, on the wall, but not many. Tate's absence is something else that Marcy's family ignores. When asked, her parents say he's away, instead of saying that he's earned multiple stints up at the Buckland Retreat over the border in Vermont and is currently a long-term resident of The Bellingham School.

In the middle of the room, surrounded by more boxes and bags, is a wrought iron spiral staircase that goes up to the second level. We all used to love running up and down those stairs when we were kids. Now, the stairs are just another place for the Coles to leave junk. Every third or fourth step has something on it.

I take a deep breath. Somehow it seems like a monumental task to grab on to the banister and pull myself up the staircase. I grit my teeth and make the climb. Seconds later, I'm upstairs in the saucer of Marcy's house, which is equally as messy as what lies beneath.

The open concept layout is a little unnerving. There are no hallways to slink down, away from a mother who is so disinterested in you that even the act of slinking goes unnoticed. There is minimal furniture, though the mess fills the void left by a lack of seating, and there are windows everywhere.

On the kitchen table, which is almost directly in front of me, is a huge pizza box, probably an extra-large from Rinaldo's over on Meadowfield Street. I know Candy Rinaldo from school. She's tiny, with little black eyes and a pointed chin. Myers says she looks like a ferret, but I secretly think that Myers gets a boner every time he sees her.

After all, like his shirt implies, he *is* a master baiter.

I casually walk over to the pizza box in the kitchen and lift the lid. There are a few cold pieces left and my stomach threatens to lurch again. I don't know why, but I recall the recent taste of tomato sauce and mozzarella in my mouth.

Was I here last night? I don't know.

Did I have pizza with Anders, Myers, and Marcy before everything faded to black? I don't know. It's far from likely, though. Pizza is on a long list of poisons I no longer allow to pass my lips.

I close my eyes and try to remember, but doing so is about as futile as trying to make Mr. and Mrs. Cole keep a clean house. After a moment I shrug, turn left and walk halfway around the saucer, past an office and a bathroom, to Marcy's bedroom. The door is cracked and I slip inside.

I shake my head. Marcy's room is exactly how I picture the child of a therapist's bedroom to look. It's a mecca of bizarre self-expression with psychedelic posters and slips of papers with weird sayings on them plastering the walls. Marcy likes to write things down and she likes to keep the words forever so she can always look back on them and remember. She also has half a dozen old oil paintings she did when we were all kids and took lessons from Mrs. Welling over near the shopping center. We all have the same bad masterpiece hanging on our walls—a wine bottle with a fat apple sitting next to it. There are stuffed animals everywhere. Marcy's a sucker for stuffed animals. Sitting on a rocking chair is a giant panda that Anders won at Riverside Amusement Park last year. Marcy begged him for it, so he gave it to her.

And all of it, *all of it*, is surrounded by a sea of laundry—and when I say a sea, I mean an ocean. Marcy's entire bedroom floor, from one end to the other, is carpeted in clothing. There are bras and jeans and flouncy tops. There are shoes everywhere, and books from school, and a laptop floating in the middle of the chaos, its cord draped up and across her bureau and plugged into the wall.

I don't even know where to start.

I mentally picture Marcy with her beautiful face and curly hair and try to imagine what she wears. She has on a top already, but she might need another one. She's wearing panties without any socks or shoes, but she might want another pair of panties and she needs something on her feet.

"Damn," I whisper under my breath. The truth is I don't know what Marcy would want and it probably doesn't matter anyway. I reach down and grab a pair of jeans, gingerly finger a pair of undies, and reach for a sweater that seems light enough for the weird weather we've been having. As I roll it all into a ball, I see a pair of shoes slowly sinking into the sea of clothing. I think I remember Marcy sometimes wearing them, so I grab those, too.

As I silently turn in a circle, making sure I haven't forgotten anything, a phone goes off and I jump.

The receiver rings four times before Mrs. Cole's business answering machine picks up.

"Thank you for calling the offices of Dr. Darlene Cole," echoes a calm smooth voice throughout the house. "If this is an emergency, please hang up and call 911. Otherwise, please leave your name, number, and the time you called, and I will be glad to get back to you as soon as I am able."

I wait for the beep then hear frantic chatter vomit into thin air.

"Darlene, are you there? Darlene? Pick up the phone. Please. I can't believe it. I can't believe something like this is happening right here in Meadowfield." I don't recognize the voice on the other end of the line. I'm sure it's one of Mrs. Cole's clients. The woman sounds like she's about to become unhinged and people who become unhinged are one of Marcy's mother's specialties.

"Darlene, please," begs the woman. "I don't . . . I don't know if I can handle this. Things like this don't happen here. People don't kill here. People don't kill here and hide the bodies in their basements." The woman on the other end sucks in a deep glut of air. "I can see them pulling them out in body bags right now. Christ, they're right across the street from me. Oh God." The woman starts crying again. Her sobs are so painful that it makes me hurt inside. Then she squeaks a little like she's being squeezed really hard. "What if . . . what if my Sandy's there? What if that . . . that man took Sandy and did horrible things to her?" Her words trail off and all I hear is bubbly sniffles and snot-filled snorts.

Sandy.

Sandy.

Sandra Berman?

Fuck me. What is she talking about? I take in a deep breath, dangerously close to how that woman is breathing into the answering machine.

Sandra Berman ran away when we were fourteen. That was three years ago. I didn't know her all that well but she seemed nice enough.

One day she was there in the cafeteria at school, and the next she was gone.

Sandra Berman ran away from home.

Didn't she?

12

HER HOUSE IS ON Covington Circle. No one I know has stepped inside it since Sandra Berman disappeared, so it doesn't seem quite right to call the huge, white colonial with the faux southern columns Sandy's house anymore.

It's the Berman house, or the house where that girl who ran away from home used to live.

That house, with its pillars and in-ground swimming pool, sits on the other side of the dingle near the Meadowfield golf course. We used to laugh at that name—the dingle—when we were kids, but the swampy patch of forest that cuts through the center of town has always been called that.

At this very moment, a woman who lives there is teetering on the edge of sanity as she watches police and firemen pull body bags out of a house across the street from her, and her daughter might be in one of them.

Sandy.

Sandra.

Sandra Berman.

Now I know why the alarms in town went off this morning. Now I know why there were sirens.

Damn Myers and his obsessive imagination with aliens, government conspiracies, and all things creepy. If it weren't for his incessant chatter, I wouldn't know that body bags mean a murder house, and a murder house means someone super scary doing the murdering.

Images of infamous killers—the worst of the worst—slosh around inside my skull even though they have no business being there. There's that man out in Chicago who dressed like a clown even though he had a famous actor's name. He lured dudes into his house, killed them, and buried them in his basement. What about the freak who injected household cleaning solutions into his victims' brains to try and turn them into living zombies, but ended up eating them instead?

I feel sick, but the serial killers keep coming.

I remember hearing about the guy with the creepy eyes who made his followers cut up a pregnant lady back in the sixties. That one I know. Manson—like the musician who wears white contacts and eyeliner, but nothing like him at all. Manson's still around. He keeps asking parole boards to set him free, and they thankfully keep saying no.

Then there's lampshade guy. His shades were made from skin taken from people.

I shudder, but the Myers in my head won't stop.

Eileen Woronos. I only remember her because we talked about her murder spree in Contemporary History. Women aren't supposed to be serial killers, but she was. David Berkowitz was, too. He told the police that a talking dog made him do it, and Ted something or other, who looked like a teacher or a coach, or someone you wouldn't mind looking like yourself when you grow up, killed for the thrill of it all.

Every few years a new murderer pops up right in the middle of the most unlikely of places, and now that place is Meadowfield. My perfect, prim, and oh so proper town has just had a Band-Aid ripped off a deep, ugly, festering wound right in its heart, and the thing underneath is unthinkable.

As I stand motionless in the silence of Marcy's house, the echo of Mrs. Berman's frantic message and all that it implies still ringing in my ears, I momentarily forget about the growing horror around me, and instead, focus on the horror that is happening to me and my friends.

We've experienced something truly terrifying, but now no one will even care because there is something bigger and badder descending on Meadowfield, and I'm starting to think that monsters are real.

Seconds later, I am back in Marcy's bedroom, fishing around her desk for her car keys. They are surprisingly easy to find considering nothing is easy to find in there. More seconds pass and I am down the spiral staircase, into the garage, and inside Marcy's car. I reach above my head and press the garage door opener clipped to the visor, turn the key in the ignition, and start the engine.

I don't even realize that I am taking her car until I am backing down the driveway.

It takes every ounce of effort I have not to palm the wheel of Marcy's boat away from Primrose Lane, down Merriweather Drive, around the dingle, past Meadowfield Middle School with its dismal memories of Grafton Applewhite's fat slurs, and head toward Covington Circle and the Berman house. I want to see. I have to see. Instead, I point Marcy's car left and head back the way I walked this morning when

I was even more confused than I am now.

I drive slowly. My eyes dart from left to right. Somehow I expect corpses to be standing in the perfectly coiffed bushes in front of the perfectly coiffed homes, wrapped in white bags with zippers down the front of them, stained brown because truly terrifying blood is never red, it's darker than that.

I stifle the urge to turn on the radio. There might be something being broadcast about what is happening on Covington Circle. I'm not sure I want to hear about it yet. I have bigger, closer, more important things to worry about, and they start with a little triangle that is still burning on my left arm.

I was branded last night with something white hot that is going to leave a permanent scar. Myers lost his eye. Marcy lost her pants. Anders lost a piece of himself and he may never find it again, and layered on top of it all is a new, fresh hell that eclipses ours. There is a gaping wound on the other side of the dingle that is only going to grow larger and angrier with each body pulled out and onto the sunny grass underneath the October sun.

Still, I need to think about my friends and what is happening to us. I can't explain any of it, and if I can't explain it, I might go bonkers.

You know what happens to people who go bonkers?

They think crazy thoughts.

They do crazy things.

They live in murder houses.

13

MYERS IS STANDING next to one of the two chained entries to Prince Richard's Maze. This particular entrance isn't on Meadowfield Street. It's on Golden Road that runs alongside the woods and dead-ends overlooking the highway.

Beryl's cousin Myrna lives near the dead-end, but Myrna and Beryl don't talk. Their feud has something to do with a nose job that happened when Myrna was sixteen, and my grandmother saying how she looked much better with it done.

I guess that implied that she didn't look good before. Thus, a verbal chasm opened up right in the middle of our family and has never closed.

Myers is hugging himself. His stick arms and pointy shoulders make him look like puberty has passed him over and left him in a weird, primordial dwarf state but without the wizened face. My head is pounding as I maneuver Marcy's car over to the side of the road and park.

"Where have you been?" he cries as I open the door.

"Dealing with your fuckity-fuck-fuck-fuck of a mother, among other things."

"She's going to freakin' murder me," he sniffs and rubs his eye hole. "Did you get the patch?"

"I got it. I got it," I tell him as I rummage around in my backpack for the black eyepatch. "Here," I say and hand him the crumpled bit of cloth.

Myers hungrily snatches it out of my hand, much like a monkey would snatch a peanut from between my fingers at the Forest Park Zoo, and quickly positions the black oval over his nonexistent eye.

He visibly exhales.

"Better?" I say, even though I don't quite get what the difference is. I once asked Myers what it felt like to have a missing eye. He told me it felt like nothing. It's only skin.

"No," he says without releasing the death hold his stick arms have around his frame. "Really. Not at all."

I exhale, too. "Things aren't right," I say. "How's your head?"

"Feels like it's going to fall off my body," he grumbles. "And don't even get me started on whatever the hell is going on with Anders and, well, you know."

"Yeah," I say. "But weirder things have been known to happen."

"Name one," he says. "I can't wrap my head around it. The last I checked, Marcy and Anders weren't a thing."

"Last I checked, they were never a thing," I say as I brush past Myers and step over the low-slung chain that leads down the path toward Big Loop and Little Loop. The truth is we've always known Marcy wanted something more, but Anders kept his distance. Otherwise all our lives would have been too weird.

Myers follows after me, chattering away about his stupid eye and our collective lack of memory. I wish he'd shut up.

"And what's going on in town?" he finally blurts out like he expects that I'm this enormous fountain of knowledge that can spew forth answers on cue.

At first, the whole idea of telling Myers about Sandra Berman and what's happening across the street from where she used to live seems so difficult that I almost don't say anything at all. I keep walking, my fingers slowly rubbing the bandage on my left arm. The stinging is still there, but I'm becoming good at not thinking about it. I have too many other things that I have to think about.

Ultimately I decide to talk, but when I open my mouth something other than the subject of Sandra Berman comes out. "Do you remember being at The Stumps?" I ask, not turning around.

"What? No," he says. "You mean where everyone parties?"

I don't expect Myers to say anything other than exactly that. Like I said, we're not the kind of kids who hang out at The Stumps. "Yeah. Do you remember anything about being there last night?"

Myers snorts. "I don't remember anything."

"Me neither," I say as I continue to walk.

"And why would any of us be at The Stumps anyway? I have less than a year left in this hellhole of a town. Why would I want to screw up my wonderful memories of Meadowfield High School by getting my face pounded in over there?"

Myers isn't kidding. The Stump crowd isn't our crowd. The Stump crowd makes fun of our crowd, except for Anders.

No one makes fun of Anders.

"I saw Grafton Applewhite," I begin.

"Hate him," Myers says. It's really hard not to hate someone who only leaves you alone because one of your best friends has imposed a moratorium on him touching you.

I lick my lips. "Yeah, well, I saw Grafton Applewhite when I was walking home and he told me that the four of us were at The Stumps last night, and we were hammered."

Myers stops. I'm still not looking at him. I want to get to Anders and Marcy as soon as I can. More importantly, my brain is so crowded without a way to process everything that's crammed inside of it, I want to shut my eyes. However, the leaves under Myers' shoes stop their kinetic crinkling which makes me stop and turn around.

"That makes no sense," Myers says. He's standing in the middle of the path with his arms still wrapped around his body, but now he's wearing that stupid eyepatch over his eye. For Myers, Halloween has come early this year.

"Tell me something I don't know." I say to him.

"I . . . I . . . that makes no sense," he says again, but his voice trails off into nothingness. He closes his good eye and furrows his brow, like he's trying to remember the essence of a dream even though everyone knows that you can't remember dreams once you wake up.

Like Anders says, they're *'Pffft. All gone.'*

Myers lets go of himself and reaches up, his thumbs rubbing his temples and his fingers splayed out so he looks like some sort of weird pirate reindeer.

"I remember," he whispers. "I remember . . ." Then Myers takes a deep, raspy breath and starts to shudder. "Big eyes," he says. "They come at night and stand at the end of your bed, and they make you get up without doing anything but staring at you, and . . . and . . ." Myers literally falls down on one knee. I don't know what to say or do.

I don't know anything.

"Myers?" I whisper, but he doesn't hear me, because now he really is in that dream that you can't remember except for the parts that you can never, ever forget.

"Put this in your mouth," he murmurs, but not to me. It's more like he's telling a story about someone else who was told to put something in their mouth.

Before I have a chance to say anything, his other leg buckles and Myers falls apart on the forest floor.

"Myers," I gasp and run back to him.

"Leave us alone," he screams as he curls into a ball, but he's not screaming at me. He's screaming at someone or something that's not there at all. Goosebumps pop up on my arm. "Leave us alone," he cries again. "I don't want to. I don't want to. I don't want to."

I don't want to either, but I have to. The wisp of a memory appears but it's still far, far away.

'*Put this in your mouth,*' the memory whispers.

'*In your mouth . . .*'

'*Your mouth . . .*'

'*. . . mouth . . .*'

14

MYERS CRIES FOR almost ten minutes. I want to be there for him even though I can't stand it when he cries, but his isn't normal crying. What he's doing is born out of some sort of terror that's way worse than being cornered in the back stacks of the library and getting a wedgie from some kid who will probably end up mopping floors in his daddy's corporation for a living.

He's crying as though a bit of his soul has been ripped away and he's never going to get it back.

I sit next to him on the path, with my knees drawn up and my arms wrapped around them. I know I should do something but I'm caught up in my own little slice of memory hell and mine is all about big black eyes.

'*They come at night and stand at the end of your bed and they make you get up without doing anything but staring at you.*'

That's what Myers said.

They.

Them.

I know who Myers is talking about but I refuse to believe any of it. Myers owns more than a few stupid tee-shirts with that big face and scary eyes staring back at you, but those kinds of monsters are his fantasy, not mine. Little gray men only three feet tall, with bulbous heads and huge black eyes supposedly abduct people at night, wipe their memories and do experiments on them. They have slits for noses and pointy chins.

They're terrifying.

But aliens didn't abduct the four of us last night. Aliens didn't steal Myers' eye, douse Anders with blood, take Marcy's clothes, and brand me with a triangle.

Little gray men didn't do this, and if they did, then we might as well fall down the nearest rabbit hole right now.

Myers is my friend, but he can also be a nut job. I remember what he's always said about what aliens do to abductees.

'*They tag you if you've been chosen. They tag you with weird scars so that they can*

find you again.'
Just like we tag sheep.
Baa. Baa. BAAAAA.
Baa. Baa. BAAAAA.
Baa. Baa. BAAAAA.

I gently rock back and forth. Not only do I now remember big, black eyes, I remember the sounds of animals, like at a petting zoo when hungry mouths are trying to devour the five-dollar box of kibble you bought.

You can't be stingy with it.

The goats get mad.

The llamas spit.

The sheep cry.

Now, everything is eyes and sheep, eyes and sheep, and all I want to do is go to sleep and wake up yesterday instead of today, when Meadowfield was a nice town in a quiet part of Massachusetts and not the nightmare it has become.

Finally, Myers slowly unfurls himself and wipes his elbow across his face. A string of snot grabs hold of his hand for a moment before letting go and dropping to the ground.

"I'm sorry," he says. "I feel sick."

I nod my head in complete understanding, then slowly get up, hold out my hand to him, and say, "Let's get Marcy and Anders and get out of here."

"Okay," he says without a smartass Myers comment to follow it up. I rearrange my backpack on my shoulder and slowly start walking down the path to where it connects with Little Loop. The sun is shining through the trees, leaving patterns of light against the forest. It occurs to me that, no matter how pretty The Maze is today, it has no right being pretty at all.

The four of us aren't pretty either. We're ugly, and the thing that is happening on the other side of town across the street from Sandra Berman's house is ugly, too. Nothing has the right to be pretty in Meadowfield today.

I walk slowly, making sure that Myers is keeping up with me and not on the verge of falling apart again. If he falls apart then maybe I'll fall apart, too. Thankfully, he doesn't. Instead he quickens his steps until he's right next to me.

After a moment of uncomfortable silence he says, "I remember eyes."

"I know," I say back.

"Big, black eyes," he says again.

"I know."

"Like in my books," he continues, but I don't want him to keep going on. I don't want to remember eyes, or sheep, or being tagged with a triangle. I can't fit things like that into my world.

Maybe we did fall down that rabbit hole after all, and we're now in a nonsensical version of Meadowfield where everything is sideways.

Somehow, I can swallow that notion more easily than I can believe that we were abducted by aliens last night. The thought of that being true is too out of this world even for Myers.

Isn't it?

15

ONCE, WHEN I WAS really young, Marcy went away to Florida with her brother, Tate, and her parents. Anders' mom and dad were still together back then and Mr. Stephenson always seemed to be lurking just out of sight. I think he didn't really like or trust kids. Maybe he thought we would pee in a corner if left unsupervised.

The Stephenson's basement was partially finished, so we used to hang out down there, playing bumper pool and video games, or sometimes pretending about stuff like little kids do.

The day that Marcy came back from Florida, Anders, Myers, and I were playing Checkers and I had winners. We didn't hear the door to the basement open at first, so Marcy was like three quarters of the way down the stairs before I even noticed that she was there.

I was so happy to see her, even though she'd only been gone for a week, that I ran up to her and gave her a big hug. I was only in third grade. It was no big deal, but Mr. Stephenson thought differently. He had been loitering in the corner of the basement tinkering on something that I didn't even bother to notice. When he saw me hug Marcy, he grabbed me by the arm and got right in my face.

"Never do that again," he screamed at me. I was stunned. Beryl never screamed. Beryl never did anything because she never cared enough.

Marcy was shocked. My face turned beet red and tears welled up in my eyes and started streaming down my face. Mr. Stephenson was so big and I couldn't figure out what I had done wrong. He loomed over me, smothering me in a cloud of anger with his fingers digging into my arm.

After what seemed like a lifetime, he let go of me and hissed, "Faggot," which I didn't understand at all, then put his hands on his hips and told us all to go home.

Later that day, when Marcy, Myers and I were all outside trading game cards that none of us are even into anymore, Anders came over and quietly sat next to me.

"My dad's moving out," he said, almost in a whisper. "Mom says I'll see him on weekends."

Marcy and Myers stared that much more intently at the cards they were holding. We were so little. How were we supposed to react? After a moment I said, "I've never had a dad. It's not so bad."

I was lying about that gaping hole in my world, but nothing would ever fill it back up so I had learned to walk around it. Still, I'll never forget that day with Mr. Stephenson in Anders' basement. He was so cruel, so mean, for no reason at all. I couldn't have been more than eight or nine. Was hugging a friend so wrong?

Memories like that stick with you forever. Every time Mr. Stephenson comes into town to see Anders and raises his hand to me from across the street like I'm some sort of long lost friend, all I think about is what he said and what he did.

Sometimes it still even stings, like the triangle on my arm is stinging now underneath its Neosporin salve.

I rub it again, trying not to think about how I'm ever going to explain why it's there.

Myers asks, "Does it hurt?"

"Yeah," I tell him, then point to the patch covering his lost eye. "Does your face hurt?"

"No," he sputters with a weird look. "Why?"

"It's killing me," I say without bothering to smile. It's a cheap shot at trying to lift the oppressive feeling that's been hanging in the air all morning.

"Wow," he says. "That's bad even for me."

"Yeah," I agree. "I know."

Minutes later we're almost on top of Turner Pond. Marcy and Anders are sitting by the water with their backs to us. They're side by side, but she doesn't have her arm around his shoulder or his around hers. They're together but alone, which only accentuates the fact that we're all together but alone today.

Marcy looks up and finds my eyes. She's been crying. Streaks of dirt have dried against her cheeks, making them look like they're painted in some weird striped makeup. Anders doesn't look up. He keeps staring at the water with a deep, dark scowl on his face. I've seen that scowl before. Mr. Stephenson wore it the day he yelled at me for hugging Marcy. Now, just like then, it's frightening.

"Why are there sirens?" Marcy asks. "What's happening?"

I don't want to answer her yet. Instead, I bend down on one knee and open up my backpack.

"Your bedroom looks like a bomb went off in it," I tell her. "I didn't know what to bring so I brought this." I hand her the clothing that I pulled from her floor along with the shoes that I saved from sinking into the muddled mass.

"Thanks," she says, although part of me thinks that if I had brought back nothing, she would have been okay with that as long as Anders is okay.

I reach in my backpack again and pull out another ball of clothing. I'm scared that all my efforts might not hide the fact that Anders was mentally gone when I left him earlier in search of clean clothes.

"I covered for you," I tell him. "Your mother was just coming in from a date or something, so she doesn't even know you didn't come home last night. I barely had time to grab anything from your room, but at least I got this." I offer him his smelly laundry clothing. I'm pretty sure the stench of sweat trumps the bloody stuff he stripped off before.

I hold the clothing out to Anders, but he doesn't take it.

"Anders?" Marcy whispers as she stands and pulls on her jeans. I try not to look at her long legs or her panties. She's Marcy. She's my friend. Friends don't stare at other friends like that. Instead I focus on Anders.

"Thanks for the clothes, West," I say for him. I barely hide the fact that there's a bit of venom in my voice, but I can't help it. "It's awesome that you walked all the way across town, covered for the four of us, got our clothes, and came all the way back."

Marcy sniffs and says, "Anders?" again, but he's still dark and brooding and staring at the water wearing nothing but his underwear.

I look up at Myers. He shrugs and does this classic Myers move that might be a little funny any other time but right now. He lifts his hand and corkscrews one finger up against the side of his head.

That's universal sign language for *'your best friend has just lost his marbles.'* I sigh and bite the inside of my cheek. None of us are equipped to handle Anders like this. We might have to tell one of our parents, or worse, the police. If we do that, all hell might break loose because nothing in the world can truly scrub all the blood away. You can never scrub away that much misery.

"I think Sandy Berman didn't run away," I whisper.

"What?" Myers and Marcy both say at the same time.

"Sandra Berman," a voice that's coming out of my mouth mutters. "Remember her?" Then, of course, I have to add something else because the truth might shock Anders out of his funk. I can be such an asshole sometimes. "I think she might have been murdered."

16

SOMETIMES WORDS can be so heavy that they sink. That's what happens. My words sink to the ground and lie there. I'm hoping Anders will reach over and pick them up, if only to hold them in his naked hands.

Thankfully, my wishful thinking pays off, if only a little.

"Sandy Berman ran away," whispers Anders in a coarse voice, low and monotone. He's still staring at the water with a face that is so much like his father's face that I don't have to imagine what Anders will look like twenty-five years from now.

He'll look like Mr. Stephenson.

I want to say something snarky about how nice it is of Anders to finally decide to join the living, but a little whisper in the back of my head tells me to bite down on my tongue and not say a word.

Marcy slightly smiles as she crouches and slips on her shoes. It occurs to me that I just announced that a girl we once knew might have been killed, but I don't think that matters to her. She's far more concerned with the fact that Anders isn't completely broken in the brain. He can talk. He can respond.

Marcy stands, runs her fingers through her curls, and shakes her head. Sunlight streams down on her from behind and makes her hair look like it's glowing. I've always known that Marcy was pretty, but she's beyond that. She's like one of those actresses in a schlocky horror film who's been running and hiding through filth and grime for days but still looks hotter than ever.

Genes. They're a funny thing.

Myers adjusts his patch and says, "What do you mean you *think* she's dead? Why would you say something like that?" Myers and I went to Hebrew School with Sandra Berman up until we were thirteen. Then we both stopped going. We couldn't take another minute of it. Myers got a whole ration of shit from his parents for quitting, but Beryl said it was my choice.

Everything has always been my choice with her. She's very Montessori that way.

I notice Anders' head slightly tilting in my direction. He's alive in there, however dim that life may be. I know we have something awful happening to the four of us, but I decide that deflection is definitely the right way to go, sort of like biting hard on your lip if you've just stubbed your toe.

One pain sometimes cancels out the other.

"The sirens," I begin. "The police cars."

"We never hear stuff like that here," says Marcy as she bends and takes the wad of smelly laundry that I handed to Anders and slowly unfolds it. She dangles a pair of jeans in front of his face. Without looking, he reaches up and takes them from her.

"So, when I was at your house," I begin. "When I was upstairs getting your stuff, the phone rang."

"Yeah?" says Myers.

I ignore him. "The answering machine picked up and it was someone for your mom."

Marcy nods and Myers says, "Yeah?" again. Sometimes it's hard not to want to hit him. I know he's one of my best friends, but still. Someone needs to hit him hard soon, over and over again, otherwise when he leaves the bubble of Meadowfield and goes out into the real world, he's never going to make it.

I continue ignoring Myers in favor of Marcy, "One of your mom's clients was crying and saying she needed to talk to her right away because she's having a nervous breakdown."

Marcy is listening, but she is far more interested in Anders, who is finally starting to stand. His underwear is still damp and it has a pinkish hue to it from of all the blood. Myers continues to stare at me, his lips slightly parted, looking every bit the part of the mouth breather he's been perfecting his entire life. Anders only stands there holding his jeans, so Marcy gently takes them from his hands, pulls a dirty pair of underwear free from the wad of laundry, and holds them out to him.

"They're dry," she whispers softly like she's at the movies and doesn't want to disturb the people who are sitting around her.

In one swift motion, Anders pulls down his wet underwear and steps out of them, right in front of Marcy and right in front of me and Myers. My mouth hangs open a little, just like Myers's. How can Anders do that in front of Marcy? Sure, we're friends and all, and maybe he's in shock or something, but, right in front of her?

She doesn't turn away. She waits for him to take the better, less wet pair of underwear from her. He holds them for a second as he stares out across the water. Then he reaches down, steps into them and pulls them up, adjusting himself when he's through. He could be anywhere—in the locker rooms at school, at the swim club we all belong to down by the meadows near the Connecticut River. He could be anywhere with a bunch of guys changing their clothes.

But he's with us.

He's with Marcy.

"So?" says Myers. He doesn't get it. He never gets any of it.

"This lady was saying that they were pulling bodies out of a house across the street from her, all wrapped in white body bags."

As Anders reaches over to take a tee-shirt that Marcy is holding out for him, I see a fire kindle in his eyes. It's the fire I normally see behind them when he's normal Anders, not broken Anders.

"What?" Myers says, as though he's heard me but is unable to process any of it because I've strung together a bunch of words that he understands the meaning of, but not when they are put in the particular order that I've put them in.

"She said she hoped her *'Sandy'* wasn't in one of those bags, because if she was, then she wouldn't be able to handle it." I feel as though I'm wielding a verbal hammer and with each word, I'm beating a verbal nail into a verbal coffin.

"Poor Mrs. Berman," Marcy whispers as she holds a pair of Anders' smelly socks. She sniffs and her eyes turn glassy.

"Sandy? Like Sandra Berman?" Myers asks, but this time he's not being annoying at all. This time the words have to be said and they have to sink in. If they do, Anders might wake up and start thinking about someone other than himself.

What's more, I need my friend in the here and now and not in some dark place on the edge of an abyss.

What finally comes out of Anders' mouth isn't exactly what I am hoping for, but it's something, and something is better than nothing.

"She blew me once," he says. "Behind the middle school." His face is mostly blank, but all I can think about is a dead girl's blue lips and Anders' little adolescent escapades.

Tears immediately well up in Marcy's eyes. She turns and walks off into the woods, leaving Anders' socks crumpled at his feet. I'm not sure if she's upset about Sandra, or upset that Anders would say such a shitty thing in front of her, especially now. It could be one or both.

None of us say anything to her as she goes, but Myers mouths, *'Marcy?'* as she slips away. He has such a pathetic look on his face he might as well be a whipped and beaten dog.

Then Anders punctuates his revelation with something that's even more inappropriate, considering that Sandra Berman might be dead, along with others who have been lying right beneath the surface of Meadowfield in someone's murder house for God knows how long.

"She was good," Anders says, loud enough for Marcy to still hear, as he reaches down for his socks. "Really, really good."

17

MYERS IS WITH MARCY in the woods. She doesn't go too far, so I can see she's trying not to cry but not doing a very good job of it. Myers has his hand on her shoulder. I don't think he's ever even touched a girl before. For that matter, neither have I. Marcy is the closest that either of us has ever come, and, well, she's just Marcy.

Anders is sitting again, but at least he's dressed. He keeps shaking his head and rubbing his eyes.

"What the fuck?" he whispers half to himself and half to me.

"You mean about Sandra Berman?"

He shakes his head again. "Yeah. No. Yeah. I mean everything."

My arm has been stinging right along, but I've been ignoring it, much the same way that Anders has been ignoring everything since we woke up this morning in The Maze.

"Does your head hurt?" I ask him. "The rest of us feel sick."

"Like a son of a bitch," he says, and I flinch. The voice coming out of his mouth isn't Anders' voice. It's his father's. Somewhere deep inside I wonder if we'll even be friends after high school, or if he's only biding his time like everyone else our age, until we're set free of this place and scatter to the winds.

"I know what you mean," I tell him. "I've already puked."

"Gross," he says, and then his stomach rumbles so loudly that I think that I may have just given him a suggestion that he's going to follow through with.

"You're a mess," I say to him. "Do you remember anything?"

Anders rubs his square jaw with one hand, his beard stubble making him look as rough as he probably feels. "No," he says, then puts both his thumbs to his temples much the same way that Myers did when we were back on the path in the woods. Anders opens his mouth like he's going to say something but closes it again. "No," he says again, with such an utter lack of conviction that I'm almost positive he's lying.

I suppose I can ask him about big, black eyes and the cries of animals, but I don't want to open that can of fake snakes right now so they can explode into the air.

Instead, I lie and say, "Me neither."

I think lying is something we all do. Sometimes it's easier to lie than to say things about our lives that might be a little too personal, even to each other. I'm sure Myers doesn't need to let us know about the intricacies of the Myers household and how damaged his mother is. I'm positive Anders doesn't want to talk about the scorecard he's tallying way down deep of how many guys his mother has boned since his father left Meadowfield. Marcy certainly never brings up the big white elephant in her household—her nonexistent brother, who is hanging in photographs in their lower-level den.

Me, well, I'm not much of a sharer. I can even keep things from myself. Sometimes living is easier that way.

I sigh and say, "We have to get out of here. Where are your old clothes?"

Anders doesn't answer me.

I close my eyes and call out to Marcy and Myers. They are only about twenty feet or so into the woods but a million issues away. "Hey, Marcy. Where did you put his old clothes?"

Marcy pushes away from Myers and turns to me.

"In The Grandfather Tree for now," she says as she slowly walks back, wiping her face, with Myers following after her.

The Grandfather Tree is an old stump, hollowed out by squirrels, termites, and rain that stubbornly refuses to come down. It's been in Prince Richard's Maze ever since I can remember, only a little ways from Turner Pond, off of Little Loop and surrounded by rocks that are almost big enough to climb on.

It's as good a place as any. We'll have to get rid of Anders' stuff at some point, but for right now, I don't think anyone is coming in search of a pile of bloody clothing, and I'll be damned if I'm going to put it all in my backpack.

"We're leaving," I say. I'm definitely not the leader of our group, but right now I feel about the least damaged of all of us, and that's saying a lot since I'm the one with a little triangle burned into his forearm.

I'm planning on getting a tattoo there anyway, once I turn eighteen. I would love to say that it will be a colossal act of rebellion but it won't. Beryl has two tattoos. There's one of a rose on her calf that's more like a rose bush than a rose, and there's another one of a monkey between her shoulders. I don't know what either of them means. I've never asked, and she's never offered. The fact that my mother has two tattoos doesn't help her reputation of not fitting into the fabric of Meadowfield. Her being inked isn't much of a shocker. It's expected.

As for me, I'm still deciding what graphic will most represent freedom because when I leave Meadowfield for college, I'll truly be free. Maybe it will be a broken chain, or something else equally symbolic. Now, all I know is that there's going to have to be enough ink to cover up the little triangle that's there—enough so I'll forget that it was ever burned into my skin in the first place.

Anders slowly blows a gust of air out of his mouth. He wobbles for a moment and Marcy immediately rushes up to him and grabs hold of his shoulders so he won't keel. He grumbles something as he stares across the pond, then brushes her away.

I'm no rocket scientist, but even I can see that Anders refuses to look at her. The expression on Marcy's face is so pained that he might as well have slapped her hard. I don't understand. Yesterday we were all best friends. Only hours ago Anders was clinging onto Marcy for dear life like she was the only thing in the world that could tether him to reality.

Now he won't even look at her.

He won't look at any of us.

18

AS SOON AS WE get into Marcy's car, she slips into the passenger's seat leaving Myers and Anders to share the back. I can tell she's upset. Marcy has always had one of those faces that can't hide emotions. She probably doesn't even know she's doing it, but every mood, every nuance, is written on her face.

"Do you want to drive?" I ask her. "It's your car."

"I want to go home and hide underneath the covers," she says, which I guess means that she's perfectly happy being driven.

I want to ask how she plans on finding the covers. Her room is approaching hoarder status, but I don't. I suppose levity isn't always appropriate in the middle of tension. Sometime tension has to naturally play out or snap.

"Put on the radio," Myers says from the back seat. It's about the worst idea I can imagine. We all feel like crap. The last thing we want is canned music thump, thump, thumping against our eardrums, while the insides of our heads are thump, thump, thumping back.

"I don't think so."

"There might be something on the news about the house across the street from where Sandra used to live," he whines. Normally we would all be scrolling through our phones, looking for information, but our phones have all disappeared—just like our memories of last night.

I reluctantly reach down and push the button on the radio.

No music. Some guy is talking, but it's not about anything important. Marcy has the radio set to the low numbers. Her parents are all about her listening to NPR and stuffing culture down her throat. They think that if Marcy is cultured, she'll get into a good college and get a good job so she can end up in a good community, like Meadowfield.

I have a sinking suspicion that Marcy wants to be far away from Meadowfield and no amount of culture is going to change that.

Myers leans forward, tipping himself so he's practically lying across the front seat between me and Marcy. "Change the channel," he says, even though he's the one who is changing it.

I look in my rearview mirror and see Anders sitting there, staring out the window with that same far off gaze that he had when he was looking across Turner Pond.

'Why is there blood?' Marcy had blubbered this morning when we woke up in the middle of Prince Richard's Maze.

'Anders, there's so much,' Myers cried. *'What . . . what did you do?'*

Way down deep, far away, the sheep start crying in my head again, and a flash of big black eyes appear and vanish.

They're all weird images that don't even remotely fit together. They're just disparate thoughts that won't go away.

And, yeah. What did Anders do?

Why would he be covered in blood? None of the rest of us had any on us. We weren't cut. We weren't bleeding. Even Anders, standing naked and unashamed at the edge of Turner Pond, didn't have a scratch on him. There should have been something. The amount of blood that Anders had been covered with this morning was epic. It was the kind of blood that you only see in horror movies when they use so much of it that you know it has to be fake, dyed Karo syrup. Nobody in real life bleeds that much.

Buckets full.

Myers keeps turning the dial on the radio. He stops as a voice says, ". . . Meadowfield, Massachusetts."

Marcy stares at the dashboard. Myers pulls his hand back. Anders doesn't even flinch. It's as though he's turned around and seen Sodom and Gomorrah get destroyed and now he's nothing but a pillar of salt.

The voice on the radio goes on. "Once again, in our developing story, officials are continuing to remove bodies from inside a home in quiet suburban Meadowfield, Massachusetts."

Marcy and Myers both make weird noises like frightened rabbits probably make when they know that the fox is actually going to win and eat them for real.

In my rearview mirror, Anders closes his eyes.

The voice continues. "Community residents are gathered outside this unassuming, two story colonial in a quiet corner of the Pioneer Valley. The owner of the home has been identified as thirty-three-year-old Dr. Viktor Pavlovich, a current medical intern at Johnstown Memorial Hospital in Tolland County, Connecticut."

"Stairway to Heaven," whispers Myers. That's what everyone around here calls Johnstown Memorial Hospital over the Connecticut border in Sumneytown. No one in their right mind goes there unless they want nothing more than a couple of stitches. Anything beyond that, and you're taking your life in your hands.

"Shhhh," says Marcy to Myers and gives him a dirty look.

"Just saying," he mutters and turns quiet, but by then, all that's left is a chilling last remark that leaves us all a little unsettled.

"Officials here believe Dr. Pavlovich may be among the dead, however, no formal identification has been made. Please stay tuned for more information on this developing story."

I reach over and press the off button on the radio. I do it with a quick, jabbing motion as though I'm positive it's hot, and if I keep my finger on it for too long, I'll get burned.

"I want to see," whispers Anders from the back seat.

"What? No," cries Marcy, as she whips around and stares at Anders. Again, he won't look at her.

Myers gulps and slumps back into his seat.

I swallow and take a deep breath. The truth is I want to see, too.

19

THE NAME, DR. Viktor Pavlovich, seems so classically cliché' that it almost sounds made-up. I half expect that when they start flashing his image across the news and on the Internet, he's going to look all villainous, with a gold tooth and a prominent scar. He may be one of the dead, but it won't matter. He'll be the new face of evil, and Meadowfield will become the epicenter of a horrific media earthquake.

Years from now we'll all still be feeling its aftershocks.

Marcy and Myers don't protest when I steer the car down Merriweather Drive and past Primrose Lane. Marcy stares longingly at the gently sloping hill leading up to her house, but she's already internalized the fact that we're not going home yet. We have something more important to do.

We want to see the Pavlovich house.

We *need* to see the Pavlovich house.

There's something about an issue more perverse than our own that helps ground us. I don't know about the others, but a multiple homicide trumps big black eyes and the sounds of sheep in my head. It even trumps the little burning triangle on my arm.

Besides, there's no way I'm bringing Anders home to his mother right now. He's obviously still in shock, although I don't know why. He might be talking, but he's not all there. I don't think any of us are. The cotton fluff inside our heads is still . . . fluffy. Thankfully, we seem to be a little better than when we first woke up this morning, but a fog is still covering everything, making it hard to believe that this isn't one, huge, never-ending nightmare, and I'm really tucked beneath the covers in my own bed, in my own bedroom.

I drive farther down Merriweather, past the swampy dingle with its memories of better times playing hide and seek and catching pollywogs, and head off toward the other side of town.

The clock on the dashboard reads 10:02. So much has happened this morning that it's hard to keep everything straight. I'm living someone else's life where things are far worse than mine. I'm driving through someone else's town where murders are an honest-to-goodness thing, and losing one's memory is the norm.

A few years ago, this girl who worked at Brightstar's Pet Emporium over in East Meadowfield was killed along with her boyfriend. They were in a car by Corbin's Island, the sewage plant near the Western Mass Electric Company on the other side of the Connecticut River. That double homicide should have been a big deal. Supposedly they were parking and making out, although I don't know why anyone would want to make out with the stench of shit choking the air, but that's where they were parked and that's where they were found, brutally butchered.

Those murders went in and out of local news rather quickly because it was the murder of an East Meadowfield girl and her boyfriend, instead of a Meadowfield couple. East Meadowfield has always been considered our town's poorer cousin. Bad things can happen there and that's a little expected. But not in Meadowfield. We've always known that once you cross the border separating East Meadowfield from Meadowfield, the rain stops, the sun shines, and there are bluebirds and bunnies frolicking on everyone's perfectly manicured lawns.

Now, Meadowfield is no different from East Meadowfield. As a matter of fact, Meadowfield is worse. Instead of a dead pet shop clerk and her boyfriend, we have the den of a serial killer who's been getting busy for a while now.

Dr. Viktor Pavlovich.

Something invisible touches the back of my neck and the hair there stands on end. If Beryl had ever deigned to make me see a doctor who had a name like that, I would have flat out refused because of the absolute certainty that bad things would happen.

Just like I think bad things would happen if the four of us went and hung out at the Stumps—but I don't have to think. I know. Like Grafton Applewhite said, we *were* at The Stumps, and bad things did happen.

The invisible thing on the back of my neck starts to move down my sides, stroking my arms with spider silk. My heart starts thumping in my chest.

"Look," says Myers, as I make a right near the back entrance to the middle school. There are flashing lights up ahead. They're still blocks away, but there are so many of them that we could be over the border in Connecticut and still see the twirling red and blue strobes. I slow the car down. There are other cars parked alongside the street, and there are people walking toward the flashing lights.

"Pull over," says Marcy as we all stare straight ahead. Even Anders is looking forward, his eyes a little glazed.

"You okay back there?" I ask him.

"Sure," says Myers. I sigh and roll my eyes. He sees me do it through my reflection in the rearview mirror, and silently mouths, 'Oh.'

Anders doesn't say anything. Marcy turns around and stares at him. I have to think that she's monumentally pissed off because of what he said about Sandy Berman.

She was good.

I suppose Marcy could take the high road and decide Anders was saying that Sandy Berman was a good person, but we all know that's not what he meant.

Still, Marcy seems to be swallowing the last of her anger. She can't ever stay mad at him for long. She's melting all over again about the possibility that Anders does actually care about her after all.

"Anders?" she says.

Nothing.

"Anders?" she whispers once more. As I pull over the side of the road, hitting the curb harder than I should because I'm more interested in staring at my friend through the rearview mirror, he blinks once and his face goes white.

Then he opens the car door before I'm even fully parked and pukes on the road.

Just like the rest of us.

20

LAST YEAR'S WESTON Kahn would have never joined a group of spectators clamoring to see a bunch of dead bodies being pulled out of a murder house. Last year's Weston Kahn would be eating a box of Little Debbie's Cosmic Brownies in his bedroom, playing video games and waiting for his miserable life to end.

This year's Weston Kahn, one third smaller, no longer hides behind a fat suit of his own creation. This year's Weston Kahn is a different person altogether.

Right at the beginning of the school year, Mr. Tomlinson, the hipster music teacher with the skinny jeans and man bun, called me into his office for a chat. This girl, Lizzie Glickman, who has black poodle hair and is the lead of Cantori, the elite choral group at school, whispered something to her friends as I walked toward his office, but I chose not to listen.

"West," Mr. Tomlinson said as he motioned for me to sit down, "I gotta say I'm looking at a new you." I wrapped my arms around myself, my hands now able to touch my sides instead of the mounds of blubber that had plagued me for almost as long as I could remember.

"Thanks," I said, not really sure that I was all that thankful. The fat kept me hidden. The fat kept me safe.

"So about Cantori," he started. Mr. Tomlinson's man bun and studied five-day-beard seemed like a desperate cry to be in, or cool, or whatever his generation calls affectations like that. "You know that there are only eight spots and lots of people tried out."

I waited for him to say something else, but he let an awkward silence nestle between us. Finally I filled it with the obvious. "I didn't get in," I said flatly, knowing with certainty that what I said was true. "I get it." I wasn't mad or disappointed. I think I was relieved.

"You're very talented," he began, but his words flew out of his mouth, up to the ceiling, and disappeared like ghosts. I think he wanted me to thank him again, but I wasn't in a thankful mood. I wanted to leave his office, push past Lizzie Glickman with her poodle hair, and leave the choral room.

"It's only that, well . . ." He looked out his window and across the front lawn of the high school where the beginning of autumn leaves gathered at the base of the flagpole like kindling. I was waiting for him to say that there were other kids, more popular kids, who would be a bigger draw at the concerts, but that wouldn't have been politically correct of him. I think waiting for me to draw my own conclusions was all he had in his arsenal.

Fuck politically correct. "No biggie," I told him. I was used to stuff like this happening. So what if my friends weren't exactly the popular crowd, except for Anders?

"I'm sure there will be tons of opportunities for in-class solos coming up this year. You never know."

I took a deep breath and stood up. "I'm sure," I parroted back, then without asking or waiting to be dismissed, I left his office. Outside, Lizzie Glickman was sitting on the risers in the choral room with Cleo Collins and Nora Jameson. They stopped talking when I trudged past them. I could feel their eyes on me.

"He's cute now," whispered Cleo. I think she thought I couldn't hear. "Who would have ever thought that Weston Kahn would be cute? He was so fat."

I closed my eyes and kept walking, wishing for all that fat to come back so I could hide behind it.

That's how I feel now as the four of us slowly follow the rest of the herd gathering this side of a police barrier near the Pavlovich house, across the street from where Sandra Berman used to live. I feel utterly exposed.

I see Mrs. Berman on her front lawn. I never knew Sandy's father, but there's a tall guy going bald, with one arm held rigidly over her shoulder. The two of them are standing, watching the commotion across the street at the murder house. No one strays near them. I think everyone is afraid of the explosion that might happen if Sandy Berman is pulled out of that house.

Christ, she disappeared years ago. How would the guys doing the dirty work even be able to identify her?

I close my eyes and bite my lip as a wave of pain from the little triangle starts sending tendrils of prickly static up and down my arm.

"Jesus," says Myers as we get closer. There are so many people, and there are trucks. I see a van from Channel 40 and another from Channel 22. Then there are others—bigger stations that broadcast nationally.

Reporters have strategically planted themselves on neighbors' lawns, busily speaking in front of cameras and pointing their microphones in residents' faces.

"I don't want to be on TV," says Anders. He shoves his hands into his pockets and stands behind Marcy. He's sort of like a giraffe trying to hide behind an antelope because Anders is tall and Marcy isn't.

"Chill," I say to him, trying not to notice that his face is the color of ash. He's definitely in shock. He has to be. Nothing else makes sense for how he's been acting. After all, it's not every day you wake up covered in blood.

I look back over the growing crowd of people and the dark red house that bodies are coming out of in a stream, and my heart turns into heavy shards of glass that start stabbing me from the inside out.

There's an ambulance there, with its back doors open and a figure sitting on the floor, miserable and hunched, facing out. I gulp. Instinctively I know whoever it is has survived something terrible.

I can't be certain, but I think the person is a girl.

If it is a girl, her legs are dangling out of the back of the ambulance. She's wrapped in a sheet and surrounded by wary people. I don't know who she is, but I don't need to know her to realize that her life right now is a living hell. Her head is shaved and it looks like someone has drawn dotted lines all over her scalp. Her face is dotted with lines, too, bisecting and quartering the flesh. The whole effect is that of a discarded doll that once belonged to a twisted little girl with a knife.

There are reporters and police and every type of town official all around her, and she looks like she is already dead and only waiting for the finality of death to catch up with her body.

"Who is that?" I murmur as I stare at her. There's something about the girl that seems familiar but I can't put my finger on it. She's not Sandra Berman all grown up, that's for sure. She looks nothing like how I remember her, dotted lines or not—hair or no hair.

Still, there's something about her that feels concrete. There's no other way I can put it. I feel connected to her, but I don't know how. Maybe it's that she's about my age and is going through some sort of torture, like the four of us are being tortured. I don't know.

Still.

She sits alone, her bare knees touching and her feet pointing inward, quietly rocking back and forth. Once or twice, paramedics try to reach out to her, but she rudely brushes them away. If anything, she seems ever so slightly unhinged, but I can imagine if she was inside Dr.

Viktor Pavlovich's house, she has every right to be unhinged.

"Who is that?" Marcy says, echoing my words. Myers has his head cocked sideways in thought. Anders stares at the girl over the crowd, his skin getting grayer as the blood drains from his face.

Across the sea of people in front of us, as they watch the door of the Pavlovich house, waiting to catch a glimpse of a dead body to feed their curiosity, the girl slowly lifts her shaved and dotted head.

A manic, horrific, and slightly demonic stare immediately finds the four of us among hundreds. Why us? What did we do? What's going on?

I immediately get dizzy as a wave of nausea washes over me.

Meanwhile, the girl's mouth drops open, almost further than a mouth can open, and a high pitched squeal comes out of her that makes the crowd of onlookers hush in stunned silence. Her elongated scream goes on forever until I want to clamp my hands over my ears. The whole time, she's staring at us—at me—and I can feel the skin leaving my bones just like the fat left them, exposing a monster beneath that should have eaten itself to death a year ago by gorging on devil dogs and Yoo-hoos.

Suddenly she stops. The lack of noise is jarring. Silence lingers because everyone is too stunned to speak. As people finally start to whisper again, confused and scared, the girl starts raging. She babbles incoherently as she flails her arms, kicking and scratching but never once releasing her eye-lock on us. We're rooted to the spot as she screams and screams while heavy hands hold her down and someone with a red-cross arm band pulls a needle out of thin air and plunges it rudely into her arm.

Thankfully, no one follows her laser stare as she continues burning a hole through me and my friends while managing an Oscar-winning freak out that the nightly news will show over and over again.

I don't understand any of this. I almost want Beryl right now, so I can fold my chubby, pre-adolescent digits into my mommy's hand and hope by some miracle that I can milk safety out of her numb fingers.

Abruptly, Anders turns and leaves, walking quickly back toward Marcy's car, his hands still shoved inside his pockets, his head pointed toward the ground.

"Wait," Marcy calls after him, and leaves, too.

For that matter, we all leave. I don't know why, but something inside my brain—the primitive part that controls flight or fights, urges me to flee.

No one notices our hasty retreat. They're too busy staring at the bald girl as she continues to unleash a meltdown that they will all remember for years to come.

And through it all, the eyes and the animal cries, the blood and a missing glass eye, a burning triangle and Marcy's lack of pants, I hear Myers wailing inside my head.

I don't want to.

I don't want to.

I DON'T WANT TO.

21

WE'RE UPSTAIRS IN Marcy's house, sitting at her kitchen table. The pizza box is still there. None of us have bothered to move it. Marcy's parents don't plan on coming home until tomorrow night so her house seems like a safe place to be. However, we're not sure if the Coles are going to hear about Dr. Viktor Pavlovich on the news and come rushing back to Meadowfield or not.

That scenario is unlikely. Every family has weird rules and Marcy's family is no different. Her parents unplug from the world when they travel, and that means leaving their phones behind. They call being phoneless their 'alone time.' Marcy has the phone number for the hotel at the casino so she can always get in touch with them in an emergency, but if there isn't an emergency, her parents' motto is *'no contact is good contact.'*

Just like Beryl, but nothing like Beryl at all.

Marcy's round house with its big windows and sun-filled rooms make me feel like I'm still back in Prince Richard's Maze. I want to be in a closet some place, deep and dark, tucked in around coats and shoes where nothing can get me.

Myers is on the house phone with his mother and she is in the middle of one of her perpetual rants. I can almost make out the drone of her screaming through the wires.

"No," whimpers Myers as he gingerly holds the phone away from his ear so that his mother's fuckity-fuck-fuck-fuck of a freak out doesn't burst his ear drums. Myers has been at it for five minutes now. He's gone from whining, to crying, to whining again. Now he's at the end stage of a Mrs. Myers swear-fest, and we're all waiting for the final results.

Our goal is for him not to leave Marcy's house until our brains clear and Anders is more like Anders instead of a total basket case. At least that's what we're all hoping for. Also, Myers is wearing a pirate patch on his face. That patch is a blatant telegraph to his parents that he's lost his eye again. It's not that Myers hasn't lost one before. Most often they're bullied out of him in one of the bathrooms at school by a major asshole like Arnie Lewis or Pavel Vagin, who everyone calls 'Vaj.' You have to be a complete dick to pull off a nickname as bad as 'Vaj,' but Pavel manages it fine. Everyone's scared of him. Even teachers.

Myers losing his eye is bad and punishment-worthy, but not calling his parents, especially after they shelled out what Mrs. Myers calls 'a shitload of money' for a new cell, is a much bigger deal. The best lie Myers can come up with on the fly is that he dropped his phone in the Coles' toilet last night, and it's now sitting in a bowl of white rice on their kitchen counter so it can dry out.

I can hear Mrs. Cole screaming while Myers tries to explain to her that sticking a cell phone in rice is one way to save it from dying if you've gotten it wet.

"I'm sorry. I'm sorry," he keeps saying for dropping his missing phone into the toilet. "I'll pay for another one." That last statement elicits another barrage of verbal sewage from the other end of the phone. Myers has no money of his own. He doesn't work. None of us do. Most kids in Meadowfield don't work during high school. We're too busy with after-school activities or donating our free time to the less fortunate, even though the four of us currently feel like the least fortunate people on the planet. "I will," he says as he wipes sweat from his brow. I don't think he can take his mother being his mother for another minute.

Finally he hangs up, hangs his head, and says, "I can't wait to go to college. Anywhere."

"Amen," I whisper. I totally get what he means.

Marcy is sitting on the granite kitchen island, cross-legged, peeling an orange as sunlight kisses her all over. I know we all feel like crap, but even crap looks good on Marcy. Beautiful people can spin silk out of shit. Marcy's like that. I think peeling that orange is her way of trying to act normal for herself and for the rest of us. It makes me feel almost like nothing is happening to us and to Meadowfield, and this is only another hangout day.

She looks up at Anders. He has his arms folded on the granite and his head cradled in them. A dark cloud passes over her face then disappears.

Myers says, "Sorry," to all of us. He's been apologizing for his mother since forever. We're all used to it. Marcy shrugs and so do I. "I'm staying. I can't go home. If either of my parents find out that I've lost my eye again, I'll be wishing I was one of those bodies coming out of Dr. Pavlovich's house. They probably had an easier death than I'll have."

"That's not funny," says Marcy. It's not. It's a little weird and sick. Who knows what happened to all those dead people? Who knows what kind of terror they went through before they finally breathed their last breath?

Anders finally picks his head up off the table. He still refuses to look at Marcy or the rest of us. "That girl," he says. He doesn't say anything else. He repeats the two words again. "That girl."

"Yeah," I say. "I don't know about the rest of you guys, but she freaked the crap out of me."

Marcy nods her head as she continues digging her nails into the orange peel, flaying it in front of us like we're in the middle of the Inquisition and she's sort of enjoying its murder. "What was with the dotted lines?"

"Who knows?" says Myers. "Fashion statement?"

"Not likely. Do you know anyone from Meadowfield who would ink themselves like that?"

Anders snorts ever so slightly, which makes me think that there's someone alive in there, slowly tearing away at the walls of a cocoon. "Looks like FunTowne trash."

FunTowne is the arcade in downtown Springfield. We've all been there before. It's another hangout for the popular crowd, like The Stumps. Kids from rival towns go there, too. Even gangs from the north end of Springfield hang at FunTowne. The place is neutral territory. Everyone has silently agreed that if you're there, you're not looking for trouble. You only want to chill, spend mega amounts of quarters, and maybe find some weed.

Since none of us party, FunTowne has always been about getting a sugar buzz with ridiculous amounts of candy, but I don't partake in candy anymore.

Myers picks up the television remote and points it at the TV on the wall in the kitchen. The Coles are a little television obsessed. There are at least seven of them that I can count in their house, and maybe eight, if Mr. Cole keeps one in his bathroom so he can shit and watch the news at the same time.

Beryl only has one television in her bedroom and one in mine. There isn't a third one in the house where the two of us can sit and watch TV together. Why would there be?

As Myers flips channels, Marcy says, "Did she look familiar to you guys?" A chill runs down my back and I close my eyes. Thankfully, no images are waiting behind my eyelids to fill in the void. I'm sure they'll pop up soon enough.

The three of us answer at the same time, and we all lie. "No," we say in unison. Then two seconds later we all take a deep breath.

"Maybe," I say.

"I'm not sure," says Myers.

We wait for Anders to recant his lie, too. All he does is lift his head from the table again, rub his eyes with his hands, and run his fingers through his hair. We all stare at him, waiting for him to come clean, because we've all known each other long enough to be able to ferret out what's true and what's not.

Finally, he licks his lips and says, "I'd do her, though," like he's talking trash to the other jocks in the locker room at school. "Crazy can be hot."

22

WE ALL TAKE showers, even Anders. I take mine in Marcy's parents' bathroom. As I scrub myself with handmade oatmeal soap from one of the vendors at the Farmer's Market held in the shopping center parking lot every Wednesday afternoon, I momentarily hear the sheep cry again. This time their mournful wails are triggered by nothing more than the thought of fresh produce grown at one of the farms over the border in Connecticut, or a lady mixing vats of oils on her country kitchen stove, to cool into fancy soaps for privileged folks in rich, suburban Meadowfield.

The thing is, Meadowfield isn't privileged anymore, unless you want to single us out as one of the few towns across America that is home to a murder house. We're all damaged now, and a crazy girl that survived some sort of horror inside that house, and whose screams I can't scrub away no matter how hard I try, is the most damaged of us all.

Suddenly, the soap makes me feel sick.

Lifetimes ago, during World War II, the Nazis had homemade soap, too. Supposedly, that soap was made out of the melted down tallow of concentration camp victims. It was formed and molded by bits and pieces of grandmothers and grandfathers, parents and children, who were murdered by the biggest and most prolific mass murderer of all times.

Jewish kids don't even say his name. I guess we're taught not to in Hebrew School. We no more say his name than Hogwarts kids say Voldemort's name out loud. To breathe either is almost like inviting evil in for a cup of coffee and a nice scone.

Blasphemy.

After I finish showering and get dressed, Myers showers, too. Anders and Marcy are already cleaned up by the time we all come back into the kitchen. The hot, soapy water has invigorated us, if only a little. Anders still looks like shit, but he's a cleaner, neater version of what he was only a few hours ago.

The television is on and a reporter is talking about the newest scourge on our society.

Dr. Viktor Pavlovich.

Marcy switches the channel but several of the stations are running live feeds from the crime scene. Reporters are talking. Neighbors are talking. When things get slightly boring, snippets of what can be gleaned about Dr. Viktor Pavlovich's life are plastered onto the screen.

He looks nothing like I imagine. Marcy says something wildly out of character the first time they show a full picture of Pavlovich's face. Part of me thinks she says it because Anders is right there and Anders has been acting so much like the definition of a douchebag this morning, she wants to hurt him.

I'm not sure it works.

"Wow. I'd do him," she murmurs, totally echoing Anders' words from before. "Crazy can be hot."

"Really?" says Myers, staring at Marcy opened mouth. She's trying hard to be foul but foul won't ever look good on her.

"What?" Marcy says. "Well he is."

"Don't be gross," I tell her.

The images of the man they keep flashing on the screen, serial murderer or not, are far from what I pictured. He's not the sinister Viktor that I conjured in my head. There isn't a scar on his face and he doesn't have a gold tooth or dark, menacing eyes that give you the willies just by looking at them. The guy on the screen is smiling and looks completely normal.

As a matter of fact, this piece of human filth is going to unseat that Ted guy as the new poster boy for mass murderers. He has dark hair and a perpetual five o'clock shadow that seems studied and neat. His eyes are an electric blue without a hint of madness behind them. His smile is infectious. Girls are going to swoon all over his picture, and guys who may or may not think about other guys in that way won't be able to stop fantasizing about Dr. Viktor Pavlovich.

I guess you'd say he looks like a movie star.

Suddenly Marcy gasps, and her eyes grow wide. "Oh my god, you guys. Do you know who that is?"

None of us say anything. Anders, barely in the here and now, only shrugs like he couldn't give a shit either way.

"That's Running Man," she announces, and immediately I know she's right.

Running Man appears on Primrose Lane every morning, right as we're leaving for school. He's a permanent part of our daily routine because Running Man is precise. He's so perfectly timed that we usually wait for him to prance by at 7:30, his body covered in designer running gear and his feet slapping the ground in more of a dance than a jog, before we set off for school. He's elegant in his exercise, not like some people who are sloppy when they sweat. Running Man looks more like a cheetah or another creature that is born to gracefully run.

That's the best word I can think of to describe him. He's graceful.

Now Running Man is on TV for the whole world to see.

Precious few details have been released so far about the bodies that are coming out of his house on Covington Circle, but phrases like 'human remains' and 'dismembered with surgical precision' have been hastily uttered before station managers quickly cut and move to something less gory to talk about.

"I can't believe we know him," says Myers, which isn't exactly true. We've never talked to Running Man before. Marcy has blushed a couple of times when he's flashed a wicked grin in her direction while we've been waiting at the bottom of the driveway of one of our houses so we can all walk to school together.

"Hey there," Running Man said to her once, as he floated by on feet that barely touched the ground.

"Um, hi," Marcy said back, then turned to watch him go. When he was out of ear shot, Marcy said, "Nice ass."

I remember that day, not so long ago. It was the first time that Anders seemed a little pissed at Marcy for no good reason. Now I'm starting to realize that there may have been a reason after all and there's no more hiding it. First thing this morning when no one could calm Anders down but Marcy, he lay practically naked at the edge of Turner Pond with his head in her lap. She was there for him. She's always been there for him.

What's worse, all he's doing is shitting on her for it.

I get it.

I don't get it.

It's complicated.

23

IT'S 11:15 AND MRS. Cole's work phone has been ringing non-stop. Every time it goes off, we all stare at the caller ID to see who it is. More often than not there are messages and the messages are frightening.

We listen as the answering machine picks them up, time and time again, with hysterical women and a few men on the other end, all desperately trying to make sense of what is going on in Meadowfield. They all keep talking about how they can't cope. The very idea of a monster like Dr. Viktor Pavlovich doing what he did, right under their noses, is rattling their senses.

A few of them ask if they should up their prescriptions. I don't know why they're asking Marcy's mom about pills. She's a psychologist, not a psychiatrist. One shrinks the brain. The other medicates it.

Marcy's mom isn't a dispensary.

None of them, not a single one, say anything about the poor dead people being brought out of the house on Covington Circle. Nobody is concerned with the nightmare these peoples' families will have to endure once the bodies are identified.

Everyone is so self-absorbed that I want to pick up one of those phone calls and scream into the receiver about how shitty they sound. They aren't the only people in the world. Their lives aren't the only ones that matter.

I want to screw up my face and tell one of them, any one of them, to go fuck off. I want to point them in the direction of the nearest designer knife block sitting in their designer kitchens on their designer granite and tell them to either cut their wrists deep or go get a fucking grip.

Christ, there are other things happening right now that are more important than how the murder house and its store of corpses makes them 'feel.'

I rub the triangle on my arm with my thumb. It hurts. Sitting here, waiting for our heads to clear, listening to Mrs. Cole's clients prattle on and on, is somehow making the pain worse.

Finally, the house phone rings twice, then stops.

"That's my mom," Marcy says nervously.

"Huh?" says Myers. "How do you know?"

"Two rings then nothing, means it's her. She's going to call again," and right when she says that, the phone rings a second time, and Marcy immediately snatches it up.

"Mom?" she whispers into the phone. "Mommy?" Marcy walks out of the kitchen but doesn't go far. We can hear her conversation anyway.

Marcy's close with her parents. Like I said before, she really lucked out with her mom and dad. They're the cool ones.

"I bet the Coles are coming home," whispers Myers. He bites on his lip and nods his oversized head with the patch on it.

"How do you know?"

"They're coming home because of Running Man," he says. "My parents would."

"Your parents are bizarre," I remind him, which isn't even a stone's throw away from the truth. Marcy's home and safe. There's no difference if her parents are at the casino or at home with her. They know she's a big girl. She can take care of herself.

"Anders?" Marcy asks as she walks back into the kitchen and stares directly at him.

Anders is now sitting in a chair, leaning back, with one leg dangling over the arm of the seat. He looks like he is going to start playing with himself and couldn't care less if any of us watch. He doesn't respond to her. In fact, he doesn't even move.

After a moment, Marcy turns away from him. "Um, he's here, but . . . he's in the bathroom," she whispers into the phone. Mrs. Cole says something on the other end of the line. Marcy nods and hands the phone to me.

"What?" I mouth to her.

"My mom wanted to talk to Anders but . . . well . . . you know," she says and tilts her head in his direction. "So she wants to talk to you."

A little knot forms in the pit of my stomach. I'm going to have to lie again. I lied to Myers' mother this morning, and I lied to Anders' mother, too. Now I'm going to have to lie to Mrs. Cole. I don't know what I'm going to say, but I'm going to have to be smart. Mrs. Cole is a psychologist. She'll know I'm lying if I don't do it right. She'll know, and she'll come home. That's the last thing any of us want. We're not ready for parents yet.

None of us.

"Hello?" I breathe into the phone when Marcy hands it to me.

"Weston, hi," I hear Marcy's mother say. In the background there are whistles and bells. She's at the Indian Casino down in the part of Connecticut that no one ever visits. "I wanted to make sure you guys are okay."

"We are," I lie. "What do you mean?" Oh, crap. I sound like I'm a psychopath just like Viktor Pavlovich. Something hideous is happening in town, but I have to go and say 'what do you mean,' like I'm not totally freaked out.

"I . . ." she begins, but I cut her off.

"It's scary," I tell her, because that's the truth. I can run with that. "But we have each other, and we're not going to leave Marcy by herself. We'll stay with her tonight." I don't know if that's true, but as the words come out of my mouth they sound true. Where else would we possibly go? The four of us are experiencing a different kind of hell than the rest of Meadowfield. Our kind of hell dictates safety in numbers.

"I left money for Marcy," she says. "Order sushi or maybe go grab some salads at the salad bar over at Fresh Acres." I have to smile when she says that. Only in Meadowfield would parents be telling their kids to eat fish and greens.

"Okay," I tell her.

"Do you want me to call Beryl and let her know you're at my house?" Mrs. Cole asks. That's a big thing. Mrs. Cole and Beryl are like oil and water. Beryl floats on the surface of everything, her mind barely skimming the top of reality. The Coles are fluid and easy.

"That's okay," I say. "She doesn't mind," which is the total truth.

"Thanks, West," she says. I guess I'm a poor second to Anders. If it were Anders talking to Marcy's mom instead of me, she would be telling him that he's the strong one and needs to protect us all. Nipping at the heels of that thought, Mrs. Cole says, "Is Anders out of the bathroom yet?"

I look over at him. His GQ face is slightly defiant, like he's waging an inner battle with whatever demons are inside his head, but he knows he's going to win.

"No," I say and then punctuate that definitive word with a statement that isn't supposed to be funny but comes out funny anyway. "He's still full of crap."

24

A HALF HOUR LATER, this is what we've learned about Running Man.

Dr. Viktor Pavlovich was born in Moscow but moved to the states when he was a toddler. He doesn't have any family here. His parents both died in a car accident and there are no other relatives.

He's good looking, like really good looking, but that hasn't always been the case. His picture from his high school yearbook shows someone who is more akin to his namesake than perfect, prancing Running Man, with his winning smile and cheetah stride.

There is talk on television of a lot of plastic surgery to get from where he was to where he is, and more talk about the fact that he's now a plastic surgeon specializing in making pretty people out of misshapen clay.

He's an avid runner, with a runner's body, and has often been seen by neighbors with attractive young women and men in his designer sports car with the leather seats and the convertible roof.

Dr. Viktor Pavlovich is also a passionate gardener. His backyard is a shrine to anything that will grow in our part of the world. Speculation as to the nature of the fertilizer underneath his plantings has been mounting, and the people on the news are appropriately freaking out.

The worst reaction is from a neighbor of Dr. Pavlovich's who's often been gifted with tomatoes and cucumbers by the healthy, good-looking man with the handsome smile and perpetual face-stubble.

In another town, like East Meadowfield or someplace up the Mohawk Trail, his neighbor would undoubtedly have curlers in her hair and a house coat. Not here, though. In Meadowfield she is perfectly made up for the reporters. Unfortunately her makeup doesn't matter. Right on screen, right in front of the cameras, when the guy who's interviewing her starts talking about Pavlovich's special brand of vegetables and what makes them taste so good, her face goes completely white, and she pukes on his microphone.

Why does the news keep showing her doing that? It's disgusting.

It's raw. It makes for great ratings. Still, I have to turn away every time that little snippet appears on screen. That news clip is probably going to sprout into a viral Internet meme about how great our gardens are in Meadowfield.

The meme will say something like '*Water with puke to get a great cuke,*' or another equally noxious phrase.

As first reported, our resident serial-killer-plastic-surgeon- garde-ner-gigolo works over at Johnstown Memorial in Connecticut. He's been there for three years now, and hospital staff questioned all act appropriately shocked when asked about their co-worker and what was found inside his house.

A pretty, young nurse who seems to get a little bit squirmy when she's questioned about the handsome doctor blushes uncontrollably. The reporter who is interviewing her picks up on her reaction and immediately starts down a very disturbing path about how the two of them, the nurse and Dr. Pavlovich, might be more than friends, which makes her blush that much more.

"Slut," whispers Anders under his breath as he slouches and watches, here but not here, in another universe but still sharing the same air that we're all breathing.

I can feel the anger bubbling up inside of me. What's more, I know I can't control it anymore, and I explode.

"What the hell is with you, Anders?" I snap at him. Marcy bristles. Myers cringes and stares at his feet. "I mean seriously. We all have crazy shit going on—really crazy shit. But you? You're like not even you. What the fuck?"

Anders shifts slightly in his chair and stares at me, dangerously close to how Dr. Viktor Pavlovich probably stared at that makeup-caked neighbor of his when he delivered to her his corpse-fertilized vegetables.

"I don't know, *Weston*," he hisses like a very scary cat, punctuating his indifference with my name as though he thinks if he uses it, he'll have some sort of power over me. "What the hell is wrong with ME? What the hell is wrong with HER?" He nods his square chin toward the image on the screen. "Look at the bitch. She probably let him do her right in the middle of his garden. She probably . . . "

THWACK.

Marcy is standing over Anders, her arm raised high. She's already cracked Anders across the face once, and she's deciding whether she wants to do it again. Immediately, Anders jumps to his feet and gets right in her face like he's ready to start a fight in the cafeteria at school because someone happened to look at him the wrong way.

His cheek grows red. His eyes blaze with fire.

I'm on the other side of the kitchen counter so I can't get between them quickly enough, but Myers is there, eyepatch and all, grabbing Marcy's wrist so she won't hit Anders again.

"HIT ME BACK!" she screams at him. "If that's what it will take to make the real Anders come back instead of you, then hit me back."

I watch Anders fists tightly fold into balls, and his knuckles grow from fleshy pink to white, but by then, Myers is struggling to pull Marcy away from Anders. He looks like he's going to do exactly what she wants him to do.

"Stop it," says Anders, but he says it like he doesn't really want her to stop. He wants her to hit him again, over and over again, so he'll have a reason to hit her back. What's more, whatever version of Anders this is, he's not the Anders that we all grew up with.

He's someone else.

"Anders, enough," I growl. By then I'm around the granite island and fitting my new, thinner body between the two of them, not wanting to be hit, but not wanting a fight to break out either.

Anders glares at me with a horrific mixture of hatred and loss in his eyes. All his pent up emotions aren't even directed at me or Marcy. They're obviously targeted somewhere else, very far away.

And right when I think he's actually going to hit me, the house phone rings again. We all stand motionless, like statues, as though the person on the other end of the line can actually see us in Marcy's saucer of a house, melting, melting, melting into a bitter, angry gruel.

Like with all the other calls, an answering machine picks up and instructs the caller to leave a message.

When the caller does, the blood in my veins turns to ice. I'm sure the same goes for the rest of us.

"Hiya, Momsicle and Popsicle," says Tate Cole with a voice that sounds like it's crept out of the mouth of a spider. "I'm just chillin' over here in Bellingham with my pudding and a spork, but it sounds like shit finally got real in your neck of the woods. Seriously, what the fuck is going on down there in Meadowfield? It sounds like I'm missing one hell of a party."

25

TATE COLE.

Tate Benjamin Cole.

If Meadowfield had a cancer living here prior to Dr. Viktor Pavlovich, malignant Tate Cole was it. Born only eleven minutes before Marcy, but light years away from her, Tate Cole was the curse of Primrose Lane. As a matter of fact, he was the curse of the entire community.

In Kindergarten at Byberry Elementary, he shoved this short kid named Lane Crocker into a row of coat hooks next to our cubby holes in Mrs. Benson's class. One of those coat hooks went straight up Lane's nose, and he had to be sent to the hospital.

In first grade he broke Myers' arm. We were playing Twister at the Myers' house and Tate was having a hard time contorting himself into the pretzel he needed to be to win. I guess he thought stepping on Myers' outstretched arm until it made a wet snapping sound was the best way to ensure victory.

He won. Myers lost big time.

In third grade, Tate stabbed Mr. Scalia, a long-term substitute for Ms. Nichols who was out having another baby, with the pointy end of a protractor. It went clean through Mr. Scalia's hand, all because Tate messed up his multiplication tables and decided it was the teacher's fault instead of his own.

Also that year, right when Marcy was beginning to go through all her own shit, Tate cornered her in the bathroom with a butcher knife. I remember that day clearly. We were playing at the Coles' house, all of us, and Anders managed to get the pointy end of the knife pointing somewhere else besides Marcy.

Anders still has a scar on his hand from that day, and the memories of a hospital visit and a dozen stitches to prove it, although his scar has faded to white by now.

By the end of third grade, which seems like a lifetime ago, Tate began a series of in-house stays at various institutions throughout New England. I don't remember all their names, but I do remember that Tate slowly but surely disappeared out of the Coles' lives, at least as far as the rest of us were concerned. What's more, we were glad he was gone.

Although little kids have a pretty high tolerance for crazy, none of us had a tolerance for Tate. He was a rabid dog, and rabid dogs need to be put down. Since Massachusetts doesn't euthanize crazy-ass kids, the next best thing is to lock them away.

Marcy never talks about Tate. None of us even think about him. The sole reminder that he ever lived in the Coles' house to begin with are the pictures hanging on the wall downstairs in the den, and the couch filled with burn holes. Tate sometimes lit cigarettes, took a puff, and burned the leather with the glowing end.

I remember he always had this sort of demented glee in his eyes when he did it, like he imagined the leather to be skin, and whoever belonged to that skin squealing in terror every time he touched them.

That was Tate—Tate Cole—the monster of Primrose Lane unseated only this morning by a new monster—Dr. Viktor Pavlovich—the monster of Covington Circle.

The four of us stare at the phone after Tate hangs up, unable to move and unable to speak. There is only so much shit you can heap on top of a pile of shit before that pile begins to tip.

Marcy looks hard at the phone, her slapping hand still in Myers' grip. Slowly, Myers loosens his hold, and Marcy's arm falls away.

"Fuck me," Myers whispers. "That's all we need."

Anders closes his eyes tightly—actually squeezing his lids so hard that wrinkles form around their outer edges. He bites the inside of his lip and bows his head.

I don't know what's happening. Frankly I haven't understood the littlest bit of my life since I woke up this morning in The Maze. Now, Tate Cole is on the phone, there's a mass murder being investigated over on Covington Circle, and Anders and Marcy are having some sort of major blowout that seems to have everything to do with them and nothing to do with the weirdness that has enveloped the four of us since our memories disappeared.

Anders backs up and plops down in the chair again. He's no longer sitting like he did before with one leg over the arm, ready to scratch his balls at any moment. He's sitting bent over with his face in his hands, and he's crying.

I think I'm the only one who hasn't cried in front of the others since we woke up this morning, but I've had my fair share of waterworks ever since leaving Prince Richard's Maze to traverse the expanse of Meadowfield in search of essentials for my friends.

Every few seconds Anders pulls in great gluts of air to fuel his despair, and I feel nothing inside, except some sort of relief that my friend may not be the cold and callous asshole that he's been play-acting at being all day.

Marcy bends down next to him and tentatively puts her hand on his knee. A bomb goes off.

"Get away from me," Anders bellows and pushes her away so fiercely that she falls back and clunks her head against the edge of the granite counter.

Then he's gone, bolting for the spiral staircase in the middle of the Coles' house and disappearing down the dark hole into the mess below.

Once again, like this morning, I know I have to go after him. He's broken in the head somehow, and I have to make sure that no one else finds a broken Anders wandering Primrose Lane. We all now know that a broken Anders can be a dangerous Anders, and a dangerous Anders can hurt someone.

After all, he's hurt Marcy—and just like this morning, there's blood. This time it's wet and sticky, and on the tips of Marcy's fingers from where she reaches around to inspect the back of her head where it collided with the hard counter.

She holds her fingers out in front of her, her hands trembling, her lips quivering, and her eyes like cartoon eyes, several sizes too big for her face.

"I'm bleeding," whispers Marcy, so softly that her words are deafening.

"Shit," says Myers.

Shit is right.

Why does everything with the four of us always have to end in blood?

26

TWO YEARS AGO a girl named Annie Berg from up in Apple came to live with her aunt in Springfield. She never talked about her mother, but I got the sense that whatever happened to her, it was nothing good. Her dad, well, her dad was the kind of guy who was a little too handsy for his own good, so ultimately Annie was sent away.

Apple's a bad place anyway. It's the sort of town where kids grow up with no trajectory out, kind of like Guilford or Montgomery Falls. Their high school is rated about the worst in the state, and turning eighteen there means you either work in the orchards, get knocked up, deal heroin, or join the army.

Annie Berg was lucky. I heard she had a boyfriend back in Apple that ultimately didn't work out, so she started dating a guy here that she met at FunTowne.

The guy she met was younger than her, but she was okay with that. I suppose you could say that Annie was a little stunted anyway. I think her life until Springfield was some sort of living hell, so she was allowed a little immaturity.

Sometimes being immature is the only way to make it through the really horrible stuff.

I'm not a selfish, self-absorbed kind of guy who thinks the whole world is like Meadowfield. I know that I'll never really understand the sort of life Annie lived in a place like Apple. I barely understand a town where kids don't regularly graduate from high school, let alone don't go off to college and start a bank account on their eighteenth birthday.

Kids from Annie Berg's part of the world don't know what a trust fund is. They don't know people like me who will probably never really have to worry about money. Sure, they understand single parents. That's a universal part of our culture, but people with money, even a little bit, are as alien to them as people from Dubai or the Upper West Side of Manhattan.

The reason I'm bringing Annie Berg up in the first place was that the guy she started dating was a guy we all used to go to high school with.

He didn't go far for college. He went to the University of Massachusetts up in Amherst. It's only a half hour drive from there down to Springfield, and he thought Annie was worth it.

That guy, Owen Carter, was a friend of ours. I know he was a little older than us, but not old enough that we wouldn't all hang out. Before Marcy had her license, Owen had his, and whenever he was visiting Annie in Springfield, he would come and get us all and we'd go out.

Hanging with Owen made me feel somehow human because two years ago, you could barely make out the human underneath all the fat I was hidden behind. He never said one word about it. He never made a fat crack, which even Myers did every once in a while. He never looked at me differently.

He was Owen, and I was Weston, and he accepted me for who I was.

Owen was killed on the Mass Turnpike on his way down to see Annie this past Christmas. Supposedly he wasn't drunk or stoned, and there weren't very many cars or trucks on the road. His car slipped, spun around, and went over the guard rail at exactly the right spot where the trees were thin and the fall was far.

At the funeral, which had a closed casket because all Jewish funerals have a closed casket, I saw Annie. She was sitting next to her aunt with this glazed expression on her face. Part of me thought she didn't understand the Jewish service or why the coffin wasn't open. The real reason Jewish caskets are closed is so that we'll always remember people the way they were in life, not in death.

However, the bigger reason why Owen's casket was closed was probably that there was no Owen anymore, except for what was scraped away from the insides of his burnt-out car in the gulley where he ultimately died.

That day, I waited for the service to end before going up to Annie to tell her I was sorry about what happened to Owen and to see how she was doing.

Her answer was so weird, so off, that I'll never forget it.

"You can't fix broken," she said to me before burrowing her face in her aunt's shoulder and slowly walking away. I remember staring after her as she went. I felt like my world had been picked up like a child's snow globe and shaken hard.

I was upset about Owen and confused by Annie's words.

'You can't fix broken.'

As I watched her trudge away from me I remember thinking that what she said felt prophetic and true.

Now, a million miles away from Owen Carter's death, everything I have come to accept about my world in Meadowfield seems broken without a way for it to be fixed. The fake people and the designer clothing, the façade of perfection that is nothing more than a cardboard cutout covering a darker truth, the single mothers like Beryl or Mrs. Stephenson whose agendas don't seem to have anything to do with their children, all of it—it's broken.

Anders is broken, too.

I want to rush over to Marcy and squeeze her tight, inspect the back of her head, which I know is probably nothing more than a little cut that doesn't need stitches, and tell her that everything is going to be okay, but I might be lying.

As I stand there staring at her, rooted to the spot by an unreal feeling that I really should be in two places at once, by her side and by Anders, something creeps up from out of nowhere and starts laughing.

I don't know the voice. I don't know where it's coming from, but that laughter is as twisted as if it's coming out of Tate Cole's mouth and as brutal as if it's seeping from the pretty maw of Dr. Viktor Pavlovich.

Laughing, laughing, laughing inside my head until I think I might go insane.

27

ANDERS TAKES Marcy's car. How messed up is that? He freaks out, pushes her, makes her bleed, and then takes her car. I didn't even realize he swiped the keys, but somewhere along the way that's exactly what he's done. This wasn't a spur of the moment kind of thing. This was something that he planned, probably even before we got back to the Coles' house from seeing what was going on across the street from where Sandra Berman used to live.

I'm only like thirty seconds behind him, with demented laughter still echoing in my head, but that thirty seconds is enough time for Anders to get to Marcy's car, start it up, and pull out of the driveway.

Where the hell is he going? He's leaving, though. That much is clear. He's bailing on me, Myers, and Marcy while he's still not Anders at all. He's some weird sort of doppelganger who looks like him, but doesn't have his personality down. He's only a poor study drawn with charcoal and rough lines.

The color is all gone.

Pffft. All gone.

As I stand on the driveway, watching the back of Marcy's car disappear down the street, the growing realization that I am holding up my body by sheer force of will, glued together by exhaustion, envelopes me in a tight fist.

Whatever is happening to us and to Meadowfield is turning me into nothing more than a pummeled punching bag. One more punch and the fraying rope that's tethering me to reality is going to snap. I'll crumble into a thousand little pieces like Myers did back on the path in Prince Richard's Maze.

But I can't.

I just can't.

There has never once been anyone there for me but myself—not Beryl, not the old, dead people who left me a rich kid, not anyone. My friends have tried to be there for me, as much as they can, but the truth is we all have issues.

We all have shitty lives in shitty houses with shitty things that go on behind closed doors that would make most people's hair stand on end. Not one of us is beaten or has alcoholic parents. We haven't been inappropriately touched by the adults in our lives. We've never known hunger or poverty.

In some ways we're all afflicted with things that are equally as bad.

We hide behind smiley paper masks when in truth we're covered with the pockmarked scars of apathy and mental illness, drugs, crazy-ass brothers, fuckity-fuck-fuck-fuck mothers, and more.

I want to curl into a ball right here on Primrose Lane, underneath the blue sky and bright sun, my thumb in my mouth and the other curled around my ear, but I can't.

Someone has to go after Anders while someone has to go back inside to see if Marcy is okay. Someone has to make sure that Myers doesn't say or do something stupid, like talking to his mother and telling her everything.

Someone has to figure out why there are things in our heads that shouldn't be there, while someone else has to poke and prod at why a living girl covered in dotted lines and brought out of Dr. Viktor Pavlovich's house this morning started clawing at the fabric of reality when she took one look at the four of us.

She knows us. We know her.

How can that be? We've never seen her before, have we?

As I watch Anders drive away in Marcy's car, hoping against hope that all he's doing is heading over to Kimmel's Bagels to get us all something to eat, I have a revelation.

No one is going to help us.

No one is going to help me.

I might have my friends, and I'm sure as hell better off than any one of those poor, dead souls over on Covingtion Circle, but if I don't pull up my big-boy pants, size 30 x 32 instead of size 46 x 32, I'll be left with them floating around my ankles forever.

Anders is gone, at least for now.

Marcy and Myers need my help, and I need theirs.

I take a deep breath and go back around Marcy's house to the door to the garage. Inside, I smell grease and oil, trash and mold. At the door leading to the lower-level rec room I stop, my hand resting on the door knob and my eyes closed.

I can do this. I can make this right. I might not be able to fix everything and I'm sure as hell never going to fix the burnt triangle on my arm. Still, I have to try.

Something really messed up is happening, both to us and to town. I wish I could Scooby Doo this shit, but I can't.

I'm not smart enough to be Velma.

Anders isn't boy-scout enough to be Fred.

Marcy might very well be Daphne, but it's taken a miracle for her to get there, and Myers, well Myers might be dorky enough without the stoner vibe to be Shaggy.

We just don't have a Scooby with us. It must be nice to be a dog. Dogs don't have any issues. They sleep all day, and when they don't sleep, they eat.

I gave up eating a year ago. As for sleeping, it remains to be seen as to whether or not I'm ever going to be able to close my eyes again.

28

UPSTAIRS, THE TV is still on, and Myers is flipping channels. Every station has its cameras pointing at Meadowfield, Massachusetts and the parade of people gathered outside of Dr. Viktor Pavlovich's house.

"They've already cornered off his vegetable garden," Myers says. "They think he really did bury some people there."

"That ruins salad for me forever," says Marcy. Any other time her words would be morbidly funny, but today, right now, they're not. She has a paper towel filled with ice pressed to the back of her head, and her eyes are glassy. For that matter, she's not even watching the TV. She's staring at the wall above where the television is mounted, but I can tell her thoughts are someplace else.

My stomach gurgles, but I ignore it. Instead I walk over and sit down in the chair next to Marcy. Myers is still staring at the TV with his mouth slightly open. My coconut's eyepatch on his eye is a little unnerving. I half expect him to say *'Arrrghhh,'* at any moment, but even if he does, it won't make me smile.

It will only creep me out.

"Give me the remote," I say to him and hold out my hand. Absent-mindedly, he reaches over and grabs it off the counter and shoves it in my direction, his one good eye never leaving the screen. The news is focusing on that girl's freak out again. There she is, right on camera, with her dotted lines, her eyes staring directly in front of her, and her high pitched scream stunning everyone into silence. Thankfully, the camera doesn't pan back or swing wide so the four of us appear on screen. If I saw myself and the horrified look that must have been on my face, with the equally mortified expressions of my friends, all of which had nothing to do with Viktor Pavlovich and everything to do with some different sort of horror, I might get sick again.

I take the remote from Myers and turn off the television.

In some way, Myers and Marcy are probably thankful. Besides, we have something to talk about, but no one wants to start.

None of us are stupid. We know it has to be done.

"What happened to us last night?" I whisper. I might as well have spoken the words into a microphone. They seem to echo off the walls, asking the question over and over again.

"We were abducted by aliens," says Myers.

Marcy stares at him, her hand still on the back of her head, her fingers glistening from where the ice is already starting to melt.

"One incredibly unrealistic theory," I grimace.

"Is it?" says Myers. "Look at your arm. They branded you."

Bringing up my arm ramps up the stinging pain more than I could have imagined, and I wince.

"Does it hurt?" asks Marcy. Everything about her is so sweet. Everything about her is gentle and kind. How could Anders have pushed her into the counter? I mean, she's Marcy. We're friends. We've always been friends.

I nod my head, but I don't want to talk about aliens strapping me to a table, burning a triangle into my arm, shoving a transmitter up my nose so they can find me whenever they want, or sticking something really unpleasant up the other end for some ungodly reason that probably makes no sense other than that aliens are known to do that.

"Probably not as much as your head," I say. "I'm sorry Anders pushed you."

"Don't be sorry," she says. "You're not him."

"I don't think he's quite him, either," adds Myers being all Captain Obvious.

I stare at him, wondering the same thing that I have found myself wondering about Anders lately. Will we be friends once we leave Meadowfield? Will we even know each other in a few short years?

"I think we took drugs or maybe we were drugged," I say. I don't know how that could be true. The four of us don't do drugs, but nothing else makes sense. I certainly don't know what being drugged has to do with the shit show we woke up to this morning, but being all woozy like we're hung over makes sense.

"How?" says Marcy.

"That's stupid," says Myers. "Why would anyone want to drug us, anyway? No one even pays attention to us. It's like we're invisible." As we're talking, Myers reaches over and flips open the pizza box. There are two small pieces left, and he slightly nudges them with his fingers. "Does pizza go bad?"

We both shrug. "Would it matter?" I ask him. Myers is a bottomless pit with a cast iron stomach. I've seen him take peanut butter and chocolate bits, pop them into the microwave, melt them into mud and drink the whole thing like soup.

He tears a paper towel off a roll that is sitting on the counter, piles the remaining pizza on it, and pops it into the microwave.

"Besides," says Marcy. "I can't do drugs. They could mess up everything."

My stomach gurgles again, and I can't tell if it's gurgling from hunger or from nausea. I stare at the floor and wait for the rumbling to pass. Finally I look up at her and say, "Do you have anything to eat?"

"Really?" says Myers. "Mr. 'Extra Meatball' wants something to eat? Now I really know something screwed up is happening."

The whole extra meatball thing is so stupid. We went out for slices sometime before the end of junior year. That's when I was still starving myself silly, and refusing to eat. I was basically living on Diet Coke. Everyone was pestering me so much about not eating that I mustered up the courage to order one meatball on the 'Extras' menu, hoping it wouldn't make me gain ten pounds.

The waitress looked at me like I had something wrong inside the head and Myers made fun of me for weeks, calling me Mr. Extra Meatball, while Marcy kept telling me how great I looked and Anders kept sticking up for me like always.

Myers' nickname for me wore thin fast, then disappeared altogether—until now.

Marcy shakes her head. Myers will never learn to keep his mouth shut. "We have some apples in the refrigerator," she says. I'm thankful that she doesn't tell me the junk drawer is filled with mega amounts of sugary candy. We've all been raiding the Coles' stash since we were little.

Candy, however, is no longer something edible for me. It's poison.

"Thanks," I say and go over to the refrigerator as Myers pops the two slices back out of the microwave. They're floppy. Nuking pizza for even 20 seconds will ruin it. He juggles them in his hands until he drops them back on the counter.

A little bit of tomato sauce splatters and falls to the floor, almost in slow motion. As it hits, it creates a circular pattern.

I stare at the stain on the ground, its faux bloody dribble becoming real—more real than anything else around me. The round splotch is more real than my hunger and more real than my friends. A lightning quick memory, viscous and cruel, slices through my brain like Dr. Viktor Pavlovich's scalpel probably sliced through an unwilling victim's face.

"Anders," I whisper. "The blood."

Marcy looks up at me, my hand gripping a refrigerator apple. "I know," she says. "Someone got hurt."

Just like that, I fall down that rabbit hole hidden someplace in Prince Richard's Maze, and another memory, darker than blood, explodes into being.

29

I CAN'T MOVE. I'm lying with my back on cold, uneven ground with an enormous weight on my chest. I'm numb all over and so tired that I can barely open my eyes. Still, I force them to stay open as big black orbs stare back at me.

"Baaaaa," I hear. "Baaaaa. Baaaaa. Baaaaa."

I want to move. I want to scream. I want the heavy weight on my chest to go away because I can barely breathe at all.

I try to scream—to cry out for everything to stop, but I can't muster the words. All that comes out of me is a low moan. Then a sick and twisted laughter starts up from somewhere close, and I'm scared for real.

Suddenly, the weight disappears and there is a blur all around me. I hear growls and hisses and something going 'hummpf.' There are voices everywhere, but they are so chaotic and my brain is barely firing on one cylinder that I can't make out the words.

All I know is that I'm lying on my back surrounded by chaos, and I'm frightened. I'm more frightened than I think I've ever been, and I want to go home.

I want to go home right now.

A thud brings me back to reality, and the apple that I have pulled out of Marcy's refrigerator rolls across the floor from where it has fallen out of my hand.

"Are you okay?" says Myers, but it comes out all mush-mouthed because he is shoving day-old pizza into his mouth.

"What?"

"You look like you're going to be sick."

"What?" I say again. "No. Yes. No." There are those lies again. We all communicate in the shadows of truth, never saying what we really feel. Never saying what we really mean.

Marcy is still holding the ice wrapped in paper towels to her head, but she manages to stand. After a moment, she takes the whole thing away and feels around in her mass of curls. "It's only a bump," she says. "I'm fine."

I want to say that I'm fine, too, but I'm not. I'm someplace else with my back pressed against the ground in the middle of the woods.

"We have to find Anders before he hurts someone," I blurt out. I don't know what I'm talking about. I don't even know if I'm awake. There is a pained expression in Marcy's eyes, and I recover quickly. "Before he hurts someone *else*."

Ten minutes later we are no longer in the Coles' house. Myers has finished stuffing his big head with pizza and Marcy has dropped the wrapped ice cubes into the sink. We are down the street at my house and I'm pulling my truck, the one I bought when I turned sixteen and a half, out of the garage.

I remember Beryl was annoyed that she had to go to the dealership with me and even more annoyed that she had to sign papers so I could buy it in the first place.

Sometimes I think that I was an absolute 'oops' moment in her life. Well, I guess that part is true. I never had a dad. I think that sobering fact has 'mistake' written all over it, but it's not something we ever talk about.

I guess kids from single parent families eventually ask the forbidden question about the other half of the duo that created them. I never have. I don't know why. Beryl is more than enough parent for me. I don't need to contend with another.

Someday, when I'm way older and I get some rare genetic disease that requires me to know my family history, I may ask. Until then, I'm good, or at least I'm as good as I can be.

My truck is white and has an extended cab. I have fuzzy white dice hanging from the mirror. I don't know what they mean, although Anders' mother has told me, almost every time that she sees me in my truck, that she had fuzzy white dice on her car when she was growing up, just like mine.

I hope that's not an indication of my life to come, where I'll be trolling around for pick-ups like she does, and then bragging about them to kids who shouldn't even know that people do things like that.

My life is sad enough.

Marcy sits in the passenger seat next to me. One of her hands is at her mouth, and she's chewing on the skin adjacent to her nails. Marcy would never bite her nails like I do. She's worked too hard to get them to where they are. Chewing them would ruin everything. I know that's how she thinks.

Myers is in the back seat again. It's his permanent spot, always behind the rest of us. As I palm the wheel away from Primrose Lane, away from Merriweather Drive, and away from the horror across the street from Sandra Berman's house, Myers belches a great big pizza belch, long and low and a little wet.

"You're gross," Marcy says to him, which is about as mean as Marcy ever gets.

"Totally gross," I tell him. I look in the rearview mirror at Myers' one good eye, the other covered by my pirate patch.

Myers stares at me for a moment, then closes his eye, leans back, and slouches down in the seat. "Everything is gross today," he says. "Really gross."

30

THERE AREN'T VERY many places that Anders can go. Our lives in Meadowfield are finite. Once we pierce the bubble of town, we're either in East Meadowfield, Springfield, or over the Connecticut border in endless fields of tobacco. Kids from other towns work the fields in the summers. Meadowfield teens don't. We're supposedly too busy studying for our college entrance exams.

As I drive, I try and imagine where I would be heading if I were Anders.

Normal Anders would have finished soccer for the day. He might be hanging out with some of the jocks, but more often than not, he'd be with us.

He isn't normal Anders, though. Since we all woke up this morning in Prince Richard's Maze, he's been someone else who I don't know at all. None of us do.

"Where are you going?" asks Marcy. She keeps rubbing the back of her head like maybe it hurts more than she's letting on.

"You're hurt," I say.

"I'm fine."

"None of us are fine," I shake my head as my truck hits the top of Merriweather and I have to go left or right. I turn to Marcy, hoping for a little guidance, and catch sight of her profile. She's so elegant and pretty. How an infinite pool of genetics reaching back millennia formed and reformed until Marcy Cole was brought into being is unreal. I know I'm only thinking such bizarre thoughts because I'm still not quite normal yet. There is still stuffing inside my head, but it's rapidly going away. Hopefully when it's completely gone, I'll never have to feel this way again.

It's truly awful.

"Today's Saturday," Marcy says, still staring forward, her hands now in her lap and folded together. "He might have gone to the playing fields."

I nod my head and steer my truck to the right, go down two blocks, and turn left by the Meadowfield town tennis courts. There are white-clad people there, with whiter-than-white sneakers volleying balls back and forth. Nobody our age is on the courts right now. Probably anyone we know is part of an ever-growing crowd of spectators and forensics hobbyists, down Merriweather and around the other side of the dingle where something far more interesting than tennis is playing out on Covington Circle.

I force the awful thoughts out of my head, quickly drive past the tennis courts, and turn left again. There are several playing fields all along our right hand side, next to Jolly O's Coffee Clutch. The Clutch is Meadowfield's version of Starbucks, but all our own. Our town is too uppity to allow franchise stores to sprout out of the ground here. We're all about unique boutiques where everything costs twice what it should but people are willing to pay anyway.

At The Clutch, perpetually single or divorced grown-ups hang out in a spectacular live version of online dating. We go there sometimes and watch the desperately lonely leave in twos and sometimes threes, and hope to God we never end up like them when we're adults.

Anders' mother goes to The Clutch a lot. She brings her laptop and sits there, pretending that she's writing the great American novel, but in truth, she's hoping to get hit on by someone with an oversized checking account.

Anders hates going to The Clutch. Everything about it reminds him of his situation, and no amount of café lattes can douse that fire.

"I don't see your car," I murmur to Marcy as I scan the parking lot for what Anders took without asking. Marcy looks, too, but in the backseat Myers is slouched down with his eyes closed. He's breathing deeply. I think he's asleep, which sort of figures. Frankly, a sleeping Myers is good right now, because his special brand of annoyance is becoming increasingly hard to handle.

"Where else?" Marcy asks as she peers across the fields, hoping that we're wrong and Anders is there after all, but I don't think we're going to find him. It looks like soccer is finished for the day, and field hockey and lacrosse have taken over.

I don't play sports. I never did. By the time I was in middle school my legs were rubbing together so fiercely I could scarcely walk let alone run. Besides, I don't think it would have been in Beryl's wheelhouse to actually sign me up for a sport. She ascribes to the notion that little Jewish kids don't play sports, which is totally untrue. There are plenty of Jewish kids on the school teams. Still, I wasn't part of the 'kids-with-parents-who-care' club, so I was hiding in my bedroom eating Twinkies every day after school, while most normal kids were practicing something or other.

Even Myers had scouting.

"Over there," says Marcy and tilts her chin to the edge of the fence where the parking lot for The Clutch slides up against the grass. Grafton Applewhite is sitting on his bike talking to Joe Richman. Joe's not a bad guy. He's in some of my classes. I'd like to say he's stooping a level by hanging out with Grafton, but I think they both probably assume Anders is stooping even further to be hanging around with us.

I slow my truck down and do a three-point-turn in the middle of the street, then head back to the parking lot, Grafton, and Joe.

When I pull up, they both look at the truck and not at me. Everyone in town judges others by what they drive. A year ago, I bet more than a few people would have thought I drive a truck instead of a car because nothing else could carry me around. Now, they probably think I'm rebelling about something.

"Yo," Grafton says when he sees it's me. Joe just nods his head. "You still look like crap. Praying to the porcelain God yet?"

What a prick. I think I'll always hate Grafton Applewhite with his pretentious New England moniker and his bullying past. "Listen, have you seen Anders?"

Joe sort of smirks and shakes his head, then turns and stares hard at Grafton.

"The dude's messed up or something," Grafton says. "The coach yelled at him for blowing off the game and then Anders hauled off and punched out Barry Kupperman."

I close my eyes and pray that I heard something completely different come out of Grafton's mouth, but I know I didn't.

"And?" I say, sounding a little too pushy, a little too popular.

"What's your deal?" says Grafton, like he suddenly realizes that I don't have Anders around to protect me and I'm long overdue for a beat down.

Marcy slides across the seat, practically crawling on top of me. Grafton and Joe sort of flinch when they see her, as though their faces might melt if they stare at her long enough. Marcy seems to sometimes have that kind of power.

"Do you know where Anders is now?" she asks. Then she punctuates her question with, "It's important. Seriously."

Grafton shrugs and turns away. Joe looks at Marcy and something in his eyes kindle. I don't know what that something is, and maybe I never will. It could be love. It could be hate. It could be a thousand different things all wrapped up into one. "Try The Stumps," Joe says. "I don't think Anders and Barry are done beating the crap out of each other."

Marcy crawls off of me and repositions herself in the passenger's seat. She automatically sticks her fingers in her mouth but doesn't chew. She wouldn't dare. Finally, she turns to me and says, "You told me Grafton saw us at The Stumps last night."

"That can't be true."

"And a murder house across the street from Sandra Berman's house on Covington Circle can't be true either," she says. "But it is."

I sigh and chew at the inside of my cheek. The thought of driving over to The Stumps is so odd and out of character for us. I used to be afraid of the kids there, who hang out behind the brambles, smoking weed or whatever. They're the same kids who hang out in the courtyard at school, dealing in attention deficit disorder pills or their parents' Percocet, under the incredibly unwatchful eyes of the school administration.

I'm not afraid of them anymore. My fear of them melted away with my fat. Now, I just feel sorry for them. They're the ones who don't know that they've peaked in high school. Their popularity is going to shortly turn horizontal, until they realize too late that their parents' basements aren't life-long residences. When they finally wake up, the bitter truth that they can't even afford an apartment in East Meadowfield or Springfield will slowly creep in and force them to start counting the long, lonely days until their parents kick and they inherit a little bit of cash.

Sometimes bitter, vengeful thoughts like that fuel me. I know it's wrong, but after a lifetime of being on the bottom rung, it's comforting to know that I have nowhere else to go but up.

"Fine," I say. "Let's go to The Stumps."

Marcy nods her head then turns and stares at Myers sleeping in the back seat. "I wish I could sleep through all of this," she whispers.

"Me, too," I say. "Sometimes being asleep is way easier."

31

BACK IN 2011 THERE was an October snow storm. Usually the hill towns and the Berkshires get some snow in early November before the skiing season starts, but having snow down in the Connecticut Valley is rare in the fall.

When it happened, it wasn't only our area that was hit by what everyone referred to as 'Snowmageddon.' The entire east coast was totally blanketed with almost a foot of snow. I remember Scott Dwyer, the weather guy on Channel 22, saying the snow was Santa's way of letting on that he had an overabundance of naughty names on his list that year. He said it was up to all of us kids to make things right or we were going to end up with coal in our stockings come the holidays.

The whole Santa reference was lost on me and Myers. We didn't have Santa for Hanukah, but some of the dim kids—not Anders or Marcy, but some of the really stupid kids—started being nicer because they didn't want their Christmases to be ruined. Unfortunately, being nice can only last so long.

Anyway, that October we lost power for almost a week. We also lost tons of trees. The leaves hadn't fallen away yet and the added weight of the snow on top of leaves cracked branches in two.

In Meadowfield, all the cleaned up foliage from Snowmageddon was dumped at the dead end of Miller Road, creating the whole area known as 'The Stumps.'

Miller Road is down Meadowfield Street on the river side of the road. I drive that way, past the high school, through one of only two sets of lights in town, by the First Church Cemetery with the huge crypt in the center that used to give me nightmares when I was little, and then hang a left at the town green.

Fucking Anders. Why did he have to take Marcy's car and leave us? Where does he think he's going? He's been so off today, so wrong, like a complete stranger has taken over his body, that I don't know quite what he's capable of doing.

He pushed Marcy. He made her bleed. That in itself is so topsy-turvy that I have a hard time wrapping my head around it.

My silent thoughts are broken apart by Marcy. She turns to me and says, "Damn Tate."

What a perfect way to take my mind off of Anders. The subject of Tate Cole is definitely worse. Damn Tate is right.

"When was the last time you saw him?" I ask her. I haven't seen Tate Cole for so long that I'm not sure I would recognize him even if I did. He's a bad dream from a life lived a long time ago. I'm sure that someday his ugly specter may rear its ugly head again. I only hope it's not soon.

Decades from now would be good.

"We see him a couple of times a year," Marcy says. "Our birthday, and . . . family days."

"Is he still mental?"

"He hates me. That's for sure."

"I'm sorry," I say to her. "What's to hate?"

She stares at her hands, folded in her lap again, and snorts in that little way that girls sometimes do. "West, why are you so good?"

I don't miss a beat. "Because everyone else around us sucks," I tell her. It's the truth. If anyone ever told the embryo version of me that life outside of the womb was no bed of roses, I might have clung to Beryl's placenta more fiercely. "Your brother can go fuck himself. You're amazing. Don't ever think you're not."

Marcy reaches up and swipes at her face. I don't even have to look to know that she's dabbing at a tear. Marcy has always been a little emotional like that. "What am I going to do without you guys next year?" she asks. "You're moving as far away from your mother as you can. Myers is probably going to end up at some techy place where he can play with computers all day long, and Anders is going to Norway. What about me?"

"What about you?" I ask. "You're going out into the world, too, and showing everyone exactly who Marcy Cole is. You're going be amazing. You'll probably become rich and famous and forget all about us."

"No, I won't." she says. "I'll never forget."

She may say that now, but even I know that childhood ends. We all grow up, spend years in therapy dealing with how messed up our parents made us, then make little versions of ourselves to try and heal the wounds inflicted on us as children.

As for me, I'll never have kids. I don't think anyone needs my genes, or Beryl's. The Kahn name can disappear quietly into the night for all I care. Besides, if obesity can be inherited, I'm sure that indifference can, too.

My future kids don't deserve either.

"Okay," I say. "Let's make a pact to rock our fifth year reunion and show all these stuck-up assholes exactly how awesome we are." I'm not sure I believe we'll ever keep a pact. Who knows what's going to happen to all of us once we leave Meadowfield?

Who knows what's going to happen to all of us today or tomorrow?

I'm sure every one of those bodies being pulled out of Dr. Viktor Pavlovich's house was someone who had dreams. If Sandy Berman is one of the dead, I'm sure she had dreams, too. Even the crazy, dotted survivor girl, who screamed when she saw us, has dreams. They might be more like nightmares than dreams but they belong to her.

Maybe our dreams will somehow involve staying in touch. Maybe they won't. Even Beryl Kahn can't predict the future, although she thinks she can.

Meadowfield Street dips up ahead, right where the big yellow Drake Mansion sits on the left hand side of the road like a relic from some bygone era. The Drakes made all their money on ice cream back in the Stone Age, then funneled it into The Drake Academy up in Greenfield Center. Lots of kids from Meadowfield end up there. The Academy is elite, so it's an acceptable place for parents to dump their kids if they're going through a divorce or just plain tired of parenting. Beryl almost sent me there in ninth grade. I didn't want to leave my friends.

Case closed.

At the bottom of the dip on Meadowfield Street is a sign that says *'Miller Road,'* and another one below it with an arrow pointing right that reads *'Meadowfield Transfer Station.'*

Part of me hopes that when I turn on to Miller Road, drive past the dirt cut-off to the dump, and make my way to the dead end, Marcy's car won't be there. I don't want to deal with Anders right now.

I don't know who he is today.

I don't think he knows, either.

32

I HEAR A CHANT floating on the wind as I get out of my truck next to Marcy's car. I run my hand along her hood. The engine is still warm.

I can't quite make out the words at first, then when I do, I get this really sick feeling in my stomach that's part fear and part knowing.

Anders.

He's doing something bad.

"Fight. Fight. Fight," I hear people crying beyond the broken brambles and branches that make up the entrance to The Stumps. "Fight. Fight. Fight."

Marcy gets out of the car with me. I turn to wake up Myers, but he looks flat out with his mouth open and a dribble of drool seeping out of one corner. I decide to leave him there. Besides, he's a major distraction. Just looking at him, with his corn niblet teeth and his eyepatch, is enough to get any number of douchebags all revved up to throw a punch.

None of us need that right now. All we need is Anders.

"Fight. Fight. Fight." I hear again. "Fight. Fight. Fight."

"Come on," I tell Marcy and wince as my triangle starts aching again. The pain is just another thing I push aside in a long list of worries. I'll deal with them all when I have a chance to breathe. Right now, I have to save Anders from what I already know he's doing, and I don't know what saving him looks like.

I'm never the one to save the day.

He is.

Marcy follows me as I carefully step on rigid branches, climbing over the pile of debris blocking the woods beyond. She stumbles as she follows me. I reach out and grab her elbow to steady her. She stares at me like she doesn't want to be doing what we're doing because she knows what we're going to find in the woods.

"Why is he being such a fucking idiot," she says. Marcy doesn't often swear. I feel like I've been momentarily sucker punched by an invisible fist.

"I don't know," I tell her. "At the very least we can try and stop him from being a dead fucking idiot."

Her eyes turn sad.

God. Things are so different. In one day, how can things change so much?

I hear yelling as soon as my feet hit solid ground. There are people off in the distance, standing in the trees.

A couple of girls are walking toward us, passing a joint between them and shaking their heads. They probably don't want to watch anymore. One of the girls looks up, stares right through Marcy to me, and says, "Stupid assholes." Her name is Penny Fisk. Penny is a cheerleader on the Meadowfield cheerleading squad. The other girl is Lindsay DeCandria. All I know about Lindsay is that her daddy is really rich and pays for her to have a horse stabled over in Tobacco Alley because farm animals aren't allowed in town.

"Who's fighting?" asks Marcy, but they literally ignore her.

"Who?" I ask them.

Lindsay DeCandria, with the joint still in her hand and the sweet smell of weed tickling the end of my nose, rolls her eyes and says, "Didn't you use to be really fat?" Then she gives me a once over, her eyes mentally removing every stitch of clothing on me like she's a human x-ray machine. "Do you have AIDS or something?" She glances sideways at Marcy as the tiniest hint of a smile cracks at the edge of her mouth.

"Fuck you." Marcy swears again. The words come out of her mouth forged in something dark and sharp.

Penny Fisk pulls the joint from Lindsay's hand and says, "Anders Stephenson is going all cray-cray. Someone needs to put him down."

Marcy and I share a knowing glance and I say, "Maybe." Then we leave Penny and Lindsay behind.

We jog through the woods to where everyone is standing in a circle, chanting. "Fight. Fight. Fight," surrounding two guys who are obviously bent on killing each other.

As Marcy and I break through the circle, acutely aware that we don't belong at The Stumps in the first place, I hear Anders growl, "I'll kill you. I'll fucking kill you."

That's too many 'fucks' for one day. I feel as though we're all channeling Myers' mother.

Anders is looming over Barry Kupperman, who has a huge nose and an even huger mouth. Barry has been itching for a chance to fight Anders since way back in tenth grade. This girl, Angie Bellamy, hit on

Anders while she was still dating Barry. Anders took the bait because that's what Anders is like, nibbled on it for a weekend, then jumped off the hook.

Barry's been itching for revenge ever since.

Now, Anders looks like he's holding a fistful of Barry's face, and Barry's eyes are burning with deadly fire surrounded by spongy meat.

Shit. Anders really has done a number on him. What's worse, it looks like Anders isn't finished. He has his bunched up knuckles held high like he's going to rain down on Barry's head again until the rest of his face slips off, too.

"Anders," screams Marcy and rushes forward before I can stop her. She grabs onto his arm, like Myers grabbed onto hers while we were still in the Coles' kitchen and she was about to slap Anders silly.

That simple act—Marcy and Anders together at The Stumps, with me not far behind, and her grabbing onto Anders' arm, is enough to suck the wind out of all the spectators.

A deafening hush falls over everyone.

All we can hear is Barry Kupperman breathing and hissing, and spitting a bloody mash onto the ground that may or may not have teeth in it mixed with snot. Barry's chest heaves up and down as Anders' bloody fist is raised high and Marcy hangs on.

Finally, Barry spits again, falls back on both knees, and starts laughing. He slaps the ground, guffawing with his mouth open and blood dripping down his chin. "Now that," he laughs as he gestures towards the two of them. "That makes perfect sense."

Barry keeps laughing harder and harder until a couple of other people in the circle start laughing, too, but I can't tell if they're laughing because they think laughing makes them sound cool, or if they're laughing because they're scared and don't know what else they're supposed to do.

"Screw you, Kupperman," Anders spits out, then wrenches his tightened fist away from Marcy with such force that she almost topples over.

"Anders," she cries again. "Stop."

"Screw you, too," he growls at Marcy, then turns to me. Only then do I see his full face and realize that the guy I knew yesterday—the one I knew a week ago, a month ago, last year or even ten years ago—has changed as surely as if he was drawn with a pencil and someone took a nubby pink eraser and rubbed away the good parts.

My friend is gone. Whoever this person is in front of me, broken and bloodied, with anger seeping out of his pores, he's not the Anders I know.

He's broken.

I think we all are.

33

"LOOK AT ALL THE pretty colors," I hear a voice say, and my stomach falls to the very soles of my feet. "Wowee."

Anders, with anger streaming out of his body, pulls his eyes from me and gawks at the strangest thing I have ever seen, even stranger than the four of us waking up this morning in Prince Richard's Maze.

It's Myers.

At The Stumps.

His bad eye is covered in my coconut pirate patch and his other eye, so big and dark and round, makes him look like a cartoon instead of a real, live person.

"Look," Myers says again and giggles. "There's red all over Kuppernose and there's red on the ground and there's red all over Anders' fists . . . and . . . and . . ." Myers looks up at the sky and twirls around and around in a circle. "Look at the blue." A gust of wind shoots through the trees and a pile of leaves flies off in a dozen different directions.

"Myers," I hiss at him. Is he out of his mind? Is he as 'cray-cray' in the way Penny Fisk said that Anders was cray-cray?

Myers stops spinning, wobbles a little, then falls to the ground and begins rolling around in the middle of all the dead things. "Pinks and purples and yellows," he sings as he flops this way and that, scooping up great piles of leaves and throwing them in the air. "Browns and oranges and bloody, bloody reds."

"What the hell?" Barry Kupperman laughs, although he should be crying as his face turns all shades of puffy. "He's wasted out of his mind."

A bunch of people begin laughing and the circle starts to break apart.

"What a freak," someone chuckles.

"Damn weirdo," snorts another, and more laugh.

Still a third says, "Fly high, man. I wish I had me some of that."

And all the time that they're talking I'm feeling this incredible sense of deja-vu, like everything that is happening has happened before and not all that long ago. I remember being in the woods, and I remember

Myers there with me, along with Anders and Marcy, and I remember a sinking feeling that something bad is happening but I can't control any of it.

"Myers," I hiss again as Barry Kupperman laughs some more.

Anders suddenly clenches his fists and whirls around. Bloody Barry Kupperman, with the big nose, who has nurtured an Anders grudge since the tenth grade, sits on the ground, snorting and wheezing and laughing his ass off. What's more, I'm fairly certain a messed up Myers is the only thing keeping Barry from popping his thumb into his mouth and crying for his mommy.

"Shut up," Anders barks at him.

"Anders, it's over," I say as calmly as I can.

Marcy pushes past Anders, goes to Myers, and kneels on the ground. She looks so lost and afraid, that my heart breaks inside my chest. "Robbie?" she whispers. "Robbie, are you okay?"

"Of course he's not okay," Anders snaps, still bristling at the sight of Barry Kupperman laughing away, blood pouring down his face and coloring the top of his tee-shirt.

"Jesus Christ, Anders," I say. "What's Myers on?"

Suddenly, my eyes grow wide. Something crucial has finally clawed its way to the surface of my brain and has started broadcasting in the same amount of Technicolor that Myers is probably imagining inside his addled brain.

We *were* drugged last night. All of us.

Now, somehow, Myers is having a flashback or something. He's drugged again, and he's not going to remember any of this like none of us remember any of last night.

"Hey," I snap at Barry Kupperman, not even a little like the meek Weston Kahn who would never dream of showing up at The Stumps. Barry, still giggling, wipes his sleeve across his bloody face and tries to stand, but wobbles because his head has almost been bashed in.

"Shut the fuck up," Barry says.

I take a step forward, Anders now at my side. I don't know if I look scary or not. I've never looked scary before. I've looked fat, and I've looked doughy, but scary has never been a look I've ever perfected. Still, Barry Kupperman flinches a little, like I might hit him every bit as hard as Anders hit him, and I'll make him hurt as much as Anders made him hurt.

In his mind, I may very well make him bleed even more.

"What?" he says.

I lick my lips. "Were we here last night?"

Kupperman gets a weird look on his face like I've asked him a monumentally stupid question. "What?" he says again. "Like you don't know?"

"Dammit, Barry," I snap. "Did you see us here last night or not?"

"Shit," says Barry. "Everyone saw you here last night." He raises his hand and points a shaky finger at the four of us. There's blood dripping from it because he's used his hand to wipe the gore away from his face. "The four of you and your friends."

Anders' head tilts sideways.

Marcy looks up at Barry while Myers continues to blow spit bubbles like a toddler.

I squint my eyes.

"You were fucking stoned shitless," says Barry. "You all were out of your fucking minds."

34

FOR A FEW SECONDS that seem to last forever, we all stare at Barry. His words are both fantasy and reality. They're fantasy because he seems to be talking about something that happened in a barely-remembered dream. They're reality because I'm absolutely positive he's telling the truth.

After what feels like a lifetime Marcy stands and walks over to Anders. She holds her palm out.

She doesn't say anything.

She doesn't have to.

Anders stares at her outstretched hand but never at her. A couple of tense moments tick by before he quietly reaches into his pocket and pulls out her car keys. Half out of embarrassment and half out of feigned indifference, he drops them into her palm. Then he takes a giant step backwards and we both watch as she goes back to Myers, somehow gets him to stand, and leads him out of the woods.

There are a few people still left who saw Barry and Anders fight. This enormous girl named Val Buenavista, who looks like she'll someday win Olympic gold for dead-lifting free weights, is sitting with Kurt LaPierre and Ebon Ross on a log, passing a bottle of something really disgusting like green apple vodka between them. They are mostly ignoring us and bloody Barry.

Theo Andropolous and Mario Fragga are behind a tree, leaning up against each other. They're both on the baseball team and both out of the closet since puberty. No one bats an eye over their overt displays of public affection. People don't care about stuff like that.

What's making me a little queasy is that Theo and Mario are making out after watching one jock beat the crap out of another. Don't get me wrong. I don't care that they're making out. I think I care more about mixing violence with sex.

For a moment, my thoughts go back to Covington Circle and a certain doctor who probably liked that disturbing blend, too.

Anders hunkers down on his haunches and begins poking at the carpet of leaves on the ground. I just stare at Barry until he opens his mouth and starts talking.

This is what he says.

Last night, around ten or so, Anders, Marcy, Myers, and I show up at The Stumps. We aren't alone. There's this hot girl that nobody knows hanging all over Anders, trying her best to crawl inside his pants. Barry says she looked like she's from Springfield, or Holyoke, or maybe even some of the bleaker parts of East Meadowfield.

We're also joined by two guys who are about a year older than us. They're wasted, too, but in a normal way, if anyone can be wasted in a normal way. Neither of them is nearly as close to the moon as the rest of us.

The hot girl is dancing and grinding around Anders and one of the guys is pawing at Marcy like she's a piece of meat.

Lots of The Stumps crowd thinks that Marcy having a guy all over her is pretty interesting, but not interesting enough to care too much.

As for me, Barry tells me that I only hang out in the trees, nursing a beer. Myers, on the other hand, is being all weird and crap, not much different than a little while ago. Mostly, people understand that he's tripping out on something and leave him alone.

However, it's a little bit of a novelty that Anders Stephenson and his pet freaks decide to crash the popular crowd's hangout wasted, so nobody starts anything with us. We're not worth the time. We're more like mild entertainment.

Kupperman says that the girl with Anders starts getting all pissy. Anders doesn't seem to want anything to do with her. She ultimately ditches him and the rest of us and starts climbing over this older dude who's wearing a hoody and circling the fringes, but never getting too close.

Older people at The Stumps is nothing new. They're only looking to party like everyone else.

Meanwhile, the dude with Marcy starts looking really cozy, so more people are taking interest but not enough to do anything about it.

Mostly, they think the whole thing is sort of funny.

Finally, we all leave, but Barry says it's more like we're led away because we're too shitfaced to wander The Stumps by ourselves.

"That's all I got," says Kupperman as he pinches his nose and holds his head back. Anders has really done a number on him. I don't know why, but it seems like my best friend is all about blood, blood, and more blood.

"Yo," says Val Buenavista after Barry spills his guts. She heaves her bulk off of the log she's sitting on. Val's holding the neck of the bottle she's been sharing in one hand and her phone in the other. "Last night, when you guys were all wasted and shit, I thought it was funny," she slurs as she takes a step forward and holds her phone out to Anders without looking at me. I'm dirt to her, or less than dirt.

"So?" mutters Anders.

"So I recorded some of it," she says. "I was gonna post it online. Wanna see?"

35

THIS IS WHAT IT must feel like to die. You float up and out of your body, hovering above everything, but you can still see what's going on. In the little square window of Val's phone is my life from last night. Anders and I drift above it all, fascinated and confused, and probably a dozen other adjectives that can't come close to describe the insanity that we're seeing.

When Val recorded us, she didn't hold up her phone to advertise to everyone what she was doing. The picture in the video she shot is dark and grainy, and I can tell that she was holding her hand down when she took it, so we're all sideways.

Everything is sideways.

"Look at Master Baiter," says one of the guys that supposedly came with us. "He's a trip, dude. For sure." The guy isn't black, but he has an afro. People from Meadowfield don't have afro's—even the black kids. They straighten their hair or braid it, but never an afro. Our town is too country-club for that.

Myers slowly twirls as he looks up into the night sky. "They're out there," he keeps saying over and over again, every once in a while grabbing at empty air with his outstretched fingers. If I had to guess, I'd say there isn't the teeniest part of him that knows he's at The Stumps or being filmed at all.

He's someplace else.

The video abruptly swings to the left and pans across everyone who's partying. There's a barrel fire going, so every time Val points her camera in its direction, the image goes bright, and we can't see anything.

Up close I hear Val say, "Do you believe this shit is for real?" I don't know who she's talking to but I hear someone close to her say, "Wicked."

The thing is, what I'm seeing on her phone isn't 'wicked' at all. If anything, it's a little sick and twisted, like porn is sick and twisted but draws you in anyway.

I reach out and steady Val's phone in Anders's hand as the video pans back to me. I barely recognize myself. Last year, I would have filled up the screen. This year I'm only half filling up the screen. I'm in the trees, in the background, and I'm holding a beer. I don't know what's more strange—seeing myself as a shadow of what I used to be, holding a beer, or not remembering a single thing about either.

Nothing on Val's little video is familiar. Everything is happening for the first time.

I'm jolted back to the here and now by a rapid swing of the camera. Val takes a little time with this next shot. She probably thinks this is the important part of her video—the one that's going to get her hundreds of likes on the Internet, even if they're only from other kids at Meadowfield High School who know Marcy Cole and think it's funny that some dude has his hands all over her.

He's gross. His hair is greasy and he has really crappy skin. He looks like any number of burnouts who hang out down in Springfield under the highway with all the street kids. Frankly, he looks a little bit homeless himself. His clothes are dirty and his long, dark hair is matted to his head.

"What are you going to do for me, Sweetness?" he purrs to Marcy as she floats on air in his arms. He's touching her in all sorts of ways that would make most girls go ape shit, but Marcy's just letting him.

Everyone is half-staring at the two of them and snickering, waiting for something more interesting to happen. The suspense is probably killing them.

"Anders?" Marcy slurs and looks like she's struggling, but so slightly and so effortlessly, that no one would even notice that she doesn't want to be in the greasy guys arms at all. Anders isn't on the screen yet, but real Anders with the phone in his hand is starting to breathe heavy. Out of the corner of my eye I can see that his nostrils are flaring and his eyes have narrowed. If anger were palpable it would be seeping out of him right now and ruining his dirty laundry.

"He's busy," purrs the greasy guy on the screen, so Marcy closes her eyes and tilts her chin up to the sky like Myers.

In the background, I hear a girl's voice. I can't make out her words at first, then the audio on the little video corrects. Obviously Val is trying hard to catch everything that's going on. I guess we must be really interesting. She's now being extra careful to film us, sideways or not.

"Come on," a girl's voice says in a sultry, seductive way that comes out more sluttish than anything. "I'll be nice. Promise."

"Oh my God," Val says in the audio. "Stephenson's going to get a hummer for sure." Suddenly, I realize that the girl who is talking is the one that Barry Kupperman said was hanging all over Anders, like the greasy guy is hanging all over Marcy.

"Let's go," the girl's voice whines, but I can't really see anything. The camera is pointing in all sorts of directions, but never at her.

"I don't wanna," I hear Anders slur through the phone.

Then the video goes black, and I hear a voice, loud and muffled and really close. "Put that fucking phone away or I'll mess you up," someone barks at Val on the video. He must be standing right in front of her. All the action is blotted out. I don't see Anders or the girl who is talking to him. I don't see me. Thankfully, I don't see Marcy being fondled by the greasy guy. I don't see anything anymore.

On the little video, Val says, "What's your problem, dude?"

"Right now, you're my problem, you fucking dyke," the deep, hoarse voice says. "Put it the hell away."

"Whatever," Val says, and then the video stops.

What?

What?

In the here and now, Anders takes the phone and hands it back to Val. Then he turns to Barry Kupperman and says, "It's over, right?"

"Yeah," says Barry, still squatting on the ground with blood oozing out of his face. "It's over."

"Good," says Anders and stomps away from me like I'm the one who's done something wrong and just the sight of me will make him want to punch a wall or something.

Why me?

What did I do?

Feeling so far lost that I'll probably never be found, I turn to Val Buenavista and say, "Who was the guy who told you to stop filming?" She shakes her head and takes a swig out of the bottle she's holding. "Please," I say, and my voice goes up half an octave.

"You're the one who brought him here," she slurs, and I squint my eyes.

"Huh?"

"The asshole with the afro. He's *your* friend."

Last night, when the four of us showed up at The Stumps, we had two other guys and a girl with us. I don't have any memory of them. Still, it's all right there on Val's video. It happened, and it can never un-happen.

There was a greasy guy with Marcy.

There was a skanky girl with Anders.

There was a guy with an afro who threatened Val Buenavista.

Myers was tripping out and I was hiding in the shadows like I always do.

But there's one thing I know for sure. Barry might think it's over, and for him, it probably is. As for the rest of us, it's not over.

It's not over at all.

36

MARCY IS SITTING in the driver's seat of her car. She's staring straight ahead, but she's probably a million miles away on a planet where only she and Anders live. Myers is curled up in her back seat. We haven't decided what we're going to do about him yet. Even though we've already covered ourselves and he's not going home for the night to his fuckity-fuck-fuck-fuck of a mother, part of me thinks that he needs to go to a hospital.

None of us do drugs, but we're not stupid. His pupils are dilated so much they look like they are going to give birth at any moment, and what will crawl out of them is an abomination.

Even though I know a hospital is probably the right thing to do—even the smart thing to do, I know we're not going to bring Myers to one. That's too many cans of worms being opened at the same time, all wriggling around in a sad mass, addled and confused like the gray matter inside our heads.

Anders is in the back seat of my truck. Like before, he's staring out the window, also a million miles away but probably light years from the planet that Marcy is on.

As for me, I'm leaning against my door. I don't want to get behind the wheel yet. I need to process what just happened. I need to know what it all means.

Everyone lives through one bad day. I don't mean bad like you get a B on an important paper when you think that you are going to get an A. I mean, a really, really shitty day that will never leave for good. For years to come, when you least expect it, a particularly terrible part of that day will crawl its way to the surface of your memory and play over again, just enough for you to be reminded how miserable you felt having ever lived it at all.

Today is that day for me.

As I lean against the driver's side door of my pick-up, I close my eyes and squeeze the muscles on my face really hard. Like an epic zit, I imagine that if I apply enough pressure, the grossness that's inside will shoot out and I'll get some temporary relief.

No matter how hard I try, my face won't pop.

I need my memories. I need them to come back right now so I know what to do next. How can they be gone? How can they vanish into thin air?

Anders with a skanky girl from another town is old news. He's done that dance before. Myers and I aren't quite ready for that sort of thing yet. Myers is still a child. As for me, I'm not the same person that I was a year ago. I'm somebody newly minted, who's half the size I used to be, and I don't know who that person is.

I might very well be someone who picks up strangers, parties with people he doesn't know, and gets shitfaced with the popular burnouts.

I'm certainly someone who sports a triangle brand that aliens may or may not have given me, although that theory is rapidly deteriorating and being replaced by something darker and much more sinister.

I'm definitely someone who will always be from Running Man's town—Dr. Viktor Pavlovich—the murderer of Covington Circle.

"Weston?"

Marcy has gotten out of her car, walked around the hood, and is now leaning up against her passenger side door so that we are facing each other. I'm so lost in my thoughts that I don't even notice her at first. When I finally pull my eyes free from whatever scary daydream is playing out in front of them, I'm once again stunned by how pretty she is.

Anders is such an asshole. Why did he have to go and push her? Why did he have to do any of the things he's done today, flip-flopping like a droplet of oil on a hot skillet?

How could he?

"I'm here," I say to her. The truth is, I've always been here, ever since I can remember. I've always been the shoulder to cry on or the friend who will listen.

"I'm scared," she says.

If I were a better person—if I were a better man—I would engulf her in a bear hug and tell her that everything is going to be okay, but I'm not that kind of person. Maybe someday I'll morph into whoever he is, but right now, I'm only a frightened child in a foreign body, scared and alone.

"Me, too," I say with my arms crossed over my chest, hugging myself for comfort instead of asking for it from somebody else.

"What are we going to do?"

"Do?" I ask her. "About what?"

Ordinarily it would sound like a really dumb question, but it's not. There are so many things we should probably do. Each of them will lead us down a different path and I don't know where to start.

Marcy swallows hard. I hope she doesn't think that I'm powering down. The last thing Marcy needs is all three of us—Anders, me, and Myers—as useless husks. I just don't know which way to turn.

I'm literally afraid to get back into the car with Anders. I have no idea what he'll do. I'm clueless about Myers. I don't get this whole drug thing, or flashbacks, or any of it. I just have to hope he'll sleep it off because that's about the only thing he *can* do.

I don't know what to make of us being at The Stumps last night with three other people that none of us seem to know. I don't even know what to make of seeing the greasy guy with the long hair pawing at Marcy.

How does that even happen?

How?

Marcy closes her eyes and says, "I'm going back to my house. I'll take Myers and stick him in my bedroom. Hopefully he won't sleep for a year or wake up and start talking about space stuff."

I nod my head. "Okay." I look over my shoulder at Anders sitting in my back seat. "What about him?"

I really want Marcy to tell me to leave Anders at The Stumps and let him figure out everything for himself. I really want her to tell me that Anders needs an enormous time out away from everyone and everything, but she doesn't. Instead she says, "Bring him. We'll figure this out together."

I take a deep breath and shake my head.

Together.

We'll figure this whole mess out together or maybe we'll never figure it out at all. Honestly, who's to say?

37

IT'S 3:15. NOT TOO many hours ago, my world was very different than it is right now. There was no blood. There was no death. Sandra Berman was a distant memory, and Dr. Viktor Pavlovich was just Running Man, the good looking older guy who Marcy sometimes fantasized about because he had a nice ass.

Anders was a good guy. He wasn't a prick. He was nice and funny. He was my brother. Now, that relationship has been severed at the knees and once something is cut like that, I don't think it can ever grow back.

Drugs? How can you even say the words 'wasted' or 'shitfaced' in the same breath as you say our names? Things like that don't happen.

Still, they *are* happening. They're happening to all of us.

Back at Marcy's house we somehow manage to get a spaced-out Myers up the spiral staircase, through the living room, and into Marcy's wreck of a bedroom. Marcy and I drag him between us, his feet barely scraping against the ground, as he mutters nonsense about space.

Meanwhile, Anders locks himself in the bathroom, the same bathroom where Tate Cole took a knife to him so many years ago while he was trying to defend Marcy. Anders showers for a second time. If I were him, I would be scrubbing and scrubbing until all the dirt of the day comes off, but I think skin would be coming off with all the filth, and a red pool of slime would be circling the drain.

Not too long ago, the four of us rented a horror movie about a girl who was possessed. Myers made us watch it. He was geeking out over how good it was supposed to be. The movie sucked. Still, I'll never forget what the possessed girl said when she tried to describe what it felt like to have a demon inside of her.

She said she felt like she would never be clean again.

If that's true, I must be possessed because I feel covered in dirt.

Marcy and I turn on the television in the kitchen, flipping channels to find anything that's not about Meadowfield, but who are we kidding? We are sucked right back into the horror as soon as we hit upon a news anchor showing familiar pictures, along with that dreaded clip of the dotted girl sitting with her legs dangling out the back of an ambulance, screaming and staring at us.

We watch and we listen, but somehow the words aren't hitting anywhere beyond the surface of a dream. My mind is floating far away, desperately trying to remember anything about last night and coming up woefully empty.

My memories have been scooped out of my head and thrown down a deep, dark drain. I'll never recall lurking in the woods at The Stumps, hiding in the shadows with a beer in my hand. The weird thing is that I don't even drink. I've tasted beer once, and it tasted like ass. I wouldn't be holding a bottle in my hands unless someone put it there.

On Val Buenavista's little video, I'm nothing more than a human coaster—a prop in a movie along with all the rest of the background noise.

". . . name is Calista Diamond," says the newscaster on the TV. "Eighteen-year-old Diamond is a resident of Bellingham, Massachusetts. No more is known about her in this developing story. Once again, we are live here in Meadowfield, Massachusetts where tragedy has struck this small New England community . . . "

The newscaster keeps talking, but I no longer care to listen. Marcy doesn't either. She's sitting on the counter again staring at her feet. In the background I can tell that Anders is still in the shower. There is a steady hum running through the household. It's the sound of water rushing through the pipes. It's the sound of water washing away the dirt that is never going to wash away.

My stomach gurgles and Marcy looks up at me.

"Eat something," she says.

"I'm not hungry."

Marcy gives me a look that only a caring parent would give to a child if that child told a huge lie and got caught. "Eat," she says again.

I stare at the empty pizza box, still sitting on the kitchen island. Knowing Mr. and Mrs. Cole and their knack for living in chaos, that pizza box will probably sit there for weeks until little bits of congealed sauce and cheese stuck to the lid will turn fuzzy, signifying that it is no longer food.

There was a time not too long ago when I would scrape that excess cheese off the cardboard, remnants of pizza sliding under my fingernails, and suck on my fingers until every last bit of it was in my mouth, down my throat, and right to my stomach where it would be morphed into fat cells to be painted on my sides, layer after layer.

There was a time when I would order two small pizzas from Rinaldo's Pizza, one Hawaiian and one with everything on it, have them delivered, tip the guy way too much, then go hide in my room and alternate eating different flavored slices while steadily flipping channels, trying to find anything that would pull me away from Beryl, and reality, and my sad, miserable life.

Not anymore.

"Why can't this be yesterday?" Marcy whimpers. She's going to cry again, and I'm not going to know what to do.

Meanwhile, the reporter on the background keeps blathering on and on and says that name again.

" . . . Calista Diamond. The eighteen-year-old resident of Bellingham, Massachusetts appears to be the only survivor rescued from the house that you see behind me," he says.

I stare at the pizza box, not really listening, not really thinking. Suddenly, the words on the lid, with a picture of the Leaning Tower of Pisa and a fat chef, all printed in red, pop out at me, like they are the biggest things in the room.

They say, 'Pizza Depot, Bellingham, MA.'

Bellingham.

Bellingham.

BELLINGHAM.

I stare at the white box on the Coles' counter as something awful walks into my head, squats down, and takes a dump right in the middle of my brain. Without even knowing what's happening, my world turns on its side. I topple off the kitchen stool I'm sitting on and hit the ground with a thud.

38

I'VE FALLEN ON my burned triangle and a sickening jolt of pain runs up my arm, but I don't care.

"Are you okay?" Marcy blurts out.

No. No. I'm not okay. I'm not okay at all.

"Where did that come from?" I babble, as I struggle to my feet, pulling the upended kitchen stool along with me.

"Where did what come from?" Marcy asks, her eyebrows creased and her face painted with confusion.

I back up against the counter until I can't back up anymore. "That," I say, raising one hand and pointing at the pizza box.

"What?" says Marcy, not even quite sure what I'm pointing at. There is so much junk piled everywhere that I could be talking about a stack of newspapers or a bowl full of browning bananas or a pile of woefully out-of-date telephone books.

"That," I say again, not using my words. "That . . . the . . . the . . . "

Marcy follows my pointed finger and shrugs. "I don't know," she says.

Still, I continue holding my arm out, with my extended finger pushing at air so vehemently that I might as well be clutching a crucifix and holding it up against a vampire.

"It's . . . it's . . . ." I jabber but the words can't form anything coherent. All I know is that the word '*Bellingham*' is printed on the box. The reporter just said Bellingham. What's more, there's something else that I can't quite remember that has me scared silly, but I don't want to look at it. If I have to look at it then I'm going to have to think about it, and if I have to think about it, my head might crack in two.

Marcy leans over and reaches out for the pizza box.

"It's empty," she says, not understanding what I'm trying to say. "Myers ate the last couple of pieces."

"The box," I cry. "Read it. Read the box."

She picks it up and turns it around in her hands.

"Pizza Depot," she says. "Where's that?"

"Read it," I say again, almost whining. I think I might cry.

"Pizza Depot," she says again. "Bellingham, MA."

I watch her face, waiting scant seconds before I see the color drain from it in a palpable way. Her eyes turn glassy. I wait for her to add two and two together and come up with the fact that the reporter on the television has just said that the survivor girl, Calista Diamond, is from Bellingham, Massachusetts. Now we have an empty pizza box from there, too. It was filled with pizza that none of us remember ordering or eating, except for Myers a couple of hours ago when he scarfed up the remaining two pieces.

Marcy opens her mouth. She's smart. We all are. We're all going to go away to college next year to make something of ourselves. That's what kids from Meadowfield are expected to do.

She says, "Tate's in Bellingham. He's at The Bellingham School."

The air rushes out of me in a great whoosh. Marcy's smart. She's just a different kind of smart than me. She doesn't add the facts together the same way I do. She adds them together using new math and coming up with a new answer that's as viable and true as mine.

I feel my legs grow weak and noodle-like. I expect them to buckle under me at any moment because I'm as huge as a house.

But I'm not.

Things are different now. I just haven't gotten the memo yet.

Tate Cole, the demon of Primrose Lane, lives in Bellingham, and now, eighteen-year-old Calista Diamond who survived Viktor Pavlovich's shredding blades is from Bellingham, too.

So is that pizza box.

So is that pizza.

How?

How?

Anders comes walking into the kitchen with his jeans on, no shirt, toweling his hair. He doesn't look at us. He looks at the floor. I think some part of him is embarrassed for everything he's said and everything he's done since we woke up this morning.

"I can't be here," he whispers.

"Fuck you," I say, not because I'm angry at him. I say it because he doesn't have a choice. He has to be here. We all have to be here. Myers is in Marcy's room, tripping out on something that none of us know square one about, and now there is a pizza box here, in Marcy's house, that has no right being here. It's from a town that's about an hour away from Meadowfield and none of us, not one of us, ordered a pizza from

Bellingham last night, even if we were totally blitzed out of our minds.

"Yeah, well, I can't be here," he says and turns around and walks away. Marcy watches him go. The pain in her eyes is so real that she might as well have pins sticking into them instead of the vision of an indifferent Anders.

"Wait," she says. "Anders, wait." She hops off of the counter, dropping the pizza box to the floor, and follows after him. I don't know if she is going to slap him or if he's going to push her again and make her bleed. I don't know anything except that a fat man, printed in red, with a chef's hat and the Leaning Tower of Pisa behind him, is lying on the floor, staring back at me.

There are secrets behind the twinkle in his cartoon eyes. There are secrets behind his fat man's smile. What's more, there are secrets in every single room of that cartoon tilted tower, in every nook and cranny, begging for me to come and look.

I don't want to look.

I have to look.

There are answers there. I can feel them screaming out to me in my head, but the screams are either so soft that I can't hear the words, or they are so loud that the answers are muffled.

As my fingers back up against the counter, trying to hold on to the ledge like a rock climber holds on to the scantest bit of rock sticking out of a cliff a thousand feet high, I know what I have to do.

I leave the kitchen, too, but I don't follow after Marcy and Anders.

I go somewhere else.

39

MYERS IS CURLED up on Marcy's bed, surrounded by her sea of clothes, covered in a pink blanket that may or may not have flowers on it. I can't tell. I don't even think I care. His eyes are open into slits, and he's mumbling. I still don't think he knows he's in a bedroom or even in Marcy's house. He's flying somewhere through time and space. I only hope he'll be able to find his way back home soon.

I wade through her ocean of clothing to her floating laptop, pluck it free of panties and single socks that have long ago lost their mates in the abyss of the dryer where all second socks go, and pray that she doesn't have her computer password-protected.

She doesn't.

Big miracles come from the smallest of things.

I sit on her laundry, cross-legged, with the laptop in front of me, and close my eyes. There is something that I have to search for, but I'm not sure what that something is. Random ideas shuffle inside my head, but none of them seem to fit together.

The first one that rises to the surface is Bellingham. There's a trifecta of connections there. Tate Cole is at The Bellingham School where he is supposedly locked away. I can picture him, with the same face as Marcy's but much harder, and that sinister look he was always so good at hiding, but not good enough. That look—that narrowing of the eyes and the tiniest hint of a smile at the corners of his mouth, was the look of someone who liked to cause pain in all sorts of ways.

But my brain isn't pushing me to search for him yet. If not Tate Cole, then that girl, Calista Diamond, is next on my list.

I'll never forget the way she stared at us back on Covington Circle in front of Running Man's house, her head shaved and dotted with lines, screaming loud enough and long enough to wake all the dead people being pulled free of his residence. The reporter on TV said that she's from Bellingham, too.

That's two for two.

A shiver races through my body and I involuntarily whip my head around for fear that Myers isn't lying on Marcy's mess of a bed anymore. Calista Diamond is there instead, waiting for me to look at her so she can open her mouth wider than a human being should ever be able to open a mouth, and let free with a sonic bullet that will drop me on the spot.

I shake my head to dislodge the horrific thoughts and involuntarily rub my left forearm. I'm again becoming painfully aware that there is a burn there that is crying out for more Neosporin.

My fingers rest on Marcy's keyboard.

What am I searching for?

What am I searching for?

Two words pop into my head, so innocuous and unassuming that most people would never pay much attention to them. However, to me, there is something vital there.

Pizza Depot.

Pizza Depot in Bellingham is an hour away from Meadowfield. In Massachusetts geography that means it's practically in another part of the state. I look down at Marcy's keyboard and quickly type in a search. All sorts of weird things come up that have nothing to do with Pizza or Bellingham at all. Several entries down on the list, something a little eerie catches my eye. It's a story about the Pumpkin Festival in Keene, New Hampshire. I don't know why Pizza Depot is associated with The Pumpkin Festival in Keene, but I know all about what happened there.

The temperature in Marcy's room seems to drop several degrees as I press on the link.

An article pops up from the Keene Sentinel. The story is two years old, but what happened there is still fresh in every New Englanders' mind.

The headline reads, *'Riot decimates annual fall festival.'*

This is what follows:

Police in riot gear used tear gas and pepper spray to disperse a large crowd at Keene, New Hampshire's 24th annual Pumpkin Festival Saturday night. Dozens of individuals were arrested, and ambulances were summoned to deal with a variety of injuries.

"State and local public safety officials are on the scene and have been working to defuse the situation," Mayor Christopher Flowers said. "We will continue to monitor the situation and provide any assistance necessary to our citizens."

It's unclear at which point during the evening things took a turn, but there were reports of people being struck by flying bottles as attendees traded insults with the police, started fires, and overturned cars.

"It's like a rush," Amanda Gagne, 18, <u>told The Keene Sentinel Saturday night</u>.

"You're revolting against the cops. It's a blast to do things that you're not supposed to do," she added, describing the night's events as 'wicked.'

Last year's pumpkin festival set a world record by lighting 50,596 jack-o-lanterns.'

A strange, uneasy feeling washes over me. I had nothing to do with the riots up in Keene. I've never even been to any of the pumpkin festivals there, even though they are within an hour of Meadowfield. Still, when they happened, I remember feeling so unsafe. Now I knew that bad things could darken good places like Keene, New Hampshire.

Or Meadowfield.

I scroll through the pictures of the devastation in Keene, where cars were overturned and dozens of people were sent to the hospital, until I find why Pizza Depot is connected with the riots.

There is a picture of the Pizza Depot delivery truck parked there, along with a dozen other food vendors, selling funnel cakes and candied apples. I click on the picture, and it fills up Marcy's screen.

Immediately, I push Marcy's computer off of my lap, stand, and go to her disaster of a desk where a house phone sits in its cradle. I snatch it up and go back to the computer, squinting as I look at the numbers painted on the side of the truck next to a red picture of a fat chef and the Leaning Tower of Pisa.

I take a deep breath, jab at the phone, and wait.

"Hello, Pizza Depot," says a man's voice. He sounds both rushed and annoyed at the same time.

"Hi," I say.

"How can I help you?"

"Um, do you deliver?" I feel like a little kid making a goof, asking if this guy's refrigerator is running, because if it is, he should go and catch it.

"What's the address?" says the guy on the other end of the line. He probably gets the same call a hundred times a day. The people ordering are probably fat, neglected teens, whose mothers are named Beryl and smoke pot all day long while pretending to talk to their spirit guides. They probably order two pizzas at once—one Hawaiian and one with everything on it.

"21 Primrose Lane," I breathe into the phone.

Immediately, I can feel a wave of anger flow through the receiver along with a barrage of words worthy of any truck driver. "In fucking Meadowfield, Massachusetts?" the guy hisses. "I don't need this shit. You're goddamned lucky your phone number is blocked, kid, or I'd be calling the cops. For the hundredth time, we don't fucking deliver to fucking Meadowfield." The man growls like he may actually have sharpened teeth in his mouth. "Grow up and stop with the prank calls. If you call here one more time, I'll kill you."

Then the guy from Bellingham's Pizza Depot hangs up on me, like I now know he's hung up on someone else dozens of times before who has pranked him to deliver pizza to Marcy Cole's house.

I know who, too.

Of course I do.

40

TATE.

I hate Tate. I've always hated Tate.

The years have stretched between us, but his memory is still there, vivid enough to leave an acrid taste in my mouth.

I want to spit it out, but there's no place to spit in Marcy's bedroom. Instead, I swallow something gooey and take a deep breath. My heart starts thumping faster and faster in my chest.

Is Tate out? How the hell else would there be a pizza from Pizza Depot in Bellingham in Marcy's house? Her parents, sure as shit, didn't bring it. They're not even home. They've been gone since yesterday, down at the Indian Casino.

If not Tate, who else would bring a pizza from an hour away and leave it in Marcy's kitchen, three quarters eaten?

For all I know, Tate could be in the house right now, hiding in a closet or squirreled away downstairs with Marcy's goldfish, ready to jump out at any moment, holding a butcher knife and more than willing to cut.

I feel scary invisible eyes at my back.

This time, I don't whip my head around. I know that Myers is still there, murmuring to himself, lost in clouds. Instead, my fingers glide across Marcy's keyboard again, but this time I don't look for pizza. I look for something much, much worse.

The Bellingham School.

A bunch of stuff comes up all at once, along with images of the town of Bellingham and the Quabbin Reservoir, the largest body of water in Massachusetts. The Quabbin provides most of the drinking water for the state. It touches the edge of Bellingham at one corner, before running alongside Apple, Hollowton, and some other places that I would never be caught dead visiting.

I scroll through the entries, my eyes jockeying back and forth as the words spill out of the screen, until I find what I need—the Bellingham School's main phone number.

I pick up Marcy's house phone again, and for a second time, I make a call to a town that I haven't thought about in years—until today.

The phone rings four times before somebody answers. "Bellingham," says a woman on the other end of the line. "How may I direct your call?" At first, I don't know what I'm going to say, and the silence lingers between the two of us until it starts to have heft and weight.

"Um . . ."

"Hello?" says the woman. She sounds a little rushed and even more annoyed, like the man from Pizza Depot. "Can I help you?"

"Hi," I say, and then I lie, because lying is something that we have all perfected. "My brother is a . . . a student there. I was hoping I could talk to him?"

I'm tempted to hang up the phone. I don't know what I'm saying. I don't know what I'm doing. Still, I need to know if Tate is there, all comfy and cozy with his spork and his pudding, or if he is somehow here in Meadowfield, a twisted Michael Myers who has escaped from his maximum security mental health facility, killing a dozen people along the way, all so he can bring a pizza to his sister.

The woman at The Bellingham School sighs and recites a practiced line. "Students are not allowed incoming calls. They can only make outgoing calls between 10am and noon or 5pm to 7pm."

"Oh . . ." I say. My eyes are squeezed shut. I don't want to see Tate rush into Marcy's room, a bloody knife in his hand because he's already gutted her and Anders. I don't want to see him swing his arm wide. If he's going to kill me, let him kill me. I don't want to fight. I want it over with.

"It's important," I breathe into the phone. Part of me wants to blurt out that I'm in Meadowfield, an hour away, and I think that Tate is no longer in the building with her. He's in the house with me.

"Who is your brother?" the woman asks, but she does it in a hushed voice like she's breaking the rules and if she gets caught, then she'll lie, probably as effortlessly as me.

"Tate Cole," I breathe into the phone. I can feel the awkward untruth slithering out of my mouth like one of those slimy earth worms that squirm at the end of fishing hook owned by a master baiter.

"I'm going to transfer you over to Tate's counselor," she says. The words don't make sense at first—*Tate's counselor*. Why would he have a counselor? Is he at camp?

The phone on the other end goes quiet except for a gentle humming. After a moment, I hear a click and someone picks up.

"Guidance," says a man's voice. "This is Eddie Bick. How may I help you?"

"I . . . I was hoping to speak to my brother," I lie into the phone. Every fiber of my being is screaming for me to hang up right now, but I don't.

"Call-out hours are between 10am and noon or 5pm to 7pm," says Eddie Bick like the receptionist before him. "We don't allow incoming calls." I must sound like a 10-year-old girl to him because he punctuates his standard riff on calling privileges at The Bellingham School by saying, "Do your parents know you're calling?"

I don't know what to tell him, and once again, every cell in my body screams for me to hang up right now, but I don't. Instead, I say, "It's really important."

"I'm sorry," he says "Thems the rules." Those last three words are uttered in such a flippant way, all I can think is that he sounds more like his name should be Epic Dick instead of Eddie Bick. Thankfully, Epic Dick makes an epic gesture of good faith. "What's your brother's name?"

"Tate," I delicately whisper into Marcy's house phone.

"Tate Cole," he says. "And you are?"

I don't stop to breathe. I don't stop to think. I say the first lie that crawls onto my tongue. "Mark Cole."

"Okay, right," says Eddie Bick, not missing a beat. "Sure. I'll leave a message for Tate to call home at the normal calling hours. He's playing ping pong right now and killing it."

Eddie Bick uses such choice words that I almost flinch.

"Okay," I say into the phone and slowly hang up. Only then do I realize that I've been holding my breath through that whole brief conversation.

Tate's not in Meadowfield. He's not here.

He's not gripping the handle of a bloody knife in his fist.

He's far away playing ping pong and *'killing'* it.

During call-out times, about the only thing he's doing is making prank phone calls to local pizza shops to ask if they have Prince Albert in a can, because if they do, they should let him out.

At least I know one thing for sure. Tate didn't bring pizza from Pizza Depot in Bellingham here to Meadowfield and Primrose Lane.

Still, if not Tate, then who?

41

"PLEASE TALK TO me," I hear Marcy say. She's in her parents' room with Anders. The door is open, but not all the way. I lean against the wall outside, not really meaning to listen to their conversation, but listening anyway.

There is silence and then a deep sigh. Finally I hear Anders' voice. "What am I supposed to say?"

"I don't know," Marcy tells him. "What do you want to say?"

I feel like I'm doing something wrong. I have no right eavesdropping.

After an uncomfortably long silence, Anders says, "I'm sorry I hurt you."

"You've been hurting me for a long time," she says. Her words are soft yet rock hard.

"What do you mean?"

"You know what I mean."

Just as I imagine how Tate Cole would sneak around the house, I crouch down and slide my back along the wall until I can peek through the crack between the door and the doorframe. This is so wrong, but like watching endless speculations about Viktor Pavlovich on TV, I can't look away.

I'm addicted.

Anders is on the floor with his legs drawn up to his chest. He's still not wearing his shirt. I don't know why. He's been exposing every part of himself today—inside and out.

Marcy is sitting on her parents' bed, leaning forward. Her elbows are on her knees and her beautiful curls are hiding her face. Anders isn't far from her. If he wanted to, he could reach out and touch her leg.

He really could.

"I never meant to hurt you," he says. "You . . . you're . . ." his words trail off.

"I'm what?" she says, and suddenly I feel like being where I am, listening to them talk, is violating a sacred trust that the four of us have.

We're all too close for that. We've been through everything together. I make a lame effort to get up and leave—to be anywhere but right there, but in reality I don't move an inch.

"Marcy," says Anders, talking softly like she did before, saying words that should be screamed from the rooftops. "I care what happens to you."

"Is that it?"

"That's all I have."

He's lying. I know he is. He's doing the same thing we all do, to ourselves, to each other, to faceless people in Bellingham who work at the State School and supposedly watch Tate Cole, but obviously not well enough as he's still making prank phone calls.

"I love you," she says to him.

Silence.

I hold my breath. She's actually said the words, and not in a 'you're my best friend' way but in a real, heart-wrenching way that would be touching if she said them any other day but today.

Like I've said before, we've always known that Marcy's had a thing for Anders, but that was quiet knowledge that we shared without talking or dwelling on it. Saying the words aloud is different. Not only do they sound funny coming out of her mouth, they herald a change in how we are all going to act towards each other.

In saying those words, she's cast a spell that can't ever be taken back.

"I can't . . . I . . . ," stutters Anders.

"I love you," she says again, like the first time was only a warning shot. This one, however, strikes home.

"Why can't things be the way they were?" he cries. His voice is weirdly hoarse. I can't see his face, but I can imagine that it's flushed and red.

"We change, Anders. That's what people do. We change every day, and at some point we look at our best friend, our very best friend in the whole world, and realize that just being friends isn't enough anymore. I don't know what will be enough, but being me without you isn't what I want."

"Why?" says Anders. "Why me? Why can't you let me go, Marcy? Just let me walk away."

I stare through the crack in the door. Marcy's head droops even more. "If that's what you want then I can't stop you."

"Marcy. . . ."

"What?" she says. "You're a boy. I'm a girl. Why does it have to be anything more complicated than that?"

"You know that it's more complicated," he snaps. "What would your parents say? What would my mom say? What about West or Myers?"

"What about them?" she says. "What about the rest of the world?"

"You know what I mean."

Marcy takes in a ragged breath, long and deep. Quietly I get to my feet, hurting inside roughly the same way that Anders or Marcy must both be hurting. I wish I could rush into her parents' room and tell the two of them that everything is okay—more than okay—but I don't know if that's true or not.

Since last night, I don't know anything.

"You care too much about what other people think," Marcy says to him, like she's accusing him of some sort of awful crime.

Anders licks his lips. "Don't you?"

She looks up. Every raw emotion is painted on her face. "I stopped caring about what other people thought about me a long time ago," she says. "I thought you did, too."

Anders makes a strange noise. I can't see his face, nor do I really want to, but he sounds exasperated, like maybe he's finally out of excuses.

"I can't," he murmurs once again and stands up. Before I even have a chance to run and hide, or shrink against the wall so he doesn't see me, he's out the door. Our eyes lock but he doesn't stop walking.

"I—I—" I stutter but that's all. I don't have the right to say anything. I don't even have the right to be there.

"Enjoy the show?" he snaps at me. "We'll be on again at 5." Then he's in the living room and down the spiral staircase again. I wait for the inevitable slam of the garage door, but I hear nothing.

The only sound is the deafening silence of Marcy's house, with Anders skulking around the basement, Myers flying through another dimension in Marcy's bed, and Marcy, sitting on her parents' mattress, quietly sobbing.

Sobbing, until she has no more tears left to give.

42

IN THE BATHROOM, the air still damp from Anders' long shower, I rummage through the medicine cabinet searching for more salve to put on my burn.

There isn't any Neosporin, but there's some petroleum jelly which might work equally as well.

Gently, I pull the Band-Aid off my arm and look down at the vivid reminder of the fact that I don't remember a good goddamned thing about last night. The little triangle, puffy and red, chatters in stinging prose as it stares back at me even though it has no eyes.

The pain will leave as pain always does, but there will be a nagging reminder left behind.

Why me? Why was I marked?

All Marcy had to do was put on pants.

Anders only needed to wash.

Myers covered his deformity up with a patch, but he's always owned the glass eye thing anyway.

Me? I've been branded for life.

Too many crazy thoughts run through my head but none of them link together to form a picture. As I dip my finger into the jelly and gather together a small, gooey mound, I start humming a nonsense tune. My hope it that it will cover over the internal noise, but the first one that comes to mind is 'Ring Around the Rosie.' That only makes me feel worse. The popular theory about that song is that it has nothing to do with children and everything to do with a disease that covered its victims in stinking sores, and the ignorant belief that the bubonic plague was transmitted through smell. That's why everyone back then carried sweet smelling flowers in their pockets in hopes of dodging death.

I wonder if carrying flowers might have worked for all the people being pulled out of Viktor Pavlovich's house.

My guess is no. They'd be dead anyway.

I shake my head to loosen all the lovely bitter thoughts my brain manages to dredge up from a well so deep it might be bottomless, but shaking my head does something else instead.

Suddenly my mind is invaded by memories.

There's laughter and chaos and then a pressure on my chest and an awful burning on my arm. The pain is so intense that I feel like whatever happened to me is happening all over again. I'm stuck in an endless time loop that will never let me be free.

A wave of dizziness hits me hard, as surely as if I am standing two feet deep at the edge of a swirling ocean, then suddenly dragged beneath the surface by a dizzying undertow.

The next thing I know, the floor rushes up to meet my back. I hit my head against its hard surface and stars explode.

"Ow," I scream out, half hoping that one of my friends will come see what's wrong. Unfortunately they're all so broken that they're probably unable to hear me. "Ouch," I cry again, but my words are suddenly chopped off as another memory comes flooding in, so vivid, raw, and real that I know, way down deep, that it's true.

The girl from Val Buenavista's video is standing in front of me, her face inches from mine, and she's poking at me, one glittered polished nail pushing into my cheek and my forehead and everywhere.

"Hello?" she giggles uncontrollably, as though she's not even talking to me, but someone else that I can't see. "Hello?" she says again. "Anybody home?"

Her finger presses into me with each dull, lifeless jab.

"Wicked," says a deep voice coming from someone who is definitely from my part of the world, where people say 'wicked' for everything, instead of 'cool,' or 'sweet.'

The girl's face is so close that she's almost blurry, so I look somewhere else, anywhere else. My eyes fall on white painted cabinets. They're unfamiliar at first. Then I realize that they are the cabinets in Marcy's kitchen. They are gooey and moving, blending with the ceiling and the floor and everything until they swirl into a deep tunnel without end.

My eyes go dim. When clarity comes creeping back, the girl from Val Buenavista's video isn't there anymore. The cabinets aren't there anymore. I'm sitting in the back seat of Marcy's car without any recollection of how I got there. The world is spinning and I'm trying to make it stop by staring hard at the seat in front of me. There's a head peeking over the top of the head rest, and two others—three in all, sitting in the front seat.

Like I'm bobbing on the surface of that dizzy ocean, my head is struck by a rolling wave, and my neck involuntarily lolls to the right. Myers is next to me, his eyes closed and his mouth open. Anders is there, too. Marcy is half on his lap and half on Myers. Her curls are in my crotch and she isn't moving either.

We all look like rag dolls, tossed in the back seat without any regard for how people are supposed to sit.

From somewhere, I hear the sheep cry like I've heard before, and I get an uneasy feeling that has nothing to do with farm animals, or farms, or even the tobacco barns over the border in Connecticut. It's the feeling of being in the presence of something that doesn't make sense.

Something crazy.

I don't do crazy. I've never done crazy.

That's why I keep my distance from Beryl. My mother is bonkers with her psychic visions and her desperate, lonely clients who want to know when they're going to find a boyfriend or lose the one they already have.

That's why I always stayed far away from Tate.

Tate.

Tate Cole.

Suddenly the seed of a thought germinates and blooms into a poisonous flower.

Tate is at Bellingham State.

Pizza Depot is in Bellingham, too.

Calista Diamond is a resident of Bellingham.

The memory of Val Buenavista's video that Anders and I watched back at The Stumps with a bloody Barry Kupperman kneeling on the ground, dripping all over the place, flashes before my eyes. In that moment I learn a simple truth that I should have realized the moment I first saw the unreal images of the four of us in the woods behind the wall of debris at the end of Miller Road.

With my head throbbing from hitting the floor and a golf ball-sized lump already starting to form, I squeeze my eyes shut and will my brain to rid itself from everything but the here and now. Then I do something that I've never done before—not once in all my seventeen years.

I call for help.

With all my might, I let free with a plea so loud that I almost scare myself silly.

"Anders," I scream. "Anders. Marcy. Anyone. HELP!!!"

43

"JESUS CHRIST, WEST. You're a fucking mess." Anders growls as he pulls me to my feet.

"What happened?" Marcy says. She's in the door of the bathroom. Her eyes are red and puffy. For that matter, Anders's are, too.

That's what we've all been reduced to—either red blood or red eyes.

"Anders," I whimper, the bump on my head throbbing in time with the burn on my arm. "That girl. That girl from last night."

"What the hell are you talking about?"

"That girl," I say again, using the same words but louder this time. People always think that talking louder will add clarity to what they are saying.

"What girl?"

"The girl from Val Buenavista's video. The one she showed us back at The Stumps."

Marcy's face turns white. An image of the greasy guy on the video, licking her cheek and groping her body with dozens of hands like one of those Indian gods momentarily flits through my head.

"What about her?" Anders says with such bile in his voice his words might as well be made out of poison.

"It's her," I say.

"What are you talking about?" he snaps at me. Snapping is the new normal for Anders.

"Weston," Marcy says. "Are you okay? You hit your head hard. You're not making any sense."

Anders still has his hand around my arm, squeezing my bicep. I wrench free from him with such force that he's momentarily shocked.

"She's the girl from the television," I manage to get out, but now it isn't my arm that's burning, it's whatever is in the pit of my stomach, bubbling and brewing like a pot on the stove that's about to explode.

"What girl on the television?" Anders growls. His unwillingness to understand forces me to shut my eyes and quiet everything around me so that I can get the words out of my mouth that need to be said.

Finally I take a deep breath. "When you were taking a shower," I begin slowly. "When you were in the shower, Marcy and I were watching the news about Running Man."

"Yeah?" says Anders, still annoyed. I can't tell if he is annoyed that I interrupted his brood-fest, annoyed that I overheard his conversation with Marcy, or just plain mad at everything and everyone.

"They showed that girl in the ambulance," I continue. "The girl with the shaved head and the dotted lines who screamed at us when she saw us."

Anders looks uncomfortable, as though I pulled a scab off of something that he is trying to ignore.

"She's from Bellingham," Marcy says. It's not a question. It's a fact.

"So?" says Anders.

I lick my lips, not sure if any of what I am about to say makes sense at all, but I have to get it out. If I don't, I think I'll burst.

"That's Calista Diamond," I tell him, staring hard into his blue eyes and hoping that he will be equally as horrified as me. "We were with her," I tell him. "Last night. At the Stumps. She's the girl who came with us."

Anders says nothing. He stares at me blankly as though the words that are coming out of my mouth aren't part of his vocabulary.

"But . . ." Marcy says.

"Don't you see," I stammer at him. Then out of exasperation, I grab his bicep and lock onto it like he had locked onto mine. "That's her. She was with us at The Stumps last night. Then this morning we were in the woods, and she was in Running Man's house."

Anders still stares at me, no words coming out of his mouth.

Finally, I burst out crying. I don't have anything left to say that will make any sense. The little pieces of last night start falling into a picture, but they aren't a puzzle. Instead, they are an abstract piece of art made from sorrow and pain, with dabs of blood and tears. Then the picture is painted over in broad strokes of murderous red from a good looking doctor, who up until yesterday, was probably having the time of his life slicing and dicing up people in his house on Covington Circle.

Maybe he went out to places like FunTowne to pick up his victims, or maybe, like last night, he hung at the edge of the partiers down at The Stumps, pretending he wanted a joint or maybe even a blowjob so that he could relive his youth.

The painting in my head, the one that will always hang somewhere in its dark and windy corridors, hopefully out of the way so that I rarely have to look at it, is ugly and bitter and is somehow connected to the four of us and how we ended up in Prince Richard's Maze.

It's somehow connected to the triangle on my arm and big black eyes and sheep.

I have to find out how. If I don't, I think I really might go insane. After all, insanity is a popular option these days.

Just ask Marcy's brother.

44

BERYL WRITES TO-DO lists. She writes them all the time and leaves them around the house. Sometimes she even writes to-do lists for me. On them are things like *'do the laundry'* or *'order Chinese.'* Other times she writes simple things that she has to accomplish throughout the day—adult things, like *'call the bank,' 'pay the credit card bill,'* stuff like that.

We're all back in Marcy's bedroom. Anders has plopped himself down on the floor. Marcy is sitting on the edge of her bed. Myers is flat out, and I'm frantically scribbling on a piece of paper I found on Marcy's desk. On the other side of the paper is a drawing of a unicorn with flowers and fairies all around its head. The drawing isn't bad. Marcy's always been talented like that. I don't care about her drawing, though.

Right now, I care about getting my own to-do list out of my head and out onto the paper before it fades away like all my memories of last night.

I look at what I've scribbled down, and I get scared. As a matter of fact, I get so scared that I drop the piece of paper back onto Marcy's desk and take a step backwards. I'm only seventeen years old. What am I thinking? Any rational person would say that we have to tell the police everything we know. We have to tell them that we were wasted at The Stumps last night and don't remember anything, even though we now know we were with Calista Diamond.

I think that little tidbit of information is crazy important. Too important to even exist, and I know what we have to do.

Almost in a panic, I stand over Anders who is starting to act like he's a little afraid of me. I make him pick up the Cole's house phone and call Grafton Applewhite.

"This is bad," Marcy whispers as she sits in the middle of her sea of clothing, slowly sinking into it. "This is really, really bad."

"Maybe," I say, feeling cold and calculating icicles form in my veins. The thing is, I'm neither cold nor calculating. I don't have the disposition for it. I am, however, a survivor. If growing up under the same roof as Beryl Kahn has taught me anything, it's that sometimes you have to be cold to survive.

We all know there's truth in that. That's why we lie. We lie to survive.

Anders won't look at me. He puts his mouth to the phone and waits precious seconds for another phone in another part of town to ring. After a moment he hangs up and says, "He's not answering."

"Try again," I growl, even scaring myself a little bit, but I know in that growl is a little sense of urgency pushing and prodding at me and telling me that what Anders has to do is a vital part of my to-do list.

Anders blows air out of his nose and punches digits into the phone again. This time, it's picked up on the other end.

"It's Anders," he says when Grafton picks up. He waits a moment, closes his eyes, and says, "Because I'm calling from the Coles' house, that's why." Now I know why Grafton didn't answer the phone the first time. He screens his calls and there is no way in hell that Marcy Cole would ever call him or even cast a sideways glance in his direction.

That ship sailed years ago.

"Asshole," whispers Marcy under her breath, and I flinch.

"Listen," says Anders. "I need a phone number."

As Anders continues to talk, I stare hard at the to-do list that I wrote. My stomach roils. This has to be done. This one thing is at the tippy top of that list.

Anders holds his hand up and makes a scribbling sign in the air. I take one of Marcy's flair pens off her desk and hand it to him. It's dark pink, but he doesn't even look at the color. He pops the cap off, cradles the phone under his square jaw, and writes a number down on the palm of his left hand. Marcy watches him do it with a painful expression on her face that's drizzled in sorrow. If she could cry, she would, but I don't think she has any more tears left to give today. I don't think she has any more tears left to give this lifetime.

Anders hangs up from Grafton Applewhite, takes a deep breath, and makes another call. This one is even harder than the first call. This time Anders has to ask a huge favor—a monumental favor. Furthermore, he can't act like a prick when he's doing it. Being a prick won't work.

I hear him talking slowly to the person on the other end of the phone. He waits and listens then finally hangs up.

"Happy?" he says to the air in front of him. He still refuses to look me in the face. I don't know what I'm feeling at the moment, other than a quickening of my heart and sweat beading up on my forehead.

"I don't think being happy is important right now," I tell him, and Myers moans from Marcy's mess of a bed. I take a deep breath, fold my arms, and stare at the floor. After a moment I murmur, "It must be nice to forget."

Thirty minutes later, still feeling clammy and rushed, the three of us sit in Marcy's kitchen, drowning in silence. I keep staring at the glowing blue numbers on the oven clock. I want this part of our day to be over. Frankly, I want this entire day to be over, but I have a sinking suspicion that today may never end. The minutes will keep ticking on and on forever but the clock will never strike twelve.

When the doorbell rings, we all jump, even though we've been waiting.

"Shit," whispers Anders, then swears again under his breath. As for me, a swarm of butterflies swirls around my insides, and I think I might actually be sick again.

"I got it," Marcy says and slowly lowers herself off of the kitchen counter. She walks around Anders, who is sitting on the floor. He doesn't look at her when she walks by. He doesn't even move. I watch her leave, chewing my lip the whole time, wondering if what we're about to do is the right thing or the wrong thing. When you're lost, there are only so many twists and turns you can make before you have to pick one and follow it to the end.

That's what we're going to do. We're going to follow one little wrinkle in our day to the end and tie it off like a surgeon ties off a vein so it won't bleed all over the place.

The only thing is, I'm not sure blood ever really disappears for good.

45

UNLIKE THE REST of Marcy's house, her mother's office is pristine. I don't understand how that one room can be so perfect, so studied, when the rest of the place is a wreck. If someone way smarter than me tried to analyze the cause, they would probably say that Marcy's mom is as messed up as everybody else in Meadowfield, but she fakes it really well.

We all have public faces but private truths.

The thing is, a façade is just that—a façade. However, if you look behind the perfect surface, you'll find disaster. Dr. Pavlovich is a prime example. His studied-to-perfection appearance hid madness beneath its sleek surface.

Mrs. Cole's office is on the main floor of the house. There is a separate entrance from outside, up a flight of stone stairs. Marcy's front lawn is a hill, with tall bushes lining those stone steps. The bushes are there so no one can see her patients come and go and mark them as messed-in-the-head.

Inside, Marcy's mom's office sits behind a stark, white door that we hardly ever open. In all the long years that I have been in this house, playing in the basement, crawling on the stairs, raiding the candy drawer that I now know has always been filled with bad things, I've only seen her mom's perfect workspace a few times.

Marcy quietly slips through that door, and Anders and I wait. Seconds tick by while he broods, and anxiety claws at my insides until I actually start biting my nails.

"Don't," says Anders.

"Don't what?"

"Don't do that."

"Do what?" I ask him. I should be happy he's talking to me at all.

"Biting your nails. It makes you look weak."

"Oh. Okay, Kurt," I say. Kurt is Anders' father's name. It rhymes with dirt and hurt, but more importantly, calling Anders by his dad's name is just plain mean. I know he's right, though. Biting my nails *is* a sign of weakness, and I've worked too hard at transforming myself to slip up now. I stare at my hand, alternating between holding my fingers stretched out in front of me as though I am admiring a manicure and curling them into a fist like an ape. The little half-moons on my nails where they touch the skin are big and translucent. My mother would call that a tell-tale sign of a vitamin deficiency. I'd call it a small price to pay for shedding copious amounts of fat.

Anders is right though. I do have to stop. Unfortunately, that desperate yearning to have something in my mouth to counteract the stress won't go away, and for the first time in a long while, I crave something bad.

Chocolate, bread, macaroni and cheese—I don't care. I want a food pacifier to quell the waves of tension washing over me.

Thankfully, the cravings rapidly recede when Marcy comes back through the door of her mother's office followed by two people.

The first is Ebon Ross. He watched Anders and Barry Kupperman go at it this afternoon at The Stumps. Ebon has been around our whole lives, in our schools, in our classrooms, but has had a wildly different experience in Meadowfield than most of us.

Ebon's black, surrounded by an ocean of white faces. His father is a doctor and his mom's a lawyer, which is a surprisingly common combination in Meadowfield. They live on top of Pill Hill—High Tower Court—where all the really rich doctors live, but that still doesn't erase what he can't hide.

I don't think Ebon has ever met overt racism here in town. We're all too polite for that. I do, however, think he's acutely aware that there's a difference between him, the few other black kids in school, and the rest of Meadowfield. I'm pretty sure he counters the fact that he sticks out here by sticking out even more. He's one of the smartest kids in school. He's a top athlete. He's been the lead in all of the school plays for the last three years, and he's vice-president of the student body council.

No wonder he drinks.

Ebon stumbles a little when he follows Marcy. I know for a fact that he's been nursing a bottle all day.

The other person behind him is lumbering Val Buenavista. I made Anders call her because she has something important in her pocket. Right now it's about the most important thing in the world to us and we desperately need to see it.

"I can't believe I'm here," Val mutters, staring at Marcy with a look that is equal parts disdain and curiosity. "If you tell anyone I was at your house, I'll mess you up." Hearing a girl talk like that always makes me feel wrong. Girls are supposed to be sweet, like Marcy, not oafish bruisers like Val.

I guess it takes all types.

"Chill out," says Ebon. He knows how to be a voice of reason when he needs to be. Just like me, Anders, Myers, and Marcy, the two of them are part of a tightly bonded clique that has existed almost their entire lives. I wonder what they would be doing if they were the ones who woke up in the middle of Prince Richard's Maze this morning.

Would they be broken like the rest of us? Would they ever heal?

Val pushes past Ebon and Marcy and juts her chin out at Anders. "Yo, Stephenson," she says. "Pissed off much?" Val slurs her words. She's been sharing a bottle with Ebon all afternoon. She's not completely blitzed. When you've been stealing from your parents' ample liquor cabinet since you were old enough to reach the good stuff, you develop a tolerance. "You beat the crap out of Kupperman something fierce."

"I'm good," says Anders, which is another huge lie. Marcy stares anywhere but at him. I don't give him that luxury. Anders almost broke Barry Kupperman today in hopes that Barry would hit him back. My guess is that he wanted to be consumed with real pain instead of psychological pain. Psychological pain hurts more.

I know firsthand.

"Uh huh," Val says. "So, like, why am I here?"

I step forward. "We wanted to see that video again. The one you took last night." I lick my lips. "Marcy never saw it."

"Seriously?" snorts Val. "I could have texted it to you."

I shrug. "I never thought of that," I lie.

Val rolls her eyes and shoves her hands deep into her triple-x man's sweatshirt. She pulls out her phone and stares at it for a moment. A viscous glint sparks in her eyes.

"Hey, Marcy," says Val in a voice that that has never been the least bit feminine her entire life. "You get lucky last night?"

"Shut up," hisses Anders.

Ebon pushes Val's shoulder, but she doesn't budge. "Don't be a dick, Val," he tells her. Saying *'don't be a bitch'* somehow seems wrong.

"Can I see it?" I ask again.

Val stares at the phone in her man hands for a moment longer, then tosses it to me. For a millisecond, the memory of Anders' mother tossing me her key fob and it hitting me in the chest before falling to the ground sprouts in my head, then disappears.

I'm not going to drop Val's phone.

I can't.

It's way too important.

46

I WATCH THE VIDEO three times, each time trying to reach as far as I can into the depths of my psyche to pull out any memories of last night, but there are none.

Pffft. All gone.

When I can't stare at the face of Calista Diamond any longer, or any of her friends, I hand the phone to Marcy. She only watches the video once, the whole time Val saying stupid things in the background that bounce off the top of my head and float to the ceiling.

Marcy holds out the phone to Anders, but he doesn't move. Instead, I take it from her hand and say, "I want to see it once more."

"Whatever," slurs Val. Thankfully she and Ebon are both buzzed. Thankfully they are both standing in Marcy's kitchen, two against three, not really scrutinizing me or the rest of us. Not really watching what I have to do.

The first item on my to-do list appears in front of me, superimposed across the white cabinets, and an urgency forms in my gut, pushing me to do what needs to be done.

My heart starts beating faster and little beads of sweat pop out of my forehead.

". . . and then you smashed Kupperman's face in," I hear Val say to Anders, like he wasn't there the first time. "It was wicked awesome, dude."

Quickly, my fingers scroll through Val's phone to see if she sent the video to anyone. Thankfully, she hasn't. The only people who know we were at The Stumps with Calista Diamond and her friends are the ones who were there—drunk, baked, or both.

I'm sure they've all found reasons to forget all about us. My friends and I aren't high enough on their popularity scale to allow any more brain space than the bare minimum.

Besides, any story that will burn through Meadowfield High School on Monday morning will be about Dr. Viktor Pavlovich, or maybe Sandra Berman, if she's among the bodies coming out of his house. A few people will talk about Barry Kupperman's face and how Anders Stephenson almost caved it in, but that's a story that's been waiting to explode for years.

No one is going to talk about the four of us showing up blitzed at The Stumps, and no one is going to be talking about the people that we were with last night. Still, I have to be sure.

As I rapidly move my fingers across the little screen, with Val Buenavista spewing copious amounts of crap out of her mouth and Ebon Ross swaying back and forth because he's probably even more drunk than I realize, I find the little trashcan icon on the bottom of Val's screen, close my eyes, and press it.

The video disappears, gone for good the way bad memories slip away more easily than others, because we are wired to forget the bad and cherish the good.

"That video's messed up," I say to Val and hand her back the phone. "Thanks for letting us see it again."

"Whatever," she grumbles.

Before I can allow any time for her to reach down and check out her phone, or even think about it, I say "Have you been down to Covington Circle yet?"

"Huh?"

"The murder house," Marcy says. She knows I'm deflecting. She's practically reading my thoughts. "Have you been down there? It's crazy."

"Not interested," says Ebon. "I'm a black dude. The police will probably try to pin the murders on me. We do stuff like that, you know."

Val snorts and raises her open palm up for Ebon to give her a high five.

"Did you?" asks Anders. He sounds dead serious. Those icy fingers stroke my back again and all of a sudden I'm acutely aware that my triangle is burning.

"That's not funny," says Ebon.

"It's a little funny," laughs Val and then starts hacking because she's already developed a smoker's cough at seventeen.

"Besides, Stephenson," he snaps at Anders. "If anyone has blood on his hands, it's you. Kupperman blood."

I swallow. Ebon's words sound more truthful than I care to admit, and a picture of Anders, covered head to toe in blood this morning in Prince Richard's Maze, swims before my eyes. What's more, the air around me starts to get heavy. That familiar uncomfortable feeling I get when guys in the locker room used to call me lard ass, or whisper about Marcy behind her back, or even slap Myers' books out of his hands while he's running from one class to the next, settles around me like a dragon curling around a golden horde.

I stifle the urge to stare at my feet. The space between the right and the left has become a safe haven for me. When I'm there, in that space, no one can pick on me. No one can call me names. No one can plumb the depths of my isolation and pluck at it to make it worse.

Instead of staring down, I lock eyes with Ebon and lie. "Marcy's parents are going to be home any minute. I think you should probably go."

"West is right," adds Marcy.

"Sure. Fine," snarls Val, then narrows her eyes at the three of us. "You know what? You called me. What do I get out of the deal?"

"Yeah," says Ebon, but it comes out drunkenly slurred even for a one syllable word.

Marcy saunters out of the kitchen with Ebon and Val both staring at her as she walks, and goes to the middle of the living room where there is a huge, brown globe on a stand next to a winged-back chair. With one swift motion, she pulls a handle up from the side of the globe, and half of the world slides open to reveal a dozen or so bottles. She turns around and crosses her hands over her chest.

"Help yourself," she says as their eyes grow wide.

"You don't have to ask me twice," snorts Val as she pushes Marcy aside and starts pawing at the bottles.

Minutes later they are gone and Marcy comes walking back out of her mother's office.

"What did they take?" asks Anders, almost as if he's normal Anders instead of messed-in-the head Anders.

"I don't know," Marcy says. "I think it was blackberry brandy."

"Hmpf," grumbles Anders, still sitting on the floor. "I hope they choke on it."

47

IT'S 5:47.

Myers woke up ten minutes ago. He came to Marcy's bedroom doorway wrapped in the semi-floral blanket that he pulled from her mattress. His skin and the blanket are almost the same faded color and I know, without a shadow of a doubt, that he's going to be sick.

He stands there for maybe ten seconds, opening and closing his mouth like he wants to say something, but can't find the right words. Suddenly, his jaundiced skin seems to pale. He drops the blanket and dashes to the bathroom.

Even though he slams the door behind himself, we can still hear him retching, over and over again.

I know that feeling. We all know that feeling, but now there is an explanation as to why.

I sit on the floor with Marcy's laptop, leaning up against one of the white cabinets in the kitchen. Anders is still there, on the floor too. His face is filled with a thousand angry thoughts all at once. Marcy sits cross-legged on the counter.

"Read it again," Marcy says to me. "Please."

I look at Anders. He drops his head even more.

I swallow hard, then clear my throat. Marcy is talking about the second thing on my to-do list. It involves research. It took me surprisingly little time to find what I was looking for.

Shockingly little.

"Flunitrazepam," I begin, reading from the website that seems more informative than all the rest. "Flunitrazepam is another name for Rohypnol." I look up at Marcy. Her eyes are closed. I'm pretty sure she's wishing she is anywhere but right here, and for the best reason of all. Rohypnol is another name for roofies. We all know what a roofie is.

Isn't the Internet a wonderful thing?

"Keep reading," she whispers. "Just keep reading."

I take another deep breath and continue. "Although most commonly found in pill form, Flunitrazepam can be crushed, put into liquid, and ingested on food." I stop again and lick my lips, then add a little commentary, if only to punctuate the obvious. "Any food," I say. "Like pizza."

Right now, there's a fat little chef standing next to the Leaning Tower of Pisa, drawn onto a pizza box. He's having a good old belly laugh at our expense. The thing is, whatever he's laughing at isn't funny. It's not funny at all.

"Shit," hisses Anders under his breath. Then he rolls his hands one over the other in hopes that I'll continue so he has words to hang onto.

"Seven to ten times stronger than Valium, Flunitrazepam, or Rohypnol, takes effect fifteen to twenty minutes after it is ingested and can last anywhere from four hours to twelve hours, depending on how much is taken. While sedated, most people don't remember a thing."

I stop for a moment. That part isn't true. I remember black eyes. I remember sheep crying. I even remember a blur of activity and voices and a searing pain in my arm.

I remember all those things, all mixed up and confused.

"And?" Anders says.

"Known as the date-rape drug, those under its influence suffer partial amnesia. They are unable to remember certain events that they experience. It is mostly used so victims won't clearly recall an assault or an assailant, or the events surrounding any given situation."

I stop reading, but only because Myers retches again. I'm no longer grossed out by the sound. After all, it explains so much. When I'm sure he's through, I read the last few lines slowly and clearly. "Flunitrazepam use causes several adverse effects including episodic amnesia, brain fog, confusion, and . . . and gastrointestinal disturbances."

I finish and slowly shut Marcy's laptop. I don't want to look at it anymore. I truly want to forget.

"That's messed up," she says. "Who would want to do that to us?"

Anders shakes his head. No words will form on his lips.

"Who brought the pizza?" I ask. It's more than a valid question. It's a crucial one. "I don't remember much of anything after going over to Myers' house after school." Both Anders and Marcy look up at me. "His mother was baking cookies for his boy scout troop. She started screaming at us so we left."

They both nod. Mrs. Myers screaming is normal.

"What about you?" Marcy says. She's not looking at me. She's looking at Anders. She sits there on the counter, her curls framing her beautiful face.

There is an uncomfortable silence. In that moment, which feels like an hour long but probably only lasts seconds, Anders looks up and realizes that Marcy is talking to him. He takes a deep breath and continues staring at the floor. "There was a game right after school—us against Mount Tom Regional. We won. I came home and took a shower. My mom was there. She said she was going out and told me not to wait up."

I snort a little.

Anders levels a piercing gaze in my direction.

"My parents were here when I came home from school yesterday," Marcy says. "We talked about college next year and my applications." She lowers her voice a little as though the next part is a secret. "Then we talked about what's going to happen next summer."

She stares hard at Anders when she tells us that, but he doesn't even flinch.

As we sit there in shared silence, the sounds of the house creaking and Myers flushing the toilet again and again, big black eyes blink in my memory and I force myself to look into them. They're huge, like saucers, and light is glinting off their slightly curved surface. There are a million secrets behind those eyes and all I want to do is take both hands and press my thumbs into them as hard as I can to retrieve just one.

I want to know what they're looking at.

I need to know.

When the phone rings again, my skin jumps right off of my bones, desperate to run away.

I know the feeling. I truly do.

48

WE'VE LET THE answering machine take phone calls all day—desperate, awkward, mournful messages from people whose brains are about to break. This call, however, is different.

As soon as I realize who it is on the other end, talking through the answering machine, I scramble to my feet, grab the closest receiver, and pick it up.

"Hello?" says a familiar voice.

Goosebumps pop out on my arm.

"Take it," I mouth to Marcy in exaggerated pantomime. She shakes her head no. She wants nothing to do with this particular phone call. Unfortunately, she doesn't have a choice. "You have to."

I hit the button on the phone that says *'speaker'* and listen as a disembodied voice comes into being right in the middle of the three of us.

"What the hell?" Tate Cole says. "Hello?"

Marcy has to say something. Saying nothing isn't an option any more. "Hello?" she barely whispers.

"Twinsy," he purrs like a cat who knows that the baby rabbit in its mouth isn't going to live to squeak another day. Marcy cringes. We all do. Calling her *'Twinsy'* is a statement of fact. He's Tate and she's Marcy, and although they shared the same womb seventeen and a half years ago, they share nothing anymore except two parents who are down at the Indian casino for the weekend. That, and the brand new stigma of being from the same town as Dr. Viktor Pavlovich.

Unfortunately, I think Tate doesn't think of the latter as a stigma. He probably thinks it's cool.

"Shit," she mouths.

"Well *you're* still breathing," Tate says as smooth as silk, every bit the psychopath we all know him to be. "That answers question numero uno." I get the overwhelming sense that a venomous snake is getting ready to slither out of the phone and kiss Marcy's lips with a forked tongue.

"What do you mean?" Marcy says.

"Thought you and the rents might have eaten some bad pepperoni and wound up dead or something," he sighs so nonchalantly that he might as well be having a conversation on the veranda at the Meadowfield Country Club, sipping a Shirley Temple because none of us are old enough to drink.

"That's not nice," says Marcy. Everything about her is the opposite of Tate. She's light and he's dark. She's sane. He's a lunatic.

"I never said I was nice," he sneers. "Besides, my bank account and the knees on my jeans both took a beating this past year. The least you could do is stop breathing."

Marcy shakes her head. "I don't . . . what?" she says.

"Nothing," says Tate, and my whole body goes rigid. His single word response means far more than nothing. It damn well means something and my teeth start grinding together.

'Thought you might have eaten some bad pepperoni.'

'Eaten some bad pepperoni.'

'Bad pepperoni.'

Everything gels. Well, not everything, but one thing becomes crystal clear. Somehow, from an hour away, in a nuthouse for kids who only have call-out hours twice a day, Tate somehow managed to get us to eat a drugged pizza.

The idea makes no sense, but it makes perfect sense.

My lip curls.

As I begin to seethe and my triangle starts sending waves of pain washing up my arm, Myers stumbles into the room. His hair is sticking up in all directions and his skin is papery and pale. His eyes flutter a little. He's still messed up. I know now that there were drugs on the pizza. The four of us were dosed yesterday around dinner time. Myers was dosed again today around noon, but there were only two small pieces left. We ate the bulk of it last night and then forgot.

Everything.

"Wha . . ." Myers begins but all three of us instinctively throw our fingers up to our mouths and make the universal sign for quiet. It's like we're in the library at school, and Ms. French, the overly-endowed librarian with the ass that guys like Grafton Applewhite talk about for hours, has invoked a silent study and we're breaking the rules.

Myers' eyes grow wide when he realizes who's on the phone. Instead of opening his mouth again, he grabs his left elbow with his right hand and lets his mouth fall into an upside down grin.

"What do you want, Tate? Mom and Dad aren't home," Marcy finally says. She stares at the pizza box when she talks, her eyes round and glistening underneath the kitchen lights and understanding creeping into her brain through her ear.

"Well that sucks," he hisses. "I suppose they're breathing, too?"

Marcy's forehead creases.

'Why . . . why wouldn't they be . . . what?"

"Don't fuck with me," Tate growls. "I'm not stupid."

"I didn't say you were."

"But you think it," he says.

Marcy sniffles a little. "I don't want to fight, Tate." As she's talking, I look up at the clock. It's now after 6pm. Call-out hours.

"I do," he says. I can hear Tate's antagonism through the phone. He hasn't changed—not one bit. I can only hope that once he leaves Bellingham he'll find another place to live that's far away from sharp objects.

Marcy closes her eyes and bites her lip. As my nostrils begin to flair, a pitiful thought surfaces. It's pitiful because we live in Meadowfield where everything is supposed to be perfect.

The thought is this: What's worse? Myers and his fuckity-fuck-fuck-fuck of a mother, Anders with his serial dater of a mom, Beryl and her apathy, or the thing that is Marcy's brother that she will never, ever be able to quit? He's literally half of her.

"Tate . . ." she begins, but he cuts her off.

"I got a message that someone called," he sneers. His tone only accentuates the fact that I hate his smarmy voice. I hate everything about him.

"What?" whispers Marcy. She doesn't know I called The Bellingham School. She doesn't know I talked to an epic dick named Eddie Bick.

Then Tate takes my hate for him and makes it that much worse by sliding a verbal knife effortlessly between Marcy's ribs and gutting her on the spot.

"I got a message that my . . . uh . . . brother . . . uh . . . Mark called," says Tate, relishing every word that is coming out of his mouth. "I don't know about you, but I found that interesting."

49

"ASSHOLE," HISSES Anders. His words are loud and clear. Our moratorium on silence is shattered and Marcy puts one hand to her mouth as though she's the one who uttered profanity, not him.

"Who's that?" snaps Tate. "Who's with you?"

"Freaking dirt bag," Anders continues, like any of us could stop him even if we tried.

"I know who that is," whispers Tate Cole through the phone. He might as well be the devil. That's who he sounds like. "Stephenson, right? Twinsy talks about you on visiting days. Not that I get very many visits."

"Stop," says Marcy. "Please." I don't know if she's talking to Tate or to Anders or to both of them.

Tate ignores her. "So tell me, Anders. You screwing my twin yet? The way I hear it, you've been wanting that piece of ass for a while now."

Myers looks confused and a gray shadow passes across his face. Behind that shadow comes a moment of recognition where he suddenly understands that what he's hearing is the truth, although up until this morning, we all thought Marcy was the one who wanted Anders, not the other way around.

Like Barry Kupperman snorted back at The Stumps, through blood, snot and laughter: *'Now this. This makes so much sense.'*

In a flash, Anders is on his feet, his fists curled into cruel weapons. The problem is, there's nothing around but us to be the object of his wrath.

"Shut up," he barks at the invisible voice.

"Not that I blame you," continues Tate, sitting at some remote phone in another part of the state. "After all, we're both kind of . . . hot . . . in our own ways."

Suddenly, Anders turns around and punches one of the white kitchen cabinets. It's not made of dry wall, so he doesn't rip open a hole. Instead, the wood splits with a loud crack. He pulls back and punches it again, this time leaving red dabs on the white surface.

Marcy yelps.

Myers says nothing. As for me, my own brand of anger bubbles to the surface and pours out of me in a torrent.

"How did you do it?" I blurt out. My words stream from me louder than I intend. Myers jumps and starts to cry, but I think he's mostly crying because he isn't quite sure what's going on. He's still drugged.

"What the hell? Are you having a party?" Tate growls through the speaker phone.

"How did you do it, you sick fuck?" I bellow again.

This time, the person on the other end of the phone, sitting at The Bellingham School, probably being woefully unattended to by a lowlife mental health counselor named Eddie Bick, makes a connection.

"Is that you, King Kahn?" he says, the words crawling out of his mouth like spiders. King Kahn is what he used to call me because he couldn't come up with a better fat slur than that. All he could say was that I was as big as an ape.

"I called your school," I blurt out. "I said I was Mark. I wanted to know if you somehow got loose. No one wants a waste of space like you set free."

He laughs through the speaker phone, much the same way that a twisted villain in a cartoon laughs at the hero he's tormenting. "Owie, owie," he cries through his laughter. "You're hurting my feelings, you fat shit."

Hot, fetid air blows out of my mouth. "I'm not fat anymore," I say. My head starts to throb and I suddenly realize that I've never really admitted that to myself before. I'm not fat anymore. I don't know if I'm normal or not, too thin or still chunky. I don't know anything other than I'm not fat.

"I find that hard to believe," he says. "But honestly, I don't give two shits about you or your girth, King Kahn. You'll always be a fat slob to me. Always and forever."

If I've learned anything from our brief interaction, I've learned that Tate Cole hasn't changed at all. He's sick and he's mean, and being locked up has done nothing but make him worse, not better.

"Stop it," Marcy cries as she cradles the phone in her hand, probably wishing that she had the strength to crush it into little pieces, crushing Tate along with it.

"No," says Tate. "I'm having too much fun."

I slide around the overstocked kitchen island more quickly than I've probably ever moved and snatch the receiver out of Marcy's hand.

"Yeah, well," I say. "Fun time's over." Then I press the red button and end the call. It's not until the silence around all of us becomes deafening that I realize that I'm taking in big gluts of air like I've run the track at school, with pounds and pounds of fat jiggling all over me.

Finally, I look up at Marcy and see something in her face that I've rarely seen in her until today.

Anger.

Her eyes are narrowed and there are little creases on her forehead and around her beautiful lips. She's angrier than I've ever seen. Suddenly, I'm afraid that the virtual blade that Tate used on her moments ago is going to appear again, and Marcy is going to use it on Anders because he broke the kitchen cabinet.

Instead, she hops off the counter, pushes me aside, and dashes into the living room where there's a table overflowing with books and letters, paper, and stacks of coupons which are so foreign to all of us in Meadowfield that I'm surprised I even know what they are.

With single-minded purpose she dives into the mess, clawing at the papers, throwing them this way and that until she is surrounded by a storm of mail.

Finally she stops. In her hand is a thin book, almost like a calendar.

"What's happening?" Myers sniffs.

Anders says nothing. He's still facing the split cabinet, his eyes closed, probably willing his world to come to an abrupt and immediate end.

Meanwhile, Marcy begins rapidly flipping through the book she's holding, finger-reading the pages like Helen Keller. Over and over again, she tears through the glossy paper while the rest of us are deathly quiet.

Finally, she stops.

"Damnit," she whispers, as she stares at the page in front of her. "Damnit. Damnit. Damnit." Marcy clutches the book to her chest and stares up at the ceiling. Tears flow again, like they've done a dozen times already today.

It's not until she shows us what she's holding that we understand why.

50

DRUGS OR NO DRUGS, my head hurts.

"I don't understand," says Myers. Why would he? He's been off in a dreamland all afternoon.

"Damnit," breathes Marcy again. It's about the only word she can manage to utter.

Anders stands motionless with his eyes closed. I know him well enough to know that he is desperately looking for a calm center some- where in the middle of all the madness. He needs to find it. If he doesn't, rage might take over.

As for me, my shoulders creep up to my ears. Every part of me is clenched so tightly that if I were to fart, I think only dogs would hear the high pitched whistle.

I'm staring at a picture of Calista Diamond. She has crazy hair. Part of it is dyed that pale white-green color that is going to go in and out of style so quickly that no one will ever remember that it was a fashion to begin with. She also has thin, twine-like braids running down one side of her face.

She looks like a mental, post-apocalyptic flower child, sitting at a cafeteria table with a bunch of other crazies.

Her picture is glossy and printed in an over-the-top quarterly publication from The Bellingham School.

What was it that the reporter said on television? *'Eighteen-year-old Diamond is a resident of Bellingham, Massachusetts. No more is known about her in this developing story. Once again, we are live here in Meadowfield, Massachusetts where tragedy has struck this small New England community.'*

Oh God. Calista Diamond wasn't just a resident of Bellingham. She was a student at The Bellingham School.

"She looks all messed up," says Myers again. He's right. People who look like her don't live in Meadowfield. No matter how pretty she is, she's pretty in a way that defies our town. No one would ever say that Calista Diamond is wholesome-looking. Girls in Meadowfield don't dye their hair wonky colors while they are trying to get into Ivy League schools. Girls in Meadowfield don't have long thin braids that look like they were purchased out of one of those trashy, trendy stores up at the Ingleside Mall in Holyoke, where they sell glass pipes and blacklight tee-shirts. "Who is she?" he asks.

"Calista Diamond," I tell him. Myers has no reason to remember her, other than as a desperate, creepy reminder that a mass murderer and his house of horrors was found down on Covington Circle, and a girl survived.

"Who's Calista Diamond?"

I gulp. "Think shaved head and dotted lines."

Marcy still can't talk. She has one hand in her mouth, almost forgetting that she doesn't bite her nails anymore. The other is on her hip.

"What?" Myers says and clutches at his stomach.

"Don't puke again," snaps Anders. His eyes are now open. His words sound like an order and Myers doesn't do anything but meekly nod his head up and down.

Then he gets it.

He really gets it.

"You mean that's the girl from Running Man's house?" Myers blurts out. "What happened to her hair?"

"Shaved," I said.

"Why?"

I don't want to say the words. I want to close my eyes and pretend he's never asked the question.

"That's what a plastic surgeon does before he performs surgery," says Anders. "It's so he can see the cut lines." His words are sharp and brutal, like the sharp edge of whatever tool Dr. Viktor Pavlovich used on his victims.

Myers' lips tremble. "That's messed up. You're kidding, right?" He looks imploringly from me to Marcy then back to me. He doesn't want to look at Anders. "He's kidding, right? Please tell me he's kidding."

I wish I could, but I don't want to lie anymore. I look down and desperately search for that spot between my feet that's such a perfect place to hide.

Finally, Marcy pulls her hand from her mouth, takes the quarterly from me, and slowly starts thumbing through the pages again. Her eyes scan the photographs, stopping for a moment to look at Tate, who is featured more than a few times.

There he is *'killing it'* at ping pong.

There he is lounging on a beanbag chair, reading a book.

Three more pages, and she stops. Her mouth turns into a tiny, horizontal line, and her nostrils flair. She looks up at Anders, not at me. "This is him, isn't it?"

Anders takes a deep breath, takes a few steps, reaches out, and pulls the quarterly out of her hands.

"Him, who?" pleads Myers. "Someone talk to me."

I stand there, shoulder to shoulder with Anders as we look down at the glossy pages at a picture of a kid with a hatchet for a face and greasy, stringy hair. He looks strung out on something, even though I know he can't be. I'm sure one of the edicts of The Bellingham School is that he can't be *'strung out'* on anything.

"Shit," I whisper under my breath.

"It is, isn't it?" Marcy says with bile in her voice. "Anders?"

And just like that, we are reliving the events on Val Buenavista's video all over again. The greasy guy is pawing Marcy six ways from Sunday and touching her in all sorts of places that she doesn't want to be touched. He's telling her to be nice like being nice is some sort of sick offering she has to give to him so he'll be nice back.

I can see it all playing out in my mind, but this time, I'm not seeing it sideways, shot from a weird angle on Val's phone. I'm seeing it through the trees. A memory is forming inside my head and that memory is of me at The Stumps, holding something cold which I know has to be a bottle of beer.

Another round of throbbing pain spirals out of the little triangle on my arm, and I simply will it to go away. I'm not ready to think about my triangle yet. I'm not ready to connect the lines. Instead, I take the quarterly from Anders, flip back to the front, and start turning the pages like Marcy.

I know exactly what I'm looking for, and I know I'm going to find it.

Twelve pages in and there it is, in a photograph of a group of students from The Bellingham School on an outing.

Calista Diamond and another girl are sitting on a huge horse with one of those weirdly cropped tails that looks like it belongs on a rabbit. Tate's not in the picture, but the greasy-haired kid is there. He's wearing sunglasses and pointing at the horse's ass, laughing, and so is another kid with big frizzy hair.

My mouth grows small.

The kid with the frizzy hair is definitely not from Meadowfield.

Kids in Meadowfield don't have afros.

51

THEY KNOW EACH OTHER.

They know each other.

Tate Cole, Calista Diamond, the guy with the greasy hair, and the other one with the afro who threatened Val Buenavista when he found out she was videoing them, all know each other.

The four of them live at The Bellingham School. They're not normal. They're addicted or insane. They threaten family members with knives or repeatedly flip the bird at teachers. They pop medications like penny candy and are connected to people who can hook them up with drugs like Flunitrazepam. Kids who live at The Bellingham School know people like that.

What's more, Tate is still in Bellingham, probably because he's only seventeen-and-a-half like Marcy and can't leave, but Calista Diamond? She's eighteen. They said so on television. Her friends are probably eighteen, too. Schools like Bellingham aren't jails. Once you become of age, you can probably sign yourself out or something.

That's what happened yesterday.

She signed out . . . or something . . . and in between leaving Bellingham and now, Calista almost ended up dead at the hands of Running Man.

Shit.

A vivid memory snakes out of a dark corner of my mind and sheds its drug-induced amnesia. It's not even a memory really. It's a truth, equal parts naked and unashamed.

I remember her. I remember Calista. In my memory she still has hair. In my memory she still has thin braids.

She got right in my face in Marcy's kitchen, so close that she was a blur, and she poked me with her glittered nails and said, *'Hello? Anybody home?'*

No. I wasn't home. I was drugged. Still, part of me was there, and that part of me remembers someone else laughing and a deep voice saying *'Cool.'*

Another sickening truth dances across my face, so vicious and real that I don't even have to question it. Calista Diamond, the greasy guy, and the guy with the afro were all here last night. In this house. In this kitchen.

They were all right here, an hour away from Bellingham, with a drugged pizza courtesy of Tate Cole.

What was it that he said to Marcy? '... *my bank account and the knees on my jeans both took a beating this past year. The least you could do is stop breathing.*'

Oh no.

My head jerks like I'm a robot who just got a brain upgrade.

Everything that's happened to us since last night has been about Tate and his hatred of his family—simply everything. The four of us eating drugged pizza and being dragged to The Stumps and somehow ending up at Prince Richard's Maze—all of it—is because Tate wanted to get at his parents ... at his sister. He wanted to get at them so badly he persuaded three of his friends to do it for him.

I feel sick to my stomach, not for the lingering drugs or the truths that are slapping me in the face over and over again. I feel sick because I can taste Tate's palpable disdain for his family like spoiled food in my mouth.

On some level, if I project myself so far out of my body that I'll have a hard time finding my way back, I can even understand it. On another level I can't.

I won't.

I close my eyes and imagine Marcy's psychotic, scheming brother shelling out his allowance and performing favors in the dark corners of The Bellingham School, all to persuade a bunch of degenerates to break out, or sign out, or whatever people like them have to do to leave the woefully inadequate vigilance of Eddie Bick, and come for his family.

How much did it cost him? How many pairs of jeans did Tate wear out at the knees?

I start shaking my head, my nostrils flaring with the disgusting smell of a plan gone woefully wrong. Tate didn't know that Marcy's parents were going down to the Indian Casino last night. He planned for his friends to show up, drug them all, and ... and. ...

She had no pants.

This morning when we woke up, Marcy had no pants. Myers was missing his eye. I had a triangle burned into my arm, and Anders— Anders was covered in blood.

It's all because Marcy wasn't with her family last night when some strangers delivered a pizza and said something like, 'courtesy of Pizza Depot, coming soon to Meadowfield,' or another lie equally as lame.

She was with us.

We all probably toasted our good fortune for getting a free meal, although I can't imagine how I ever let pizza pass my lips. I'm Mr. Extra Meatball. Regardless, the four of us ate from a poisoned apple and passed out while Calista and her friends let themselves in through the door in the back of the garage that's never locked and hit the lottery, not once but four times over.

"Fuck me," I say out loud. I think we all are harboring the same sentiment.

Marcy slumps to the floor and puts her head in her hands.

My colorful choice of words just about sums it all up.

52

MYERS IS STILL wearing his Master Baiter tee-shirt from yesterday, but it's starting to smell ripe. The rest of us have had the luxury of a second set of clothes, but all Myers has done is cover his eye hole with a pirate patch.

Marcy gives him one of her dad's shirts. He is swimming in it, and the whole effect makes him look a little homeless.

Anders is brooding again. He could be brooding about blood, or bloody Barry Kupperman, or even the fact the Marcy told him that she loved him and he doesn't know how to cope. It could even be about three juvenile offenders who took a joy ride from Bellingham last night, maybe even in a stolen car, stopped for pizza and Flunitrazepam, then came hunting for Marcy and her family.

Frankly, I could keep listing the things that Anders could be brooding about for the rest of the night and be right on all accounts.

We have such a capacity to hold chaos in our heads. We cradle it there, cupped in our gray matter, while it swirls around like a tornado, breaking things at every turn.

One thing's for certain. Amidst all the chaos, none of us know what to say to each other. There are too many mental balls juggling in our hands and none of them make sense.

Myers is still groggy and drugged and completely confused.

Marcy is rapidly falling apart with the realization that everything that has happened to us since last night has something to do with her family and three residents of The Bellingham School.

As for me, I keep going back to a fourth resident—Tate Cole.

None of us ever really talk about him, or his anger, or that awful day so many years ago when he cornered Marcy in the bathroom with a knife and Anders had to intervene. What kind of kid—what kind of person—does something like that to his twin? I can't speak from experience. I'm an only child. So is Anders. So is Myers. I think our parents realized that one and done was a good policy, especially after they figured out that kids are nothing more than sucker fish attached to their sides, syphoning off whatever we can get.

What's more, once we greedily drink our fill, we turn our backs on our creators, vowing to move as far away as we can from the things that made us.

I guess that's the circle of life. At least we don't resort to matriphagy. The only reason I know all about matriphagy is because of a paper I wrote in Advanced Biology for Mr. Kirkpatrick. Matriphagy is when the offspring of a species eat their mothers. I got an A for the paper. Kirkpatrick likes me, but he did jot down a note in the margin on the last page asking if I was saving up for psychotherapy.

I know he was only being funny, but it made me wonder if he had ever met Beryl. If he had, I don't think he would have written that note in the first place. Words can hit too close to home sometimes, even when they are never meant to cause damage at all.

Just like Marcy's words. I can't even imagine the bomb that she detonated when she said what she said to Anders. '*I love you.*' That's what she said, and he's probably now caught in an emotional typhoon. Honestly, I don't have to imagine it at all. I'm watching it unfold right in front of me. If I had to guess, I would say that Anders is brooding because of what she said more than anything else. He's not thinking about Prince Richard's Maze or waking up without a memory, or even being covered in blood. He's not thinking about Running Man or Calista Diamond or beating the crap out of Barry Kupperman down at The Stumps.

He's thinking about Marcy, and it's eating him alive from the inside out, like when a mother crab spider's baby spiderlings devour her until she falls over, immobile, and they consume her entirely.

I get it, but at the same time, there's a hint of jealousy there that I can't ignore. Fat kids don't have people who fall in love with them. Fat kids hide in their bedroom and shore up mental walls so they don't have to talk to their mothers. Fat kids stare at the space between their feet and find solace in the fact that the bigger they get, the more invisible they become.

Fat kids . . . and I stop myself. I'm not fat anymore.

I'm not fat.

I'm not fat.

I'm not.

I close my eyes.

Am I?

Marcy slowly stands, wipes her mouth with the back of her hand, and glides into the kitchen like a ghost.

"I'm hungry," she says.

None of us reply but she's not waiting for a reply. She's sucking everything up inside herself, shoving it into a little mental box and locking it tight. That's how Marcy rolls. That's how she has managed to stay relatively sane here in Meadowfield when none of us have sane lives.

Our town, our world, might look really pretty on television, but the truth of it is, our lives are hard. Just like hiking the Grand Canyon looks like an amazing time when you're watching other people do it from the safety of your own home, but doing it for real? It's hard. It's dirty. It's like living in Meadowfield where everything looks beautiful on the outside.

Even our serial murderers are beautiful. Perfect, prancing Viktor Pavlovich with the fancy sports car and the string of beauty wannabees who eagerly got in his passenger seat because he was hot.

Calista Diamond should know all about that. She almost got close enough to him to get burned.

For real.

53

I SIT AT THE KITCHEN counter staring at the to-do list that I wrote. The next thing on the list is something I don't want to do, but I don't think we have a choice.

Way across town in the fading light, the sun is setting on Prince Richard's Maze and on an old, rotted-out stump that everyone calls The Grandfather Tree. Wrapped into a ball inside that tree's guts is a wad of clothing covered in blood.

It's not my blood. The blood doesn't belong to Marcy or Myers. The syrupy red paint doesn't even belong to Anders, but it's still blood.

That ball of clothing can't be there. That ball of clothing can't be anywhere where people can find it. Not now. Not ever.

"We have to get rid of Anders' clothes," I say.

"Why?" asks Myers.

"Because we don't have a good answer for why they're covered in blood," I tell him without looking at Anders.

Marcy has pulled some boxes of cereal out of one of the cabinets in the kitchen, plopped a gallon of milk on the counter, and littered the granite island with bowls and spoons.

I don't eat cereal anymore. Cereal is part of an ever-increasing number of evils that I've decided will never again enter my body.

Cereal is a carbohydrate.

Carbohydrates turn into sugar.

Sugar turns into fat.

Fat can never happen again.

Anders slumps over a bowl that's bigger than the rest of ours. It's more for mixing food than eating food. He has one arm curled around it while he's shoveling corn flakes into his mouth with the other. I don't even think he's chewing. A steady stream of milk is dripping down his chin and falling back into the bowl, only for him to scoop it up again.

We all watch him for the better part of a minute, until he takes the remains of the bowl, soggy broken flakes and all, tilts his head back, and drinks the rest of it as though he's totally alone in the world, wearing nothing but dirty underwear and anticipating that he's going to be able to let out a long, low belch in private.

The thing is, Anders isn't that gross. He's nothing like how he is acting today. He's never seemed so lost in all the years that I have known him.

He drops the bowl back onto the counter, wipes his mouth with the heel of his hand, and thankfully doesn't belch.

"I'll do it," he says. "I'll get rid of them."

"No," says Marcy.

"Not up to you," he says.

"It's not up to you, either," she tells him. "Don't you get it? We're all in this together, whatever 'this' is. So we're all going to see it through."

Anders stiffens. It's a new look for him. Anders Stephenson trying to hold in a powder keg of anger is something that none of us are used to seeing. After a moment, his shoulders drop and he lets a quiet sigh slip from his lips.

"Fine," he whispers.

"Good," says Marcy.

I clutch my to-do list in my left hand and stare down at the bandage I have on the triangle. The fact that I've been able to blot out the pain emanating from the burn is almost surreal. It's been there all day, a persistent stinging without end, but I've stubbornly refused to acknowledge its presence.

Whatever I'm doing must be obvious. Myers says, "Still hurt?"

I look up and my friends are all staring at me—beautiful Marcy, angry Anders, and Myers in a ridiculously oversized shirt. I catch all their eyes and hold them in mine as the light outside turns a deep burnt orange that is only reserved for this time of year in New England, and without realizing it, I start to cry.

Marcy's face scrunches up, but it's not because she's going to cry, too. It's because I know she finally, finally feels the totality of my pain. Not only the pain in my arm, or the weirdness of the drugs. She feels everything.

Myers buttons his lips. No snarky comments spill out of his mouth. No sarcasm.

Anders is there, too. I see a glimpse of the protector that I've always known. He's always been there for me, for all of us, and he's still there. Right now his pain is as big as any of ours, but he's still the old Anders deep inside. I know he is.

So my tears fall, getting harder and faster, spilling out of my eyes so freely that I can't do anything but let them fill up imaginary buckets at my feet that will be swiftly taken away by walking broomsticks, only for more buckets to be filled and more broomsticks to take them away.

This time, however, no magical wizard is going to suddenly appear and make everything better with some sort of lame morality lesson.

What's left is only me and my friends, the decisions we make, and the lies that we tell ourselves and others out of sheer self-preservation.

I cry, and I cry, and I cry. Suddenly, Marcy is there, right in front of me, pulling me to her in a tender embrace. Myers is there too, his floppy sleeves curling around the two of us as best as he can.

Finally Anders gets up, comes to stand in front of our mass of tears, limbs, and emotions, and engulfs all of us in his lanky basketball arms. He squeezes, in probably the most real and profound way that he has ever hugged anyone, ever.

"We'll get through this," the old Anders whispers, his mouth pushed into Marcy's hair and his arms grasping onto all of us in an embrace that none of us want to ever end. "That's what we'll do. We'll get through this. Together."

54

THEY SAY THAT everybody is searching for their fifteen minutes of fame. I'm not. I've never wanted that kind of publicity. Others want it though, like people who are only famous for being famous without ever doing anything to earn the notoriety. They plaster themselves all over social media in a desperate attempt to add meaning to their lives, because, let's face it—none of us really know why we're here, or why we're put through some of the hell that's heaped upon our heads like foggy whipped cream christened with a blood red cherry.

I'm not so sure Calista Diamond was after her fifteen minutes of fame when she left The Bellingham School yesterday. I think she was more into letting her inner demons out to play. The way I see it, Calista wasn't looking to force feed herself to the masses. Unfortunately, that's exactly what she did when she landed in the middle of Meadowfield and somehow ended up inside the lair of Viktor Pavlovich.

I don't think she expected a monster to shave her head, mark her with black ink for a fantastically brutal death, and churn her special brand of crazy into something even crazier. I don't think she thought beyond what was going to happen to her once she found herself locked inside that house down on Covington Circle.

I think she expected her life to end.

Pffft. All gone.

That's not how it happened for her.

She wasn't sliced into bits, maybe in a lunatic's insane attempt to make her into his version of 'pretty.' Somehow, she got free, and when she did, her quiet, crazy life was turned on end.

What she found out in front of Viktor Pavlovich's house was noise and people, cops and reporters. There were camera flashes and Eye Witness News choppers overhead. There was so much chaos that even a normal person would have probably gone mad from all the fanfare.

It turns out, Calista was about as far away from normal as you can get.

I keep saying 'was,' not 'is,' because sometime today, long before

Val Buenavista and Ebon Ross ever showed up at the Cole's house with a cell phone featuring a video from last night at The Stumps, Calista Diamond died.

I'm so stunned as I watch the television in Marcy's kitchen that I start to think that I've gone mad. How can this be real? How can any of this be real?

This morning, shortly after Calista had to be pinned down and sedated in the back of an ambulance in front of thousands, she was transferred to an out-of-the-way hospital for observation.

She couldn't be brought to Stairway to Heaven over the border in Connecticut. It was too close to home. Also, that's where Running Man worked. The place was probably crawling with the press. That would have been a mistake.

They couldn't bring her to Baystate in Springfield. The hospital is too big and there would have been too many people. News reporters and murder junkies would have descended on the place, flooding the hallways in a gross attempt to get a look at the girl who lived.

In the end, she was taken to a small hospital called Wang Memorial up in Apple, the creepy town that Annie Berg had moved away from. I had never heard of Wang Memorial before. People in Meadowfield don't go to hospitals like Wang. If we have a hangnail, we go straight to Boston to a top-notch specialist who doesn't take insurance, because he or she is better than that.

That's how Meadowfield people think. If something costs more, it's superior.

Anyway, while up at Wang Memorial, Calista went even more bonkers than she already was. She managed to get a gun away from one of the officers who was probably taking her to a nice, comfy, and most likely padded room where she could rest and get her head on straight. It was all for her own good. As far as the news said, she wasn't being charged with anything. She was the victim, not the assailant. She did nothing wrong.

The grainy surveillance footage that has been cut, edited and streamed on television so fast that you would think the whole thing was planned, shows that Calista thought something entirely different.

"I'm not going away for murder," she screams, waving the gun wildly around, pointing it at anything that moves. A young cop, chunky, even though he probably had to go through cop training, climb a rope, or even do a dozen push-ups, stands there with his hands stretched out in front of him, like maybe he thinks he can catch a bullet between his fingers. The footage doesn't show his face but I'm sure it's riddled with terror. He's probably the one who was stupid enough to let her get his gun.

"Put it down, Calista," orders a woman cop with her hair cut short and two hands pointing her own gun at the crazy bald girl.

"I'm not going away," screams Calista again, "It's not my fault." She points the gun at the woman, and then at the guy, then back at the woman again. "He deserved it," she cries. 'He good goddamned deserved it."

Then something insane happens.

Calista Diamond turns the gun around and points it at herself. She screws her face into a knot, and although we really can't see the details, I'm sure she's crying big, angry tears. The chunky cop doesn't move. He's frozen in that weird position with his hands out in front of him and his knees slightly bent.

"Put the gun down," barks the woman cop one more time.

Calista sniffs, closes her eyes, and says, "Oh, fuck it," although what they show on screen is her saying, "Oh, *BEEP* it."

Then she stuffs the muzzle of the gun in her mouth and pulls the trigger, effectively ending up the same way that Dr. Viktor Pavlovich planned for her to end up all along.

Dead.

It's just that she didn't die by his hands. She died by her own.

"Oh my God," Marcy says, stunned. She is holding a box of matches and little plastic bottle of lighter fluid that she found in her Dad's part of the basement. The four of us, together, are getting ready to go back to Prince Richard's Maze where everything started this morning, and get Anders clothes from where they're hidden in The Grandfather Tree.

We're going to burn them until there is nothing left but ash.

"That didn't just happen," whimpers Myers.

"Damn," says Anders as he stares at the television.

The reporter, who's from national news and not a local station, continues to speak. "In a new twist in the ongoing tragedy unfolding in Meadowfield, Massachusetts, the sole survivor rescued from Dr. Viktor Pavlovich's house has taken her own life." More words follow, but I stop listening to them as they drone on.

I don't understand the sick media coverage that won't end.

I don't understand why puking on a microphone is news.

I don't understand why Calista Diamond killed herself and her suicide is being broadcast on national TV for everyone to see, like we live in a weird sort of reality where horrific images are what feed our world.

Soon, the station is going to cut to a commercial, and the commercial is going to be selling ice cream or diapers, and then it's going to go cut back to the lead story of the day and show the brutal footage all over again.

I think I'm losing my mind.

Either me—or the rest of the world.

55

MARCY HOLDS THE lighter fluid in one hand and the television remote in the other. The screen is blank. She's thankfully turned it off because we've all had just about enough. Besides, I have a sinking feeling that this is only the beginning. A new worry, glaring and urgent, comes rushing to the surface.

"We're screwed," I whisper. "We are so screwed."

No one says anything. Our little Kumbaya moment that we all shared before we found out that Calista Diamond blew her brains out up at Wang Memorial in Apple is a distant memory.

The idea that we'll ever get through whatever 'this' happens to be is starting to grow transparent, like smoke.

Smoke disappears. What's left behind is fire, and fire is deadly.

"Shit," whispers Anders under his breath.

"What?" says Myers. I should feel bad for him. He's woefully behind the rest of us. I suppose that has to do with him eating a couple pieces of cold, drugged pizza this afternoon. I shouldn't blame him for not putting the inevitable together.

"How much time do we have?" I ask. I'm not looking at Myers or Anders. I'm looking at Marcy. Nobody matters right now except for those whose last name is Cole.

"I don't know," she says. "It will be quick, though. I think it will be really fast."

Myers, in Marcy's dad's oversized shirt, wraps the loose sleeves around himself. He actually squirms in an absurd way like he's getting ready to have a tantrum. "What are you talking about?" he whines.

Anders stares down at his feet, probably trying to find that hiding place between the two of them where he's never had to venture before. He's never had the need. "Before the police come here," he says.

Myers' one real eye grows so round and wide that I think it's going to fall out of his head like his other one probably did somewhere in Prince Richard's Maze last night. "Why . . . why would the police come here?" he whines, growing smaller and smaller until he seems as though he might actually disappear down the sliver of a crack in the hardwood floor of the Cole's kitchen.

"Because we're in high school, and we were drugged." I snap. "Because, even coming down off of the effects of getting wasted, we've been smart enough to put two and two together and figure out that Calista Diamond, her friends, and freaking Tate all know each other." There's an acidity to my voice that's fairly close to the acerbic way that Anders has been talking all day. I'm well aware that the words are burning when they come out of my mouth. They aren't burning like my scar, but they're burning.

Marcy licks her lips. "West is right," she says. "Tate is at The Bellingham School. His friends all left The Bellingham School and came to Meadowfield. Tate's family is from Meadowfield. Tate's twin is from Meadowfield." She takes a deep breath. "I don't know if it's going to be the police, or reporters, or maybe even someone who wasn't totally shitfaced last night at The Stumps, but people know we were with that girl last night. That . . . that Calista person. First she was in Running Man's house. Now she's dead. Of course there are going to be questions."

"We don't have the answers," I say. "We don't even know her, or that guy with the greasy hair or the other one with the afro." Marcy looks pained when I mention the greasy guy. Her face turns red.

"Don't we?" says Anders.

We're all quiet.

Anders' words unleash a huge bomb that explodes over everything and leaves little invisible pieces of shrapnel flying in all directions.

'Don't we?'

'Don't we?'

Do we?

Marcy puts the lighter fluid down on the kitchen island and turns around so that her back is facing the rest of us. She bows her head and her shoulders start to tremble. The first thing I realize is that I'm not the only one having memories of the last twenty-four hours. I think we all are but don't want to admit it.

Then, without warning, and brutally honest, Anders' words tumble into my head and open up a combination lock that has been hiding the events of the last day behind it since I woke up this morning.

Another memory falls into place, vague and amorphous, but still there, like a dream, or a memory of a dream where you have to fill in the missing pieces as best you can.

I'm downstairs in Marcy's basement with Anders. He's flipping through an old Playboy magazine that is part of a collection her father keeps in a bin underneath the stairs. The glossy pages are foreign to me. Nobody buys magazines anymore. Everyone goes on the Internet and looks at stuff.

In my memory, he's making comments about some of the pictures, but I know that can't be true. Anders has never been like that. I guess we've all grown up thinking that it's crass to talk about people like they're sex objects.

Meadowfield people are more civilized, or we'd like to think that we are.

Myers certainly isn't. He's there, too. He's wearing his Master Baiter tee-shirt and eating something out of a bag. I don't know what it is, but Myers is a bottomless pit so it could be anything that he's found in the Cole's junk drawer. Anything at all.

As for me, in my memory I'm hungry but I'm also relishing the hunger pangs. Since losing weight I have come to regard my hunger pangs as close, close friends. We go everywhere together. The more insistent they are, the more powerful I feel. I might not be able to control much, but I can control them.

I feel as though I can control them forever.

'Knock. KnockKnockKnock.'

I remember the knocking and I remember wondering why anyone would be knocking on the door from the basement to the garage, but I don't think much about it. Myers doesn't move. Anders doesn't stop flipping through the pages of the magazine. Marcy is nowhere, but I think in reality she's upstairs in her bedroom probably sifting through clothes or trying on shoes.

So I go to the door, but in my memory, I float to the door, my feet barely touching the ground, and I open it.

A greasy guy is standing there wearing sunglasses. I've never seen him before and my brain registers a whole lot of things all at once. First, I think he needs zit medicine. His face is covered with red welts. Second, I notice his hair and realize that the greasy look isn't as much a fashion statement as it is an unfortunate outcome of never being taught that you have to bathe on a regular basis.

I barely notice the sunglasses. They are stupid and affected. I gloss right over them.

He's smiling, but his smile is almost demonic, or at least it is in my memory. I don't know if that's one of those things that I'm making up in my head, or if his smile is really like that. The third thing I notice, behind his smile, is that his teeth are gross and jagged. They look as though the greasy guy has gone out of his way not to brush or floss or do any of the things that you are supposed to do to take care of your teeth.

They seem mossy green.

Finally, my eyes fall on the box he's holding. It's big, and square, and white, and I remember thinking it's a pizza box.

I don't understand why there's a greasy guy at the garage door holding a pizza box. How did he even get into the garage to begin with? Who ordered pizza?

I remember him talking, the words coming out of his shark mouth with his snaggle teeth, but I don't know what he's saying. All I know is that suddenly Anders is calling for Marcy and shortly she's down the spiral staircase wearing jeans and the same top she woke up in this morning, and the whole room seems to light up with her presence.

I even remember her saying something about her parents being so cool for ordering a pizza for all of us, and Marcy giving the guy some money for a tip and thanking him.

Suddenly I gasp. Another memory slams into me. This one is even more important than all the rest and it makes sense in so many of the right ways that I can barely breathe.

'Put this in your mouth' a voice whispers in my ear, and I don't want to. I don't want to put anything in my mouth. If I do, I'll get fat again, and if I get fat again, I'll surely die.

'Put the goddamned pizza in your mouth,' hisses the voice, but this time it's menacing. Then the big black eyes appear, right in my face, and I know what they mean. I finally understand.

'Do it,' the greasy kid barks at me, his sunglasses inches away from me. *'Do it or I'll cut you.'*

56

NO MORE LIES.

We have things to say to each other—important things.

It's not like we've intentionally hidden them away. We haven't had the words, or we haven't remembered, or we have remembered but refused to believe our own minds.

Also, there are missing pieces that we might never understand, but we have to try. People are going to come looking for us soon, all of us, because we were at The Stumps last night with three runaways from The Bellingham School.

We don't remember being with them. We barely remember anything. All we have is the fading image of Val Buenavista's deleted video to prove that it's true, along with random snapshots of memory that may or may not be real.

There's no comfort in thinking that The Stumps kids won't remember us from last night. Of course they will. When something bad happens, a mob mentality takes over and good people get thrown to the wolves.

When Grafton Applewhite was going to beat the fat out of me in middle school before Anders stopped him, a mob formed then, too. It didn't matter that I had done nothing wrong. It didn't matter that Grafton Applewhite was a douchebag. All that mattered was that people were going to see blood and mobs feed on blood.

No. There's isn't any comfort in thinking that everyone at The Stumps last night could care less about us or how doped up we were.

They'll care.

As soon as they all realize that the girl on the news who blew her head off for all the world to see was hanging on Anders last night, fingers will point, and they'll point at us.

God. We are so screwed.

At this very moment, Dr. Viktor Pavlovich's murder madness is the most popular thing on television. His house of horrors is going to be front and center for days before focus is drawn elsewhere.

Until then, everything about Running Man is going to remain squatting like a big, fat toad, bloated with flies and hungry for more. Unfortunately, the four of us are the definition of 'more' and there is a swampy trail leading from Tate Cole to Calista Diamond and her friends, to Pizza Depot in Bellingham, Marcy's kitchen, The Stumps, Prince Richard's Maze, and for some random reason, Covington Circle.

Why are the four of us part of that trail?

I don't know.

I don't know.

I don't know.

It's now 7:35 and the sky is dark.

The four of us are sitting in my truck in the empty parking lot of Meadowfield High School. It's as good a place as any to talk. At least we're not at Marcy's house, or Anders, or Beryl's, or under the fuckity-fuck-fuck-fuck nose of Myers' mother.

If someone comes looking for us, we're gone.

There is a lone streetlamp off in the distance with a neat and tidy trashcan underneath it. The pie of light that it casts makes the metal bin almost glow and it occurs to me that Meadowfield is so perfect that even our trashcans are polished and pristine.

Jesus. Look inside and you'll still find used condoms and needles, empty beer bottles and cigarette butts. You'll find the same things as you'll find in East Meadowfield or Springfield, or even outside the back door of a sad little hospital up in Apple called Wang Memorial. That's where some equally sad custodian is still scrubbing bright pink Calista brains off of the floor and the walls.

Just because a trash can looks nice on the outside doesn't mean that what it holds is nice, too. Peel back the petals of the prettiest flower and there will still be tiny gnats eating it from the inside out.

Spiderlings.

Myers sits in the front seat this time. Anders and Marcy are sitting in the back. The darker it gets outside, the more Anders seems to mellow. The more hidden we all are, the more normal he seems to be.

Still, there's something he has to say. There's something we all have to say but none of us are willing to start.

Myers finally mumbles something.

"I can't hear you," I tell him.

He takes a deep breath. "I don't know how to fight," he says.

My mouth curls. "What does that have to do with anything?"

Myers sighs again and rubs the oversized sleeve of his shirt across his face. It's dark in the car and all I can really see is his shadow, but the light from the lone streetlamp still manages to glint off his one good eye.

"No one ever taught me," he continues. "That's why people pick on me. There must be a target on my back or something that says, *'Easy Pickings.'*"

Marcy leans forward and puts a hand on his shoulder. "You're not that bad," she says. Marcy is always so good. Why does she have to be so good?

Myers sniffs again and says, "I remember trying to fight."

My head tilts like a dog's when it hears a high pitched noise from far away. Does a fight sound familiar? The idea that Myers was in some sort of fight seems so absurd that I want to burst out laughing. Still, beyond the absurdity is a tiny bit of truth.

His words seem right.

"You don't fight," says Anders flatly.

"I know, right?" continues Myers. "But there was some reason that I had to fight and I don't remember what it is." He gulps and taps himself. "It's like that reason is sitting right here, you know? Right in middle of my chest, and it hurts, but I don't know why. I just know that I had to fight or something bad was going to happen."

"Like what?" I ask, starting to feel a little bit of a burn in my own chest because his words sound so real.

"I don't know," he sniffles. "I can't remember."

Again, there is a bubbly, burning sensation inside. It's not the same type of burn that I feel on my arm. This one seems more fueled by emotion and mental pain.

"Try," I prod.

Myers turns and faces in my direction. He sniffs and gulps at the same time, then takes a deep breath. "So, like, you know those pictures in the brochure back at Marcy's house? You know the kid with the afro and the other guy?"

"Yeah."

"I don't remember them," he says. "I know you guys all say they were on a video that Val Buenavista had on her phone but I don't remember that either."

"Okay," I say as evenly as I can. I can tell there are more words coiled in Myers' mouth, and if I can quietly coax them out, maybe some truths will come along with them.

"I don't remember them," he says again. "All I remember is big black eyes." Myers sniffs again and adjusts himself in the front seat, one leg folded under his body like we are sitting on Marcy's bed in her disaster of a bedroom.

"The thing is, I don't think what I'm remembering is big black eyes anymore." I bite my lip. I know what's coming next. Myers turns and looks in the back seat, trying to draw sympathy from Marcy and Anders, but they're only shadows in the dark, quietly listening while struggling with their own demons.

"Then what?" I ask.

Myers licks his lips. I don't see him do it. I hear him. "I think I'm remembering sunglasses."

57

THIS IS WHAT MYERS tells us.

He doesn't recall anyone coming to the basement door at the Coles' house last night. He doesn't remember anything after we left his mother's kitchen, her screams chasing us away because she thought we wanted to eat her cookies.

He doesn't remember the pizza from Pizza Depot and he doesn't remember eating it last night, or even today. Myers has had a double helping of Flunitrazepam. I'm surprised he remembers his own name.

He doesn't remember Calista Diamond, the greasy guy, or the guy with the afro. It does no good to tell him that I do remember her, laughing at me, poking me in the face like a helpless marionette that's lost its strings. That part of his memory is gone.

What he does remember is being in the woods at The Stumps, surrounded by a lot of people and not caring one bit. He says he remembers feeling naked like in one of those stress dreams you have about being bare-assed in the middle of the cafeteria, but instead of feeling ashamed, he likes the way it makes him feel—free and alive without a care in the world.

As we sit quietly in my truck, the only vehicle in the Meadowfield High School parking lot, Myers tells us that he remembers staring up at the stars in the sky and wanting to pluck them from the black expanse and cradle them in his arms.

For him, the heat of the barrel fires at The Stumps keeps coming back in an endless loop of memory that his subconscious thinks is important. All day long, he's been thinking that he's been kissed by the surface of the sun, which I know is crazy, but everything today has been crazy. He's almost convinced himself that he's touched the stars last night.

He didn't.

None of us did.

His abstract memories are fueled by drugs. That's what drugs do. They give you wings. They mess you up. They make you forget, or least that's what Flunitrazepam does.

"There were animals crying," he tells us. He remembers the sounds of sheep, just like me, but he doesn't remember why or even how there could be sheep anywhere near Meadowfield. Then he remembers being in the woods again, and this is where Myers starts to cry a little when he talks. It's not the kind of crying that always makes me angry. His face isn't scrunched up into a ball. He isn't gasping for breath or screwing his fists into his eyes to make the water stop. He's simply crying, softly, as he tells us what happened next.

"Baaaaa," he says. "That's what I heard. Baaaaa. Baaaaa. Baaaaa. I don't know where the sheep came from or why there were sheep in the first place. All I know is that I kept hearing the crying." Marcy sniffs a little but Myers continues on. "And the laughing," he says. "There was laughing." I don't tell him that I remember laughing, too. It's the kind of laughter that sounds as though it's coming out of a painted mouth with sharp teeth. It's the kind of canned creepy laughter from one of those amusement park rides where they put you in a little cart on a track and send you into the dark. It's the sort of laughter that makes you hope you won't tinkle in your pants. "Yeah," says Myers again. "Laughing."

Marcy sniffs some more and says, "I remember laughing, too."

"Oh my God, thank you," he cries. "I thought it was just me. I thought I was the only one."

"No," I say, because I have the same memory. "You're not."

Instead of Anders chiming in and telling us that he remembers the laughter, too, he says, 'What else?"

Myers has released so much darkness that he might crumble if he pulls out anything more, but he has to. He has to process this for himself as much as for the rest of us.

"Screaming," he says quietly. "There was screaming, too, and there was me thinking I had to fight." I am listening to everything Myers says, but in tandem, my thoughts are also back at The Maze, lying on my back on the forest floor, hearing the baaing and the laughing. Maybe even the screaming. "And then I think I did fight," he says. "Not for long. Someone punched me in the stomach and then pushed fingers into my face and my eye popped out." Myers gulps. "It popped out and whoever I was fighting went away."

While I try to imagine someone's hands in Myers' face with big, fat thumbs, pressing hard into his eyes, I feel a heavy pressure on my chest, like stacks of lead weights, and the sunglasses are in my face again, along with something else.

A whisper.

"Fucking stupid sheep," the voice says in my brain. *"You do what I tell you to do, right? Because you're a stupid sheep."*

I shake my head to try and make the voice go away but it doesn't do any good.

"Are you okay?" Myers asks. "Weston, Are you okay?"

No. No, I'm not okay. There is someone sitting on my chest with his face so close to mine that I should remember the foul smell of his breath, but I don't. He's holding my arms down and I'm letting him while transfixed by his eyes. They're huge and black and I can't understand why they're so big.

But I do understand.

They're big and black because he's wearing sunglasses.

What's more, as his hands press my arms into the ground and I don't struggle because I'm so drugged, he bends over until his mouth is right next to mine.

"Baaaaaa, you goddamned sheep," he hisses. *"Say it. Say you're a sheep. Baaaaa. Baaaaa. BAAAA."* I don't say it, though. I don't think I can talk. I can barely even move my lips. I feel his grimy fingers pressing into my arms until he finally pushes them both above my head and pins me there with one hand. A bright light suddenly appears, and I think it's the sun or the moon or anything bright enough to be blinding, then along with the brightness comes words that I will never forget as long as I live.

"Sheep are property. You're mine now. And you know what we do with our sheep?" I don't know. I don't know anything. I barely even know my own name. *"We brand them,"* he hisses, and a searing pain burns into my left arm with such force that maybe I pass out.

Hopefully, I pass out.

Who would want to remember something like that?

58

"WEST?" SAYS MYERS. The light from the streetlamp is making my side of the truck glow. He can see my face. It must look awful. "Are you okay?"

"It's nothing," I lie.

"It's not nothing," he says.

"I'm fine," I hiss at Myers, although he doesn't deserve my anger. I don't know where to aim it though, and he's an easy target. He's always been such an easy target.

"It's just that . . . "

"I said I'm fine, Robbie."

Myers instantly shuts up. Calling him by his first name is a really shitty thing to do. Marcy sometimes calls him Robbie, but Marcy is sweet and she doesn't mean anything by it, but me or Anders calling him that is barely an inch away from his fuckity-fuck-fuck-fuck of a mother flipping out and sending him to bed without any supper, or worse, washing his mouth out with soap.

She still does things like that. Christ, he's seventeen years old and she still pulls the same old crap on him that she did when he was five.

Immediately, I regret snapping at Myers, but just like the scar that's on my arm, the damage is done.

I now have to live with the consequences of my words, like I have to live with a half memory of a greasy escapee from The Bellingham School sitting on my chest, his nasty hair hanging down over his hatchet face, torturing me and burning me forever.

Branding me like I'm a sheep.

My nostrils flair and anger spills out of me in waves so dense and powerful that you can probably see them. Still, I don't say anything. I don't even know what I would say or how I would start.

I feel violated. I've never had this feeling before. Sure, I've been as-saulted—verbally—by my indifferent mother or by kids at school, by anyone who ever made fun of fat people. The blubber always shielded me from the verbal stones that they hurled. Eating made the pain go away.

Now there's nothing that can make this pain go away.

Not ever.

The four of us are quiet, smothered in Myers' memories as well as our own, all different from each other yet all the same. I look out the driver's side window and stare off in the distance at the Meadowfield High School flagpole planted in front of the circular driveway. The flag isn't at half-mast yet. It's only Saturday night. Come Monday morning if school is in session, which it may not be because the residents of Meadowfield will still be reeling with the amount of death found in Running Man's house, the flag will surely be lowered halfway down the pole. It will stay like that for a long time—maybe a week or two—until someone's parents, who are snobby and selfish enough to complain that the morbid symbolism is affecting their child's education, will make the school raise it back up.

I wonder if Meadowfield High School will have special workshops on how to process the grief that Dr. Viktor Pavlovich caused.

I wonder if there will be armed cops at the front entrance and the exit by the library.

I wonder if metal detectors will be installed because of stupid people thinking that surgical scalpels might now get smuggled in by ugly, plain girls who are plotting to go postal on any perky, pretty cheerleaders they see.

I wonder how everything will change.

Wading in my own thoughts, I barely hear the click of the back door. The light in the cab of the truck blinks on and Anders steps out and pushes the door closed behind him.

I expect Marcy to call after him, but she doesn't. I look through the rearview mirror and catch her shadow in the back seat. She's not even looking at him. Her head is bowed and all I can see is the outline of her curly hair.

"What did I do?" says Myers. He's so used to blaming himself for everything—the wrath of his mother, the cruelty of our classmates, that he naturally thinks he's the cause.

"It's not you," I tell him. I try to be nice. I try to be compassionate, but I think I only sound angry—like Anders.

A moment later I open the driver's side door and let myself out, too. Anders is ten feet away from the truck, hunkered down in a crouch, staring at the black pavement like the sun is shining, and he's watching carpenter ants burn or sink into tiny puddles of asphalt.

"You leaving again?" I ask him. He doesn't say anything. "You can't. There's no place for you to go. There's no place for any of us to go. We have to get rid of your clothes."

I walk up to his hunched form, trying to quell the idea of kicking him hard because if anyone needs a good ass kicking today, it's him.

Only then do I realize that he's crying, too.

"I can't . . ." he begins. "West . . . how . . . I can't. I just can't."

I take a deep breath. I know what he's talking about. I think I've always known. For the first time today—probably the first time forever, I decide I need to say something about the unspoken thing that we never discuss. Anders Stephenson is my best friend. He's one of my very best friends in the whole world. He's always been there for me. Now, I have to be there for him.

I lower myself down so I'm also resting on my haunches in the middle of the empty parking lot. A year ago I would never have been able to be comfortable like this. I would have toppled over into a heaping pile of lard.

"Hey," I say to him as gently and as honestly as I can. "She really is beautiful, you know."

Anders turns his face away. He doesn't want me to see him like this. He doesn't want anyone to see him like this.

Finally, he takes in a ragged breath and pushes it out into the night. Anders lifts his head and stares off at the flagpole, flapping gently in the evening breeze.

"That's just it," he says, quietly acknowledging what we've always known about Marcy, ever since third grade when her parents, our parents, our teachers, and everyone explained to us as best they could that Mark Cole didn't exist anymore. Anders wipes away his tears and chuckles in a way that would be endearing if it wasn't so sad. "He is beautiful, isn't he?"

59

MARK COLE DISAPPEARED when we were in third grade. His disappearance coincided with his twin brother, Tate, crossing over into Crazy Land, but Mark Cole's disappearance had nothing to do with Tate being mental.

Tate was always destined to end up a bad seed.

The introduction of Marcy was the most natural thing in the world. Marcy was always there anyway. We all knew it. It's just that her outsides finally started to mirror her insides. She began wearing dresses and letting her curls grow out. Her parents even allowed her to get her ears pierced—only one on each side.

After all, this *is* Meadowfield.

Mark became a distant memory so quickly it's like we all forgot that he ever existed. Marcy was just Marcy. Sweet, beautiful Marcy.

Anders was always protective of her, like he was over all of us. Maybe other groups of kids who grew up on the same street might have drifted apart with the wealth of crap we all had to deal with, but our circumstances only made the four of us stronger. Of course our bond didn't stop me from eating thousands of calories a day to drown out the fact that I had a distant, uninvolved mother, or Myers and Marcy from getting picked on at school, but through it all, we had each other.

That's all that really mattered.

When we were in middle school, Marcy started taking some sort of medication for kids committed to fully transitioning, so that her body would slow the onset of puberty. The rest of us grew peach fuzz, then real stubble. Anders shot up like a weed and cemented his reputation as a jock. Marcy remained Marcy, without any tell-tale signs that she wasn't genetically born that way.

Then, a year and a half ago, right on her sixteenth birthday, Marcy started hormone therapy with her parents' blessing. That's when everything really changed. I mean, she was always pretty, but Marcy didn't only blossom into the girl that we all knew she was.

She turned into the definition of a high school boy's wet dream.

I knew she was beautiful. We all knew she was beautiful, but knowing and admitting are two different things. Besides, I've always realized that what's on the inside is more important than what's on the outside.

Being fat will teach you that pretty damn fast.

It wasn't until the end of junior year, after we all took our initial college exams and began talking about what comes next, that our lives began to change. Anders started testing the waters with little comments here and there about how he had loads of family over in Norway. He began dropping hints about maybe taking a year off before going away to school, but I didn't really think anything of it.

Honestly, I thought he was full of crap.

Marcy never said a word about Anders going to Norway, but we all knew she wasn't happy. Well, Myers and I knew. Anders seemed to be clueless. He's such a guy. He's always had that jock thing going that Myers and I will never understand, and he's always had girls, too—lots of girls that he goes through like I used to go through bags of potato chips.

This past summer was normal enough. Except for some completely unnoticed tension between Anders and Marcy, which I can now go back to and fill in the blanks, we were all fine.

We were fine until last night when a bunch of lunatics drugged us, dragged us around town, and somehow landed us in Prince Richard's Maze.

'Baaaaa.'

'Baaaa. Baaaa. Baaaa.'

My mouth grows small as the sheep quickly skip through my head, in one ear and out the other. I slowly stand in the parking lot of Meadowfield High School and hold my hand out for Anders.

"Dude, you'll figure things out." I say. "To be honest, I'm kind of jealous."

Anders shakes his head and takes my hand. As he gets to his feet, he says "I'm not talking about this, okay?" He doesn't say it in a mean way or a way that makes me think that the subject is off the table. He's just putting the conversation on pause because we have other things to worry about.

I think that's fair. Besides, I don't think I'm the one he has to talk to. The person he needs to have a serious one-on-one with is himself. He has to finally sort out his feelings and come to the conclusion that what people think, doesn't matter. Only what he thinks matters. When he's done with that conversation, he has to have another one with

Marcy. I don't know how that one will end up. It's really not my business.

Right now, my business is the four of us and putting together the rest of the pieces of what happened last night. I'm starting to get the idea that I'm not going to like what I find, but I have to look.

We all have to look.

One thing's for sure. Calista Diamond is dead. She would have been dead whether she blew her brains out with a rookie cop's gun up at Wang Memorial Hospital or if Running Man sliced her into thin strips like sushi. Somehow we're part of what happened to her.

Now we have to figure out why.

60

MARCY AND MYERS are quiet.

Myers has unloaded his addled brain as much as he can. He sits in the front seat, slouched, with his head almost touching his chest. I don't think he's sleeping. I think he's hiding by folding in on himself instead of seeking out the safe place between his feet.

To each his own.

As I slowly drive my truck through the side streets of Meadowfield, I quickly glance in the rearview mirror at Anders. He's barely visible, but I can still feel him, all messed up and confused. There must be a storm inside his head right now, and he doesn't know when it's going to end. I don't know how a guy like Anders is going to come to terms with the fact that he's into a girl like Marcy. Who can blame him?

It's all confusing until you stop thinking and start living.

Marcy isn't talking at all. She's staring out the window as we drive through the tree-lined streets of the older part of town. Huge brick colonials, some with pillars in front, are the norm here. This is where old money Meadowfield lives. Don't get me wrong—Primrose Lane is beautiful, but none of us who live there can say our families came over on the Mayflower. None of us can cite great, great, a dozen times great grandmothers who voyaged to the new world centuries ago. People on my side of town are only two or three generations-worth of wealthy. People in old Meadowfield have family crests hanging in their living rooms and own centuries-old moss-covered crypts in the huge cemetery behind the stark white church in the center of town.

As I slowly drive my truck, passing by majestic homes with their lights on, I can imagine that inside the beautiful facades, frightened families are huddled around their big-screen TVs, drinking martinis, totally engrossed in the saga of Viktor Pavlovich.

Meadowfield doesn't know how to deal with such things. We're mostly populated by people who are ill equipped to handle the messier truths of life. The four of us, in one way or another, have been dealing with those messier truths for so long that I think we've developed an extra layer of skin to make us a little bit tougher.

Maybe everyone in town has the same extra layer as we do, but is so adept at lying, they hide their misery just like us. Sometimes it's hard to know how other people might feel. Maybe Val Buenavista is such a bitch because she's trapped inside the body of a linebacker. Maybe Grafton Applewhite gets beaten with a soup ladle by his mother or has spent years trying to live up to his father's unreasonable expectations of what a man should be.

You never know what other people go through. Contrary to what they say, we can't walk in other peoples' shoes. We don't have that kind of power.

Five minutes later, I pull my truck down Golden Street alongside Prince Richard's Maze. The four of us haven't said a word since Anders and I got back in the car. Like before, I don't think we'd know what to say even if we wanted to talk. Instead, we've nested into our collective silence like it's a fluffy pillow that promises the best night's sleep ever. Who wants to mess with something like that?

After I park my truck up against the woods and quiet the engine, we still sit there in silence. I stare through the black trees into an abyss. I'm not afraid of going into the woods at night. That brand of visceral fear has all but drained away from me, and probably from my friends, too.

We've already had enough scares to last a lifetime. I think something really frightening would have to happen in order for us to register any kind of emotion. As for me, I feel dead inside about what we have to do next.

I'm just following a to-do list, and this is the next thing to be done after deleting Val Buenavista's video and finding out about Flunitrazepam. I go over the steps in my mind.

Drive to town but take side streets so no one will see you.

Park your truck in the shadows of the trees next to Prince Richard's Maze.

Open the door.

Get out.

Close the door quietly so none of the houses across the street will notice the truck in the dark.

Carry a bottle of lighter fluid and a lighter into the woods.

Follow Little Loop until it passes the cut-off to Big Loop.

Veer off into the woods at the same place you've veered off a thousand times before.

Don't let your sneakers crunch the leaves too much in case there are others in The Maze doing God knows what.

Find The Grandfather Tree.

Reach inside and pull out Anders' bloody wad of clothing.

Take it out.

Burn it.

It isn't lost on me that we are potentially destroying something that shouldn't be destroyed. I feel like the four of us are systematically covering someone else's tracks, but those tracks seem connected to our own feet. It's as though we are intentionally eliminating evidence, but evidence of what? After all, none of us know why Anders woke up this morning covered in blood. None of us know why it was only on him and not on the rest of us, and we certainly don't have a clue where it came from.

Still, it feels as though his blood-stained clothing can't be found. I don't know why, but what we are about to do seems right.

As a matter of fact, it seems vitally important.

"So?" I say, with my hand on the driver's side handle. "Are we going to do this?"

"I'm afraid," Myers sniffs.

"We don't have any room to be afraid," I say. I'm not mean when I tell him that. I'm speaking the truth.

"Let's get this over with," Anders says and opens the door.

As the light flicks on, I see Marcy's face. She should look as though she's ready to bolt down the street any second, running as fast as she can away from us, Prince Richard's Maze, and everything, but she doesn't. She scoots across the leather, going out the same door that Anders opened because it opens to the street. The other side is a matted tangle of brush and dead October leaves. She probably wouldn't be able to get out that way, anyway.

Her face is hard and determined and maybe even a little scary.

For a second, a vision of Tate flashes before my eyes.

Tate had a twin. His name was Mark. Mark's gone. Now there's only Marcy, and no thanks to Tate, Marcy is very much alive.

61

HOW DO YOU ignore your own brain turning on you? How do you make the jabbering stop? As soon as we step over the chain that blocks cars from entering The Maze, I feel like the woods are alive with voices.

It's the same soundtrack that I've been hearing all day long. There's laughter and sheep crying. There's screaming and more. All the little snippets of memory that are floating around in my skull are trying to come together into a coherent tune, but instead of coming together, they keep smashing against one another like in one of those old Asteroids games where giant rocks float around a black screen until they collide and break apart into smaller rocks.

I feel like I'm living in that game right now. I'm floating in a great black expanse of nothingness, and every thought that I have keeps sliding up against the next one and then splintering into twos and threes.

Marcy and Anders are walking ahead of me and Myers. Marcy is actually first. If we had our cell phones we could flick on a flashlight app, but we don't. All we have is the moonlight peeking through the trees and our own memories of these woods to guide us.

That's all we really need. If we were blind and the trees only had braille bark, we would still be able to find The Grandfather Tree easily enough. This is Prince Richard's Maze. Every kid in town knows the trails here. We all know the offshoots and the shortcuts. The Maze's geography is secret knowledge to those in Meadowfield of a certain age. Of course, we'll grow up and forget. Too many other things will take over our lives when we're out of this town, and the lingering memory of the patch of woods between Meadowfield and Springfield, looming over the highway and the Connecticut River beyond, will disappear forever.

For me, I'm not so sure about that forever part. I have a feeling I'm never going to forget Prince Richard's Maze. Even if I do, as soon as I look down at my left arm and the little triangular reminder of what happened here during October of my senior year in high school, the memories will come shooting back.

This place will forever secure its gnarled roots deep inside of me.

Every time I think about it, all I'll want to do is suck my thumb until the memory goes away.

"Ow," snaps Myers. "Watch it." I've inadvertently let a taut branch whip back into his face.

"Did you lose another eye?" I say. I'm not trying to be funny. I don't even know why I said it.

"Maybe," he sniffs. "Do I get a cool dog with a harness if I do?"

"Your mother would probably freak."

"About me losing another eye?"

"No," I tell him. "About having a dog in the house. Maybe it will want to eat her cookies or something."

"Maybe it will give her something else to scream at besides me."

I don't answer Myers. He picked open his own scab and is waiting for me to pour verbal vinegar on it so his pain will be that much more intense. I don't want to be the person to cause him any more pain. I don't want any of us to be in pain.

"She's a bitch," I say as we make our way through the woods. "Graduate and leave. Don't even send her a mother's day card or acknowledge her birthday."

Myers snorts. "That's kind of harsh," he says.

"I'm feeling harsh."

"If you say so," Myers says right as Anders turns and tells us both to be quiet.

Meanwhile, Marcy is traversing The Maze with single-minded purpose. Step after step she goes deeper into the woods, the only sound being the soft crunching of dead leaves under our sneakers and the slosh of lighter fluid in the plastic bottle that she's holding.

How much of the liquid will it take?

How much of the fluid in that little bottle will we have to splash on Anders' bloodied clothing and light with a match before we can obliterate the memory of his soiled pants and shirt forever? My guess is that Marcy's dad's lighter fluid could come out of an endless stream in the side of a rocky hill, gushing free for hours and hours, days and days, and it still wouldn't be enough.

I don't know if it will ever be enough, but we still have to try.

We have to try no matter what.

Five minutes later we're in front of The Grandfather Tree. Underneath the moon the rotted bark hangs on its sides like wrinkled skin. The jagged openings in the huge stump look like eyes, a nose, and a mouth, and the broken branches sticking out of its sides are arms.

I stop for a moment, a wave of fear bubbling up inside of me. Anders left his bloodied clothes insides its guts and now the Grandfather Tree has tasted blood. This is the part of the movie where the unreal becomes real and the huge stump comes alive. It will take Marcy first, because she's the closest. As it stuffs her inside its gaping maw, Anders will grab onto her feet to try to pull her back, but he won't be able to, and he'll get eaten alive along with her.

Myers will be next. He'll try to fight, but by his own admission, he doesn't fight, and the monster that the Grandfather Tree has become will get him, too.

Finally, I'll be the only one left, and the tree will scoop me up like one of those talking trees in the old Wizard of Oz movie—the ones that grew apple bombs to fling at trespassers. It will take its time, doing horrible, unspeakable things to me. After all, it lives in Prince Richard's Maze and that's what happens in a place like this and a town like this, where everything is supposed to be all sunshine and roses when it's really darkness and thorns.

Such morbid thoughts are the only ones that keep me company as Marcy reaches inside one of those dark holes—a mouth, an eye, I don't know—and pulls back Anders' bloodied wad of clothes. She throws them on the ground and begins shaking the bottle of lighter fluid.

"Not here," I tell her and open my arms. "There are dead leaves everywhere. We'll set this part of town on fire."

"Is that such a bad thing?" murmurs Myers.

"Yeah, well, Meadowfield has already had one tragedy today." I say "Let's try and not make it two."

"Then where?" Anders snaps. "I can't look at the blood anymore."

"None of us can." I say. After a moment an idea comes to me that seems a little too convenient. "Let's burn them by Turner Pond."

"Sure. Fine," Ander says. "I want this over with."

There's no need to respond. We all want *'this'* over with, too.

62

THE REFLECTION of the moon rippling across the water of Turner Pond is beautiful. We've never been in Prince Richard's Maze at night before except for last night, and none of us fully remember last night other than the horrific snippets that should be burned along with Anders' clothing.

Off in the distance I can hear cars going back and forth on the highway. More likely than not, those cars are filled with autumn leaf peepers, coming back home from Vermont after a day of gazing at amazing vistas of burnt oranges and yellows. They are blissfully unaware that the highway they are driving down, heading to Connecticut and beyond, is cutting right alongside the infamous town of Meadowfield, Massachusetts.

The people in those cars are probably listening to the radio while their kids are asleep in the backseat. They don't even realize that, for a brief time, they are skirting the edge of our town. They'll never feel the specter of death tickling the base of their necks or whispering horrible things into their ears about how so many people died on Covington Circle.

Even if they do feel the darkness, they won't know what it is. They'll chalk it up to a momentary gloomy patch in their otherwise glorious day, and be thankful when they cross over the border to Connecticut, leaving Meadowfield behind forever.

The people in those cars have no idea that four high school students are in the dark woods to the left of them—the ones that loom over the highway. They have no idea that we are standing on the edge of Turner Pond, or that a beautiful girl is spilling out the contents of a bottle of lighter fluid onto a pile of bloody clothing.

The fluid streams out of the bottle like piss. Marcy waves the liquid back and forth over Anders' shirt and his pants. She soaks his socks and his underwear, probably using more of the flammable chemicals than she needs to use. I hear the plastic sucking in and out, in and out, as she squeezes the bottle.

A foul odor fills the air.

"Do it," whispers Anders.

Marcy keeps squeezing the bottle until it's empty. Meanwhile, Myers grabs a long stick, dead leaves still clinging to it, and pokes at one of Anders' bloody socks until the cloth catches in a little fork between two branches. He lifts the sock up and holds it in front of Marcy.

"Helping," he shrugs.

Marcy nods her head, steps back, and lights a match. The sock bursts into flames quickly, and Myers yelps. He drops the stick with the burning sock to the ground and Anders shakes his head.

"Damnit," Myers says.

"It's fine," I tell him as I reach down, grab the end of the stick that isn't burning, and thrust it at the rest of the liquid soaked clothing.

Minutes later, all that is left are ashes and the taste of smoke in our mouths. Without saying a word to each other, we all kick the ashes to the edge of the pond and let the water suck them in. Whatever is left of Anders' bloody clothing sinks away to mix with the mud and the slime down below.

Next spring, when algae covers the pond, no one but us will know that the green slick is blood-fed.

No one will think on it for a second.

"What's that?" says Myers and cocks his head.

"What's what?"

He's quiet for a moment. "That," he says again, and this time I hear it, too.

"Is that a phone?" asks Marcy. "That sounds like my ring tone." Without waiting for us to respond, she starts jogging down Little Loop.

"Wait," Anders shouts out. "Marcy, wait." He races after her. Myers and I follow.

A few hundred feet into the dark, maybe more, Marcy stops.

We all do.

The woods are silent.

"That was a phone, wasn't it?" She says in a whisper. I don't know why she's whispering. There's nobody around.

"I don't know," says Anders, but his voice sounds strange, as though a bony hand has reached around his throat and squeezed. "I . . . I . . . "

The ringtone starts again. This time it's close. It's off to our right, straight through the foliage, and we all turn our heads.

"It *is* a phone," she yelps and takes a step toward the dark woods. Only then does Anders shoot his arm out and grab her hand.

"Marcy, don't," he says to her, but he doesn't say it like I would or Myers would. He says it as though there is something unimaginable inside the woods, and if Marcy goes into them, she may never come back out again.

Myers and I are transfixed as Anders holds onto Marcy's hand with such strength and such tenderness that I feel like I'm watching something miraculous take shape before my eyes.

"Anders, please," she whispers, but doesn't pull away from him. "Let me go. I think that's my phone."

Anders doesn't let her go. Instead he grabs hold of her with his other hand and falls to his knees, right there in the dark, right in the middle of Prince Richard's Maze. He holds onto her hands tightly like he never wants to let her go.

"Oh God, Marcy" he cries with real tears, in such a mournful way that I can feel his pain right in the middle of my chest.

"Anders," she whispers. "What's wrong? What's happening?"

Anders Stephenson, my best friend, our protector, with the basketball frame and GQ face, takes in a deep glut of air and begins shaking, like he started shaking this morning when we all woke up in the woods and he was covered in blood.

"Oh God," he sobs again as he gently pulls Marcy to her knees so they are close enough to touch foreheads. "I remember. I remember what happened last night."

63

MYERS AND I DON'T say anything as we watch Marcy and Anders crouch on the ground, their heads inches away and their arms clutching on to one other. They're having a moment, or they're having *'the'* moment that will define them from now on.

"I remember. I remember," he keeps saying over and over again, and Marcy nods her head like she understands.

"Shhhh," she tells him as he keeps saying the same words, like if he says them longer or louder, they might mean something different.

Suddenly Marcy stiffens and pulls away from him, but not too far. They're still close enough that if they leaned forward their lips could touch. Who cares? It wouldn't be such a bad thing. Maybe it would be a great thing for Anders and Marcy and all of us.

"I screamed, didn't I?" she says to Anders, totally ignoring the fact that her ring tone starts going off again in the woods. It rings six or seven times before stopping. Seconds later it starts ringing again. "I did," Marcy whispers and lets out a quiet gasp. "There were hands. I remember hands, and they were grabbing at me. Someone pulled my shoes off and then fingers were on my waist, pulling at . . . pulling at my pants. I remember hearing laughing and me trying to make the fingers stop and . . . no matter what I said . . . no matter what I did, it wasn't enough, and I screamed."

"You did," Anders nods, holding on to her. "You screamed, and I couldn't do anything. I remember I couldn't do anything to help you, and I felt like the worst kind of person in the world."

Myers stands next to me, the long sleeves of Marcy's dad's shirt wrapped around himself again. His breathing is shallow and ragged. "I tried to fight," he whispers. "I did. I tried to fight, but it was like I was fighting in a dream. Then I couldn't breathe." He turns to me. "West, I was punched in the stomach and the wind was knocked out of me so hard. I remember not being able to breath and thinking that I was going to die."

I start shaking my head. I don't want to hear this. I don't want to hear any more of this. I throw my hands up to my ears and close my eyes, praying for everything to stop, but it won't stop. The memories come flooding in—the final ones, the crucial ones, and God help me, I don't want to know.

I don't. I don't. I don't.

The phone starts ringing again in the woods and I take off running away from Marcy and Anders, and away from Myers toward the sound of that phone. I go right through the brush, the branches scraping at my face and my arms, clawing at me, tearing at my skin.

And as I run, I remember everything as though it is happening all over again. This time I remember it all, and my lips curl up to expose my teeth.

We were with the greasy guy. His friend with the afro and Calista Diamond weren't with us anymore. Either we had left them back at The Stumps, or they had left us. I don't know which. All I know is that we were in the car again, in the back seat, and then we were in The Maze.

"No wonder Tate hates you so much," I heard the greasy guy say. He was talking to Marcy and she was sitting on the ground, her head lolling around on her neck as though she couldn't hold it up even if she tried. "You're way prettier than he is. That must really piss him off."

Anders was on the ground, too. He was trying to stand, but he couldn't quite get his legs to hold his body. "Leave her alone," he bellowed, but the guy only laughed and pushed him over with one hand.

"Fucking you up like Tate wants is going to be so much fun," the guy said. "Too bad none of you will remember any of it." There was a whoosh in the air. It was the sound of him pulling his belt out of his jeans.

"Stop," I cried, but I was probably mumbling because I could barely focus on what was going on. All I remember was thinking that I had to save Marcy. Whatever I did, I had to protect my friend.

"Not a chance," said the guy, and this time he was wearing his awful sunglasses. Who wears sunglasses at night? What kind of person does something like that? He turned to Marcy and said, "You ready for me, Sweetness?" and Anders growled something that was equal parts incoherent and insane.

"Leave her alone," Myers cried from out of nowhere and charged the greasy guy, but Myers was so small that whatever he thought he was trying to do was almost comical. The greasy guy grabbed him by his hair and punched him really hard. Myers immediately fell to the ground, and I think I fell to the ground, too, because I was at the very edge of passing out from whatever was coursing through my system.

Still, Myers got back up and ran at the greasy guy again. He was met by two hands wrapped tightly around his face. Myers started screaming as fingers pressed into his eyes until his glass one popped out.

"Holy shit," cried the guy as he bent down and scooped up Myers' eye off the ground. Then he pushed Myers really hard. Myers lost his footing and fell. This time he didn't get back up. Meanwhile, the greasy guy pulled his sunglasses off and stared at the funny shaped piece of plastic in his hand, because glass eyes aren't really glass, they're resin. "Would you look at that," he whistled. "I got me a third eye." Then he laughed in that sinister laugh that I had been hearing in my head.

"Stop it," Anders howled again, still unable to stand. His words were totally ignored. The guy barely even flinched. He turned back to Marcy and crouched down in front of her.

"We don't need these, now do we?" he said and pulled her shoes off of her feet. Marcy was still floating and barely understanding anything. I wanted to cry out for him to stop what he was doing but I couldn't. I didn't think I had enough energy to push the words out of my mouth. "And I don't think we need these either," the greasy guy said.

That's when Marcy screamed. I didn't know what he was doing to her, but I could imagine his disgusting, dirty fingers pulling at the waistband of her jeans, dragging them down until they weren't covering anything anymore.

"Noooo," I heard Anders again, but it sounded as though he was far away on the other side of the world.

Then there was a gasp and all the sound in the woods seemed to disappear and be taken up by one single statement that was so obvious to the rest of us but such a revelation to the greasy guy, that he was momentarily shocked.

"Fuck me," I heard him bark at Marcy with such cruelty in his voice that I wanted him dead. I wanted him to die over and over again until he couldn't die anymore. "You're a dude. You're a goddamned dude."

64

WAIT, WHAT?

That's what I kept thinking in my head. It had been so long since any of us thought of Marcy as a boy that the words stung as badly as if he had flung them at us instead of her. I mean she was born a boy, but Marcy was a girl. Every part of her was a girl except for one last thing that was getting taken care of right after her eighteenth birthday.

How could anyone say such a hurtful thing to her?

'You're a dude. You're a goddamned dude.'

"Stop it," I screamed as loud as I could. "Just stop it."

Meanwhile, Myers was on the ground. My head rolled to the right and I saw him there. His chest was heaving up and down, and I couldn't tell if he was crying or passed out.

I saw Anders, too. He was trying to get to his feet again. The greasy guy with the sunglasses turned to him and I remember being scared.

"Well this is a pickle," the greasy guy said in such a sickly, smarmy way that my stomach did a flip-flop. My arms and legs were numb and I could feel my brain slipping away. "But here's the thing. If I'm going to get my rocks off with a dude, then I want a real dude, not some messed up pre-op tranny."

Shut up. Shut up. Shut up. "Shut up," I managed to squeeze out.

The greasy guy laughed that weird laugh again and said, "How 'bout it, pretty boy. I bet you'll love it."

No, No, NO, I thought as I struggled against the veil slowly shrouding me in darkness. *Leave Anders alone. Leave my friend alone.*

The next thing I knew there was a huge weight on my chest and hot breath in my face.

"You know, when I lived on my daddy's farm we used to screw with the sheep," a voice said as the pressure pushed me into the dead leaves on the ground. The greasy guy was on top of me, with his hair hanging down and his breath right in my face. "You've ever been to a farm, pretty boy?"

Pretty boy?

Pretty boy?

Who . . . who was he calling a pretty boy?

Spittle fell on my cheeks. "They're filled with sheep," the greasy guy hissed. "Fucking stupid sheep." He laughed some more then started bleating right in my face.

"Baaaaaa. Baaaaa. BAAAAA."

I didn't understand. Anders was the jock. Anders was the pretty boy. He'd always been the tall, good looking one with the blond hair and the square jaw. He'd always been the one with people fawning all over him.

"That's right, pretty boy," the greasy guy whispered right in my ear, and I suddenly realized that he wasn't talking to Anders, or Myers, or even Marcy. He was talking to me and he was calling me a pretty boy.

Weston Kahn, who used to sit in his bedroom with his hand shoved into a box of Fruit Loops.

Weston Kahn, whose legs used to rub together when he walked.

Weston Kahn who passed by a group of girls in the choral room at school while Cleo Collins said, *'He's cute now. Who would have ever thought that Weston Kahn would be cute? He was so fat.'*

He was talking to me. I was the pretty boy, and part of me was so confused and maybe even a little happy that I barely heard the greasy guy say, "You do what I tell you to do, right? Because you're a stupid sheep."

I didn't care that he said I was a sheep.

I didn't care that he was holding my arms down.

I didn't care that there were big, black sunglasses right in my face.

I didn't care, as he bent right down to my ear and said, "Baaaaaa, you goddamned sheep. Say it. Say you're a sheep."

I didn't even care when he leaned back on his haunches as he straddled my chest, pulled off a ring from his left hand, then flicked a lighter right before my eyes. 'Sheep are property. You're mine now. And you know what we do with our sheep?"

I didn't care.

I didn't care at all. Someone in this world said I was more than just a hunk of fat and this time it rang true.

"We brand them," he hissed, as he pinned both of my arms above my head and drove the hot surface of his ring into the pink flesh of my forearm. "We brand them for life."

I screamed and suddenly the weight on my chest was gone. There were sounds everywhere but I barely even heard them because my arm was on fire, the likes of which I had never felt before.

As tears poured out of my eyes and lucid thoughts finally decided to take a holiday or at least a well-deserved siesta, I heard grunting and growling and I didn't know what it could be.

My eyes opened one last time.

That's when I saw Anders standing over the greasy guy with a rock in his hand. He was hitting him again and again, his arms turning black and slick as he kept driving it down, down, down.

"Leave my friends alone," Anders screamed, drugged and deranged, as each rock fall broke something new in the greasy guy's head and dark liquid sprayed out of him in the moonlight. "Leave them the fuck alone."

65

BACK AT MARCY'S house there is a to-do list lying on the kitchen counter. It's missing the next chore we need to get done because the next item is something that I never even considered.

The missing item is 'bury a body.'

The greasy guy is lying face down in the leaves, not far from where we all woke up this morning. Only, he didn't wake up with the rest of us. He's never going to wake up again.

The woods are bright enough from the moon that I can see where his head isn't exactly round anymore. It's concave, and covered with black goop that I know isn't really black.

As I stare at his corpse I realize that it's almost a miracle that we didn't notice it this morning. Only some mounded up piles of leaves and branches separated him from where we found ourselves with our memories gone and our world turned on its side.

I'm sure that when the sun rises tomorrow morning the leaves all around the corpse will be covered in red sap.

That can't happen. Either the sun can't rise or the red leaves and the mangled body of the greasy guy who caused all of us so much pain can't be there.

We have to get rid of the blood.

We have to get rid of the body.

My mind makes a mental leap way too far and I decide that we have to bury the greasy guy, in the woods, in the ground.

There simply isn't any other alternative.

I don't know what makes me come to that conclusion, but I can't think of any other way to distance the four of us from last night other than to make that distance a vertical six feet.

The simple truth is that Anders killed a boy who is from The Bellingham School. It doesn't matter that Anders doesn't really remember doing it or that he acted in self-defense, because he didn't.

He brought down a rock on the greasy guy's head, caving in his greasy skull, because he was defending me.

He was defending all of us.

He shouldn't have to own that.

Myers is standing next to me. Tears are streaming down his face, and once again, I allow them to happen without wanting to lash out at him for being such a baby. Once you see a dead body, you can never unsee it, no matter if you have one eye or two. Myers' one eye is now indelibly printed with the greasy guy's dead image.

He'll never forget it and neither will I.

Thankfully, Anders and Marcy haven't followed us into the woods. I'm sure they are still back on the path, content to be wrapped in each other's arms where there is tenderness and love—where their world makes sense inside a world that makes no sense at all.

The world outside of the two of them has people like Tate in it. The world has psychotic murderers like Viktor Pavlovich and psychopaths like the greasy guy who thought a fun night on the town involved drugging and raping someone as sweet and kind as Marcy, and maybe doing something worse to her—or me.

I don't blame them for not coming into the woods. I don't blame them for not wanting to look at the greasy guy ever again. He's gone. That's all that matters.

As for Anders, I can't ever let him think of himself as a murderer. He doesn't deserve to carry around the weight of that burden for the rest of his life. I know what it feels like to carry weight. It's a nightmare.

It's better that the greasy guy be erased. At least that's what I decide.

A half-hour later the four of us are back in my truck. Myers is riding shotgun again. Anders and Marcy are in the backseat, but something has changed. Anders' arm is draped protectively around Marcy and her curly head is leaning up against his shoulder. A barrier has given way inside Anders, and I think if anything positive can come out of what happened to us last night, the two of them together might be it.

As nice as that thought may be, there is something very not-nice that has to happen first. We all know it, but I'm the one who says the four fated words that will change our lives forever.

"We need a shovel," I tell them. That's all. We need a shovel to dig a hole in Prince Richard's Maze, away from Big Loop and Little Loop and away from Turner Pond. The hole has to be excavated from the ground in a remote part of The Maze where no one goes. Next Spring, poison oak and poison ivy will hopefully grow out of the ground over the unmarked grave, and no one will ever know that the poisonous plants are covering an equally poisonous person who deserved every bit of what he got.

Only digging that hole and putting the greasy guy in it, along with all the bloody leaves, will make him go away forever so that we can forget about him and what happened to us last night.

Hopefully, Marcy, Anders, and Myers will be able to completely erase his memory. As for me, maybe I will talk Beryl into signing a waver so I can get a tattoo this year instead of next, so that I don't have to look at the triangle on my forearm every day and be reminded of why it's there. Otherwise, I won't have the luxury of being able to forget the sheep's cries and the big black eyes. I won't have the ability to ever forget that a psychotic rapist, barely a year older than me but firmly on the adult side of the fence, was the first person to ever make me believe that the fat part of my life was gone and what was left behind wasn't so repulsive.

I want a better memory than that.

I deserve it.

66

I PARK MY TRUCK across the street and down three houses from the Coles' house. Primrose Lane is thankfully quiet. There are no cars in any of our driveways and the lights in Marcy's kitchen are on. If any of our parents bothered to care, they would think we are all in her kitchen, watching television and wondering if we know anybody who was pulled out of Running Man's house.

The truth is, we sort of do, if our brief and messed up interaction with Calista Diamond after we were thoroughly drugged last night constitutes knowing someone.

There are no reporters or cops in sight. No one has realized yet that we are connected to the psychotic girl who blew her brains out up at Wang Memorial in Apple.

I'm grateful for that.

"I'll be right back," Marcy whispers as she slides out of the back seat and quietly clicks the door closed behind her. She's going to get a shovel in the Coles' garage. It's probably one that her father purchased a dozen years ago from the local hardware store but has never used. We all have lawn men to do work like that in Meadowfield. Owning a shovel is only for show.

That, and burying bodies.

"Are we really doing this?" whimpers Myers. He's rubbing my coconut's pirate patch like it's his real eye. It's not. Underneath the black cloth is nothing, and his fake eye is back in The Maze with only a dead body as company.

"We have to," I tell him. "I don't think we have a choice."

"We could go to the police," he says.

Anders snorts in the backseat. "And tell them what? That I murdered someone? Maybe we should tell him that it's my fault Calista Diamond is dead, too. Maybe if I screwed her like she wanted she wouldn't have ended up with Running Man."

"Anders," he begins, but Anders cuts him off.

"Or better yet, maybe I should have let him get his rocks off with

West and then he'd be alive right now and I wouldn't be a murderer."

I shake my head. "You know that's not true."

"Do I? Seriously. Do I?"

I don't answer him and neither does Myers. I stare out the window at Marcy's house. Myers stares at that secret spot between his feet. Anders stares into empty space. We know what we have to do. We don't have any other choice.

"What about after?" Myers asks.

Anders and I are both quiet. I don't know what's going to happen after. I'm barely holding on to what's happening now. We'll deal with after when after comes, and hopefully, the only thing we will tell anyone if we're ever asked is that we don't remember anything about last night.

Let Tate Cole answer the hard questions, although I doubt he'll say anything either. He'll just continue eating his pudding and 'killing it at ping pong' with Eddie Bick until he turns eighteen and gets transferred to some big-boy facility where electric shock therapy might be just the thing he needs.

Jesus. Do they even do that anymore? What about lobotomies? It's a pleasant thought to think of Tate Cole being strapped to a chair, with electrodes attached to his head and someone wearing a white lab coat dialing the voltage up to its highest level. It's an even more pleasant thought imagining someone as equally skilled as Running Man shoving a sharp instrument into the orbit of his eye and poking around inside until the part of him that makes him so psychotically evil is turned to mush.

As I bask in my thoughts, each one viler than the last, Anders says, "Where is she?"

"I don't know," says Myers.

The back door opens. "I'm going to get her." He unfolds himself from the back seat and gets out of my truck.

Seconds tick by before Myers says, "No offense, but I'd rather be with someone who can actually protect me," and he gets out, too.

I sit alone in my truck without any real motivation to move. My mind wanders back to what the greasy guy said to me as he sat on my chest. I play the scene over and over again in my head. I want it to stop, but each time I hope it will end, the memory rewinds and starts over again, getting more vivid and more real.

What seems almost laughably unreal is what Dr. Viktor Pavlovich did in his house on Covington Circle. For a moment, an old image of Sandra Berman pops into my head. I hope she's not one of the bodies in that house. I hope she really did run away and is living another person's life far away from Meadowfield where she can be happy and free.

Happy, because kids don't run away from home unless life there is unbearable. They don't run away from home unless they can't take one more second of their fuckity-fuck-fuck-fuck parents or indifferent mothers.

Five more minutes pass as I let myself marinate in my thoughts, all of them gross, all of them thoughts that I would never have even entertained twenty four hours ago, before I decide to go after Marcy, Anders, and Myers.

If Mr. Cole even owns a shovel, it's as likely to be in his underwear drawer or the kitchen closet as in the garage. Chaos is the norm in Marcy's house. I can't even imagine what it would be like if Tate had never gone away. Frankly, I don't have to imagine. I know. The Coles' house would be a burnt stain in the earth. Marcy's crazy twin would have torched the place years ago, maybe while using a cigarette on the couch in the basement, all the time watching Tyrone float in his bowl.

Foul, bitter thoughts like that one keep running through my head as I cross the street, jog down a few houses, then slink alongside Marcy's garage to the back door that's always open—never locked.

Marcy is standing on the garage steps leading into the house. Anders and Myers are leaning up against the wall with their arms folded across their chests.

The guy with the afro, the third of three that left The Bellingham School yesterday, bought a pizza at Pizza Depot, and doused it with Flunitrazepam, is standing next to Marcy with his arm around her shoulder and a knife pressing into her throat.

"It's about goddamned time," he hisses at me in a voice that's both bitter and evil. "I was about to call the cops."

67

THE GUY WITH THE afro applies pressure to the knife and the tip of it pushes into Marcy's throat. A little trickle of blood slips down her neck.

"Let her go," I say so calmly and evenly that I might as well be one of the teachers at school quietly reprimanding Pavel Vagin for flicking snot at Myers.

"Shut the hell up, pretty boy," he snarls at me, and I flinch. There are those words again, the one that the greasy guy breathed into my face last night in Prince Richard's Maze—the words that I never thought would be associated with someone like me. In that moment, I realize that he's probably been referring to me as *'pretty boy'* since he and his friends drugged us last night. We haven't had names. We've been the hot girl, the pretty boy, the jock, and the master baiter.

I cast my eyes sideways. Anders is pale. Myers is standing next to him. Mr. Cole's oversized shirt is now hanging down almost below his wrists, but not far enough that I can't see that his fists are clenching and unclenching, clenching and unclenching.

"She didn't do anything," Myers says, and I feel like I'm in an alternate universe where people like me and Myers are the ones who protect our friends, and jocks like Anders shrink in their own grief.

"What's with the patch, dude?" he snaps at Myers. Then he pushes his lips together and says, "Your mommy going to dress you as a pirate for Halloween?"

I don't even give Myers a chance to respond. "What do you want?" I say in that calm tone.

"I want this to be fucking yesterday," sneers the guy. Obviously, he doesn't realize that what he wants is pretty close to what the rest of us want. The thing is, there's no going back to yesterday where Meadowfield was decent and we never woke up in Prince Richard's Maze.

Calista Diamond is dead.

The greasy guy with the sunglasses is dead.

Running Man is dead, and everyone inside his house is dead, too.

There's no going back to yesterday. There's barely even room to go forward.

"I have money," I say. I probably sound really stupid, like some desperate victim on a crime show who is trying to weasel out of a tight spot.

"Yeah, we'll get to that soon enough," the guy with the afro snarls, then gets a slight pained look in his eyes. "Right now, I just want to know where Frankie is."

Anders closes his eyes.

Marcy bites her lip.

I take a deep breath.

"Who the hell is Frankie?" Myers hisses, fire coming out of his mouth right alongside his words. The guy only stares at him as though he's monumentally stupid and that everyone in the world should know who *'Frankie'* is.

"Don't be a douchebag," he says, "Or I'll slit her pretty throat."

He adds a little more pressure to the handle of the knife and more blood slides down Marcy's neck.

I want to murder him.

Bad.

"Don't," cries Anders. He takes a step forward, but it's a baby step. It's the step of someone who is walking on a tightrope but has never stood on a tightrope before, and there's no safety net below. "Please."

"Why? She your girlfriend or something?"

Anders swallows, and his Adam's apple bobs up and down. "Yes," he says. A tiny smile flashes across Marcy's face. A zillion pound weight sheds from Anders' shoulders.

"Too bad," the guy with the afro sneers then bends down so his lips are right up against Marcy's ear. "You know what?" he says. "You're hot and all, but if I hated my sister as much as Tate hates you, I'd want her all fucked up, too."

"Tate's a psychopath," Marcy says as though the nightmare we're living has done nothing but render her bored.

"Maybe," says the guy with the afro. "We weren't in Bellingham for being normies. Still, a deal's a deal. He put a lot of time and effort this past year into making sure that when we had a chance to get out of that hell hole, his whole family would end up in pieces."

"So?" says Marcy again in that same unaffected voice. I hope she's not broken in the head like Anders was for most of the day. She needs to be sharp. She needs to be as brutal as the knife he's pushing into her neck, or maybe she'll end up like Tate wanted her to end up.

"So?" says the guy. "So Frankie was going to have some major fun with you while Calista and I robbed that old dude for some cash, but I guess we all know how FUBAR that plan went."

That old guy.

Running Man.

"Pavlovich?" I whisper.

"Yeah," he snaps. "Pavlovich. And I thought Bellingham was a shit show. You should have seen what I found in his basement. Walk-in freezers full of people, all cut to shit."

Myers whimpers, his hands still balled into fists.

The guy with the afro pulls his knife from Marcy's neck and waves it around in the air, presumably to illustrate his point, but he doesn't let her go. He holds onto her as tightly as ever. "He drew all over them and sliced them up," he says. "Like I really wanted to find that crap when I snuck in though his basement window?"

"Too bad for you," says Marcy and I get nervous. She's going to get herself killed.

"Too bad for me?" he roars. "Too bad for him." He puts the knife to her throat again and I die a little inside. "He had Calista upstairs in the kitchen. I thought she was screwing him, because, you know, she screws everybody. Then she screamed. So I went up the basement stairs, cracked the door and there he was. He had Calista in a chair, with her hair all gone, and he was drawing on her face with a sharpie."

"That's sick," I say.

"Sick?" he laughs. "You want to know what's really sick?" He pauses for effect, only accentuating how touched in the head he really is. "I stabbed the fucker, probably a dozen times. That's what's really sick." He pulls the knife away from Marcy's throat and slices it through the air over and over again. "Of course, freaking Calista had to go freak out and call 911. What a stupid bitch. What a goddamned stupid bitch."

With his words, I see everything clearly. The greasy guy, Frankie, took the four of us to The Maze while Calista went with Running Man back to his house. The guy with the afro probably followed them, snuck into the basement window with the hopes of stealing some cash, found his handy work, then caught him upstairs doing to Calista what he did to everyone else who died in that house.

Running Man was going to slice up her beautiful face, like Tate wanted Marcy's whole family to end up, so the guy with the afro killed him, most likely with the same knife he's holding now. Calista was wigged out about everything and probably so scared out of her mind that the first thing she thought to do was call the police.

911.

That's all it took. Just three little buttons on a phone was all it took, and Meadowfield's resident crazy was come undone.

The guy with the afro reaches up and wraps his fingers around Marcy's throat. "You know what?" he whispers. "It was kind of fun playing inside his guts. I think that's the kind of fun I want to have again."

"Go ahead," says Marcy in a husky voice, her words dropping almost an octave. "But we know where Frankie is."

The guy with the afro blinks twice and his knife hand falters a little.

"Yeah," says Myers because it's true. "We know exactly where Frankie is."

The guy's fingers loosen around Marcy's throat. His forehead wrinkles.

"Let her go," says Anders. "And we'll take you to him."

As for me, the rest of my to-do list sitting upstairs in Marcy's kitchen suddenly gets a few last minute additions.

"Fine," I say, although anyone who knows me knows that my voice is tinged with a thousand disturbing emotions all at once. "If that's how it has to be, we'll take you."

68

THIS IS HOW IT ENDS.

69

THE NEXT MORNING, bright and early, the four of us go to the cops and tell them the truth. The Meadowfield police force is battle fatigued from having to deal with the fallout of Running Man's reign of terror, and we almost feel bad that we add heaping platefuls to their misery, but there isn't any other way. After all, it's only been one day since an anonymous phone call was made from inside Dr. Viktor Pavlovich's house which ultimately led to one of the most brutal and heinous serial murderers that Western Massachusetts has ever seen.

We're just icing on top of that crazy cake.

It doesn't matter that the truth we tell them is littered with fiction.

Most truths are.

Tate Cole had a vendetta against his family forever. Most of it was because he was messed in the head, and some small parts of it could have been because Marcy was trans. Whatever the reason, Tate wanted them all hurt or dead, and went to extraordinary lengths to talk three of his friends into skipping out of The Bellingham School once they all turned eighteen to get the job done.

They came to Meadowfield—Calista Diamond, a boy named Frankie Keller, and a third named Billy Yorns. The three of them delivered a pizza to Marcy's house laced with a drug called Flunitrazepam—the date rape drug.

Calista, Frankie, and Billy never expected the Coles to be gone, or me, Anders, and Myers to be there with Marcy instead. We were only added excitement in an excitement-filled night.

After we were all drugged, the three of them took us in search of a good time which ultimately led to The Stumps. While there, Calista hit hard on Anders, but he wasn't interested.

We even tell the police that there's a video out there, probably sitting in the deleted files on Val Buenavista's phone that proves what we're saying is true. If they look hard enough, analyzing each image, frame by frame, they might even catch a glimpse of Dr. Viktor Pavlovich in the background. He was there that night, probably looking for his next kill way too close to home.

This is where our truth turns into fiction, but only a little, or at least that's what we will tell ourselves for the rest of our lives.

We explain to the police that all eight of us ended up at Prince Richard's Maze after the Stumps. Me, Anders, Myers, and Marcy, Frankie, Billy, Calista, and Running Man.

We were drugged, but we still remember pieces of an argument that mostly centered around who was going to get a turn with Calista first. In a rage, Dr. Pavlovich picked up a rock and bashed in Frankie Keller's head. When he's was through, he did the same to Billy Yorns.

After all, murder was his thing.

Then he filled their pockets with stones and let them sink into Turner Pond.

We tell the police we hardly remember anything after that except for what Dr. Pavlovich put us through. It's amazing how effortlessly the four of us lie to them. We lie because the truth can never come out.

Not ever.

I tell them that Running Man branded me with a triangle from Frankie's Alcoholics Anonymous sobriety ring, which he obviously only wore for show. I don't know why he burned me the way he did. I only remember the pain and waking up the next morning with a permanent scar on my left arm.

Myers tells them that Running Man was disgusted by the fact that he had a glass eye. It made him less than perfect. Running Man seemed all about perfection, so he took his eye from him.

Marcy tells them that Running Man was far more interested in her than in Calista because Calista seemed like she wanted it and Marcy seemed purer than that. She tried to fight him, but he succeeded in getting her pants off. It was only then that he realized that Marcy was genetically male.

Running Man didn't want her anymore.

Anders' tells them that that most of his clothes were gone. He doesn't make up an explanation as to why. He doesn't remember. No one can argue with that. Besides, his story sounds more realistic that way and realism is key.

Finally, we tell the police that when we woke up the next morning, we smelled fire and thought the woods were burning but they weren't. We heard the town fire alarm and police sirens and thought that they were coming to save us in Prince Richard's Maze, but they didn't.

We were all alone.

Throughout the day and into the night, we slowly remembered the important parts of what happened to us. During that time, Anders got into a fight with Barry Kupperman at The Stumps, but all of that nonsense was just residual effects from the drugs. They don't need to know the real reason.

Nobody does.

We tell the police that we spent the rest of the night scared out of our minds, not knowing what to do. Finally, early this morning we decided we had to tell someone.

That's all of it.

That's our lie that we tell the police.

We say it over and over again until we believe it ourselves, probably like Sandra Berman's parents will always believe that one of those body parts inside Running Man's house is from their daughter, regardless if she's identified or not.

What we never tell the police is that we brought Billy Yorns to the woods to show him where we said Frankie was waiting for him.

We never tell them that I picked a rock up off the ground and smashed it into the back of his head, nor do we tell them that Myers took a turn, too.

We never tell them that Anders was next, and he relished every second of it.

We never tell them that Marcy struck the killing blow, hitting him more than a few times until her arms couldn't hold the rock over her head anymore.

We never tell them that we dragged the bodies through Prince Richard's Maze, scooping up handfuls of pebbles along the way, stuffing them in their pockets, and making sure not to touch our cell phones that were also with them, along with Myers' eye.

We never tell them that we watched Frankie Keller and Billy Yorns melt away into the waters of Turner Pond, or that we knew the pond would be dredged anyway to confirm everything we said, or that it would all be pinned on Running Man.

We never tell them any of those things.

70

WOULD YOU?

The End

Acknowledgements

I would like to thank my wonderful readers David Gilfor, Nick Gilfor, Shira Block McCormick, Tamara Fricke, Lauren Levin, Michelle Scalia, and my mother, Joline Odentz, whose nickname "Jolly" appears in every one of my books.

I would also like to give special thanks to Brigadier General Thomas Heath and the fine folks at the Enfield, Connecticut Police Department for spending the time to speak with me concerning matters I know nothing about.

Finally, I would like to once again give thanks to Lois Winston, Ashley Grayson, Debra Dixon, and the team at Bell Bridge Books for their tireless support.

About the Author

Author and playwright HOWARD ODENTZ is a lifelong resident of the gray area between Western Massachusetts and North Central Connecticut. His love of the region is evident in his writing as he often incorporates the foothills of the Berkshires and the small towns of the Bay and Nutmeg states into his work.

What We Kill, a taught thriller set in fictional Meadowfield, Massachusetts, is his sixth publication with Bell Bridge Books. Other works include the young adult zombie romps *Dead (a Lot)* and *Wicked Dead*, the thriller *Bloody Bloody Apple*, the creepy anthology *Little Killers A to Z*, and the holiday horror short story *Snow*.

The mysterious has always played a major role in Howard's writing. He is endlessly fascinated by the psychological aspects of those who are thrown into thrilling or otherworldly circumstances.

50350495R00139

Made in the USA
Middletown, DE
29 October 2017